CIRCLE OF
BLOOD

Debbie Viguié has been writing for most of her life
and holds a degree in creative writing from U.C.
Davis. Debbie loves theme parks and enjoys travelling
with her husband, Scott. Debbie grew up in the San
Francisco Bay Area and now lives in Florida.

Other books by Debbie Viguié in the
Witch Hunt trilogy

The 13th Sacrifice
The Last Grave

CIRCLE of BLOOD

Debbie Viguié

arrow books

Published by Arrow Books, 2014

2 4 6 8 10 9 7 5 3 1

First published in the US in 2014 by Signet

Arrow Books
Random House, 20 Vauxhall Bridge Road,
London SW1V 2SA

www.randomhouse.co.uk

Addresses for companies within The Random House Group Limited can be
found at: www.randomhouse.co.uk/offices.htm

The Random House Group Limited Reg. No. 954009

A CIP catalogue record for this book
is available from the British Library

ISBN 9780099574576

The Random House Group Limited supports the Forest Stewardship
Council® (FSC®), the leading international forest-certification organisation.
Our books carrying the FSC label are printed on FSC®-certified paper. FSC is
the only forest-certification scheme supported by the leading environmental
organisations, including Greenpeace. Our paper procurement policy can be
found at: www.randomhouse.co.uk/environment

MIX
Paper from
responsible sources
FSC® C016897

Printed and bound in Great Britain by Clays Ltd, St Ives plc

To Juliette Cutts, my sister in spirit.
The family you choose is just as important
as the family you're born with.

ACKNOWLEDGMENTS

There are so many people that I need to thank. First, thank you to my magnificent agent, Howard Morhaim, who always has my back. Next, I have to thank my fantastic editor, Danielle Perez; it has been an honor and a privilege to work with you, and your insight and dedication continue to astound me. You are truly one of the great ones. Thank you to the entire team at Penguin for their continued support of this series. Thank you to my husband, Scott, for all the love and support. Thank you also to the circle of friends and family who love me and keep me safe: Rick and Barbara Reynolds, Ann Liotta, Calliope Collacott, and Chrissy Current.

1

The room was dark. No one was home, but that didn't mean that she was alone. Shadows slithered down the walls and voices whispered all around her. They told her to stop, told her that she was a fool and that she didn't know what she was doing. Something deep inside her was thrashing like a dying animal, and it took everything she had to keep her concentration.

Sitting on the floor of her bedroom, she sliced her hand open with a butcher knife she'd gotten from the kitchen. It wasn't a ceremonial object, but the important part wasn't the blade itself but the blood. Her blood.

She smeared the blood on the floor around her until it formed a circle. When it was completed she wiped her hand on her skirt and took a deep breath.

It was now or never. If she didn't do this, she'd be a prisoner forever, and she wanted so desperately to be free. But the thing that slithered around inside her hated the very word. It made her hands shake so bad she almost couldn't light the candles that were around her.

On the circle she placed two candles. One was blue for protection. The other was yellow for memory. Then she lit a white candle and placed it inside the circle in front of herself. The candle represented her, her higher self, who she wished to be.

Next she lit three black candles and placed one on the other side of the candle from her and the other two to the left and right of the white candle. Black candles repelled negativity, were used for protection and binding.

Her hands were shaking so badly now she knocked the third candle over. She quickly snuffed the flame that leaped to life on the carpet. And she understood exactly what the thing that was clawing at her stomach wanted. If it couldn't have her, it would kill her.

But she wouldn't let it, not today of all days. It was her birthday. She was thirteen. Mr. and Mrs. Ryan were at work, but they had already given her the present she had asked for. She picked up the necklace that had been sitting next to her on the floor. It was a silver cross and they hadn't even balked when she'd asked for it to be made for her based on a centuries-old design.

She twisted the top of it off, revealing a tiny, hidden chamber in the heart of the cross. It wasn't large, but it didn't have to be.

She shuddered as she could feel the shadows reaching out to her, touching her with icy hands that inspired dread and sorrow and terror as they always did. But now, for the first time, they also inspired anger.

She wouldn't let them control and manipulate her anymore. Everyone was dead: her mother, Abigail; all killed when their coven had tried raising that demon that had destroyed them.

She would not be joining them. She was choosing life. A new life. New family, new religion. Even a new name.

"I put away the old self, the old life. I renounce the witchcraft and the acts of evil I have witnessed and participated in."

Around her she could hear screaming. Inside her belly the creature that had been with her for what felt like a lifetime writhed in agony. It needed her fear, her will to survive, and she was going to deny it.

"I seal myself to God and as Christ shed His blood on the cross, I, too, shed my blood on this image of the cross to bind my life to Him."

She lifted her injured hand and squeezed three drops of blood into the hidden chamber of the cross. Three, a holy number, a sacred number to so many different peoples. She screwed the top of the cross back on and put it around her neck.

She could feel heat radiating from the cross into her skin.

"I turn my back on the darkness."

Things were throwing themselves at her now, but her circle of protection kept them at bay. There was howling and scratching outside the circle. Inside the circle the thing within her was making her sick, trying to confound her mind so she couldn't remember what it was she was doing, so she couldn't remember how to rid herself of it once and for all.

"I choose a new life, a new world. And nothing of the old belongs in it. I am no longer Desdemona Castor. I choose to forget the evil that she has done. I am Samantha Ryan. Behold, I am become new."

She blew out the white and black candles and then immediately doubled over in pain. She wretched and something black oozed out of her mouth and slid across the floor, seeking escape.

*She picked up the blue candle and set fire to the black slime,
incinerating it. And slowly the screams faded from her mind.*

*When it was gone she blew out the flame on the blue can-
dle and then the yellow candle. Yellow, for memory. Very
deliberately she took the knife and cut the candle in half. The
two pieces toppled to the floor and she slid to the ground as
tears of relief burst from her.*

Desdemona Castor sat up with a shriek. She had been
dreaming about the moment when she ceased to be
and the imposter known as Samantha Ryan had taken
her place. She swung her legs over the side of the bed
and put her hands together, forming a ball of energy
between them that grew and twisted until finally
Freaky, in the form of a sleek black panther, was sitting
on the floor staring at her with eyes that glowed red.
She reached out to pet his head as she shook off the
remnants of the nightmare.

"Never again," she promised the big cat.

They were in an abandoned house on the outskirts
of New Orleans. A little magic when they arrived the
night before had made it habitable and obscured them
from detection. On the nightstand was a picture of the
cross necklace from her nightmare. *Come and get it* was
written in blood on it. The cross had been stolen by
witches months before when she was a homicide detective in Boston and had still been going by the name
Samantha Ryan.

Whoever had stolen it had left the picture for her in
a grave in Salem, taunting her, daring her to come and
find them. When she did, she would destroy both the
cross and the witch who had stolen it.

The night before, when they had arrived in New Orleans, she had attempted a summoning spell to bring the witch to her. It had failed. The witch in question was either very powerful or had taken precautions against such spells. It was no matter; Desdemona would find her, and when she did, nothing on earth would save the witch who had crossed her.

Desdemona rose and got dressed. It was time to hunt a witch.

An hour later she was haunting the dark streets of the French Quarter. The bars and clubs had emptied out and the shadows reigned supreme. She stalked through them, unafraid of anything that might be lurking within. No mere mortal was a match for her, and few witches had enough power to pose any kind of threat to her.

A gunshot rang out through the air and she tensed. She started to turn toward the sound, but she forced herself to continue walking on her path. She wasn't a cop. That was the usurper's job and self-identity, not hers. That wasn't who she truly was. Local police could handle the human drama just fine. Besides, what did she care?

As she walked she searched for evidence of the witch she was seeking. She would head to the Garden District next if she couldn't find what she was looking for. Witches by their very nature loved places steeped in history. A police car sped by a few minutes later, followed by an ambulance.

The streets were grimy, and without throngs of people the place felt desolate. She stepped over a puddle on the ground that seemed to be congealing blood. The energy in the place was palpable and so very different from that of other places she had been.

There was no sense of the earth beneath her, just concrete. Instead the energy was pulsing off the buildings, the collected fears and dreams of so many creative and desperate people. Life was one big party until you died; here, sex, death, and jazz seemed to permeate the air.

It was nearly dawn when she finally felt power shimmering in the air. Those with the talent for magic interacted with the flow of energy around them and they could sense others with the same ability. She turned into a small café that was open for early-morning breakfast. She took a table and her eyes zeroed in on an older man with gray hair who was engrossed in his meal. She ordered beignets and coffee.

When her food came a few minutes later, she was still closely watching the man. So far he had refused to acknowledge her presence, even though he most surely had felt her power as well.

She considered confronting him then and there, but the importance of keeping magic a secret had been well drilled into her as a child. She had once blinded a schoolyard bully only to be tortured by her mother as punishment. She could wait until the man left the café.

The coffee was only lukewarm, but she had no need of distracting herself by yelling at the waiter. Instead, keeping her eyes focused on her quarry, she wrapped her hand around the cup and pushed energy out of her body through her hand and into the cup. She could hear the liquid begin to boil and she released it.

Twenty minutes later, she was finished eating. The

man finally got up and exited the café in another ten minutes. She waited a beat and then rose to follow him.

She stayed about a block behind. He couldn't help knowing that she was following him. She would let him choose the place of their confrontation. Finally she saw him turn up an alleyway between two buildings.

She tensed, the energy ebbing and flowing through her. She debated briefly about how to enter the alleyway in case he was waiting to ambush her. Finally she took it slowly, hand raised, fire dancing along her fingertips.

She stopped a couple of feet in.

The man was standing over the body of someone else sprawled on the ground. The stench of blood filled the air and she could feel the life energy leaving the man on the ground as he died.

She stared with narrowed eyes at the man she'd been following. He just shrugged and looked at her with steely eyes. "And what, then, is it you'll be wanting of me?" he asked in a lilting Irish accent.

"What are you?"

"A man, last I checked," he said, a smile twisting his lips.

"Are you a witch?"

"Druid, actually," he said shortly.

A surge of power rippled through the air, followed by a gasp and the sound of shattering glass.

Desdemona turned impatiently. There, standing behind her, was one of the magic users whose life she had spared back in Salem, a young girl with flaming red hair who was shaking uncontrollably, a broken vase with fresh flowers at her feet.

"Please, please don't kill me," the girl begged.

Desdemona turned back. The man had vanished. Her eyes dropped to the corpse and she blinked in surprise as she recognized the frozen features.

The dead guy was her waiter from the café.

What was he doing here? she wondered as she crouched down to get a better look at the corpse. He must have left the restaurant before she and the older man did. Had the other man killed him or just found his body? In either case he hadn't seemed particularly rattled or surprised.

She looked at the body closely, looking for any obvious, mundane cause of death. There was nothing she could see in the way of marks on the body, no holes, no bruises. There wasn't any blood on it or on the surrounding ground, either. Just by looking she couldn't rule out poison or something like a heart attack.

When Desdemona was thirteen she had renounced her old life and taken on a new name, Samantha Ryan. Samantha had grown up and become a police detective in Boston, where she had solved many homicides. Samantha's carefully ordered life had been turned upside down, though, when she'd been forced to go undercover in nearby Salem to apprehend a coven of dark witches who were murdering people. They had been trying to raise a demon and she had barely stopped them.

Using magic again had opened a door that she had kept firmly shut for years, allowing memories and even old personality traits to slip through. For years, the part of her that was Desdemona, the witch, had been locked away inside Samantha's mind, struggling to get out.

Following a move to the San Francisco Bay Area and

an encounter with another dark coven of witches trying to release a different demon trapped beneath a mountain, Desdemona had finally been freed. The irony was, just as Samantha had not remembered a great deal of her childhood, shutting out the memories, so Desdemona had tried to block memories from her teen and adult years that belonged to Samantha.

Yet, even though she had denounced that part of herself, she could feel herself still trying to solve the puzzle before her. She felt like a cop, and she hated it. That was the imposter, not her. Muscle memory existed, though, that led her into certain old habits, unwelcome as they were.

She heard the slightest whisper of fabric and she lifted her left hand behind her. She pulled energy in from the environment as well as from the girl who was trying to sneak away.

"I compel you to come here," she said quietly.

She heard feet sliding along the ground, their owner struggling so hard not to comply as if she actually had a choice in the matter. At last the girl was standing next to her, whimpering.

Desdemona didn't bother looking up from what she was doing. "Why are you here?" she asked.

"I work at the flower shop down the street. I was doing an early-morning delivery, and I just happened to walk by."

"Not here in this alley, here in New Orleans," Desdemona said.

She could feel the girl struggling, straining to pull away, but she might as well have been a gnat for all the effect it had.

"I . . . I don't know. You told me to leave Salem and I went to stay with some friends in Tennessee for a couple of weeks and then I felt something sort of calling to me, drawing me here."

"A word of advice," Desdemona said as she stood. "When you feel something irresistible calling you to a certain place, that's the last place you should go."

"I . . . I didn't know. I didn't know you'd come here."

"Neither did I. Look at this man. Tell me, have you seen him before?"

As though against her will, even though she wasn't being compelled to, the girl bent down to get a closer look. Curiosity is a powerful thing in any person regardless of who you are.

"No, I don't think so."

"He's not a witch, nor does he have our powers," she mused.

"I—I'm not a witch."

"No, of course you're not. Even if you were, you wouldn't be very good at it. But still, look at him and tell me what you see, what you feel."

"I don't understand."

For the first time Desdemona looked up and met the girl's eyes. She saw terror there, running rampant, practically paralyzing her. The curiosity was visible, too, but to a much lesser degree. The memories of Samantha were present in Desdemona's mind, but it took effort to focus in on them and to pluck out the information she needed.

Back in Salem the dark coven had brought about the resurrection of Abigail, Desdemona's own coven leader from childhood, killed when Desdemona was twelve.

The new coven leaders had not warned all the members what exactly they were doing or that they would be ripping energy from them in order to restore the dead woman to life. The action had killed several of the weaker members and left others badly injured and terrified, suddenly aware of exactly what they had gotten themselves into. Samantha had taken pity on them and, without blowing her cover, had managed to give a few of them a way to escape the coven.

The girl in front of her had been the first to accept Samantha's offer of amnesty in the graveyard after the resurrection of Abigail. Samantha had given her enough energy not just to rise from the ground but also to run from the place and never look back. She had never known the girl's name.

That was easily enough solved. Desdemona didn't bother asking; she pushed her way inside the girl's mind and took it.

The girl gasped and sank to her knees, a stricken look on her face. She'd never had someone walk through her mind before; that much was clear. In a moment Desdemona knew everything she needed to know about her.

"Claudia."

"Yes?"

"I want you to look at this body and tell me what you see, not with your eyes but with your powers."

The girl hunched her shoulders and turned agonized eyes onto the body. "There is a faint shimmer about him."

"Very good. What else?"

The girl strained but finally shook her head. "I don't see anything else."

"If you can't see, then you should hear." Desdemona tilted the girl's head slightly to the side so that she could see what had been standing there the entire time.

The dead man's ghost was present, a look of terror and confusion on his face.

Claudia tried to jerk away, but she was still under Desdemona's control.

"It's a ghost," she whimpered, fear filling her voice.

"Yes. I'm surprised you've never seen one before. Tell us, spirit, how did you die?"

The ghost shook his head, refusing to speak to them.

"Very well," Samantha said, lifting her hand toward him. "If you will not tell us, you will show us."

Then the spirit disappeared and reappeared a moment later several feet away. It began walking. It halted, then half turned as though sensing someone behind it. "I did what you asked!" he screamed.

Then he seized up, bending nearly double. An invisible force lifted him about a foot off the ground and then dropped him. He went straight down, and she could tell from the reenactment that he'd been dead when his head hit the pavement.

The spirit lay there for a moment and then got up and repeated the entire thing again.

"Why—why is he doing that?"

"It's a ghost's natural function to replay his death over and over like a bad recording. Some grow more sentient and become more creative. He was in shock, those moments just after the soul has departed from the body, when it doesn't understand what has happened to it. I just pushed him out of that slightly faster."

"Somebody was following him. They killed him. It was someone with the powers," Claudia said.

"Very good. Now the only questions that remain are who and why."

"He said he did what they asked. And yet whoever it was killed him anyway."

Desdemona shrugged. "He was clearly only a tool and a disposable one at that."

"How sad," Claudia murmured.

Desdemona looked up at her and smiled. "How touching you should think so since you, too, are disposable."

Claudia took one look at her smile and began to scream.

2

Don't kill her, a voice whispered deep inside Desdemona. She scowled. There was nothing that could stop her from killing Claudia if she chose to. As she imagined the girl spontaneously combusting, burning from the inside out, she realized that she really wanted to. It had been ages since she had held life and death in the palm of her hand, another creature's fate dependent solely on her whim.

Use her. Find out what she knows, the voice whispered.

She hissed under her breath. That annoying voice that sometimes came to her usually didn't make so much sense.

"You know how they used to kill witches?" she asked, tilting her head to the side.

Claudia was ashen, trembling from head to toe. She shook her head.

"Oh, come on, of course you do. They'd tie them to a stake and then set them on fire. They'd burn them from the outside until there was nothing left. It's a terrible way to die, but one of the first things that's destroyed is your nerve endings, so you stop feeling the pain, the heat, all of it."

"That's awful," Claudia sobbed.

"Yes, but not half as awful as what I'm going to do to you if you don't tell me everything I want to know. I can burn you from the inside out and I can make the pain last much, much longer."

"Please, I don't know anything," the girl begged.

"I'll be the judge of that."

"I don't, really."

"How many other witches have you met here in New Orleans?"

"I—I don't know."

Desdemona *tsk*ed. "Come, come, you expect me to believe that?"

"I don't know how many witches, honest. I'm not—not a witch . . . not since you . . . please, don't kill me."

Desdemona rolled her eyes. "How many others with power have you met?"

Spittle was dangling off the girl's chin, and her eyes were wild. The terror coming off her was almost overwhelming in its intoxicating effect. "A lot. There's a lot here. I don't know why. There seems to be more every day."

"Interesting. Why do you think that is?"

"I don't know. Some of them try to talk to me and I get scared. I want to leave, but—"

"But you can't?" Desdemona guessed.

The girl nodded, spittle flying.

"Almost as though some invisible force compels you to stay?"

"Yes, yes."

"Interesting. What type of people are they?"

"I don't know. All kinds. I don't know if they're witches, but they seem to come from all over and be all different kinds of people. Rich, poor, young, old."

"And there's nothing tying them together?"

"Not that I can tell."

It was interesting. If a magic practitioner were calling all these people to him or her, from all different places and all different walks of life, that person would have to be very powerful. It was very indiscriminate as well, which would seem to indicate a need for these people's powers and not necessarily their will or ability to use them.

Something stirred in the back of Samantha's mind. Something had happened not that long ago in Salem, where mass numbers of people had been drained of energy, used as human batteries. But if her shadowy memory served, those had been just ordinary people, not ones with power.

Which meant that whoever had called these people here to this place must have much bigger plans than resurrecting a single person.

She felt as though her thoughts were flowing like quicksilver, as if she was almost free-associating rather than thinking. It was as though a part of her, her subconscious, had struggled to work it out and now it was whispering to her—

"No!" she shouted as she realized that it was that other version of her, the one who had been a cop and witnessed those events in Salem, that was trying to talk to her, warn her about something. She wouldn't listen;

she couldn't. That other self was weak, foolish, afraid. There was nothing Desdemona would take from her.

Isn't that weakness, too? the hateful self whispered.

If Desdemona could have figured out what part of her carried that wretched voice, she would have ripped it out days before. The only thing it had to offer her was fear.

And Desdemona had sworn to herself that she would never be afraid again. "Have they seemed to gather in one place? Have you felt a call to any place specific in the city?"

"No, I haven't. I don't know about the others, but I heard that some of them, some kids and homeless, are actually camped out at an old abandoned amusement park that closed after Katrina. It's called Jazzland."

"There's a witch in town, a very powerful witch."

"I've heard there's a witch who lives in the Garden District. Everyone knows about her. I haven't seen her, so I don't know how powerful she is."

"Or even if she has powers," Desdemona mused. "No, the witch I'm looking for would cloak herself more in secrecy, in shadow. Have you heard any whispers, rumors?"

"No, I swear it."

The girl didn't know anything else, of that Desdemona was certain. She still wanted to kill her, but she realized it might be useful to keep her around. The girl had only been there a few months, but she was already far more familiar with the city. She, and her powers, could prove very useful indeed.

"Claudia."

Claudia jerked at the sound of her name.

"You belong to me now—do you understand?"

"No."

"You live only because I wish it. If I were to stop wishing it, even for a moment." She snapped her fingers and Claudia stifled a scream.

"Do we have an understanding?"

"Yes."

"Good. You will learn for me all that you can about the witches who are already in the city and the magic possessors who are coming here. You have no other role, no other purpose in life, but to serve me."

"My job—"

"Is over."

Claudia licked her lips, the distress mounting in her eyes. Desdemona started to think the girl was going to have a heart attack on the spot. In fact, she could actually feel the girl's heart, skittering out of control, fast, erratic.

"How will I live?"

Desdemona smiled at her. "I'm sure you'll find a way. Now go. I'll be in contact with you soon."

It wasn't exactly true. She would be in contact with her constantly. Being aware of the fact that Desdemona had that much control over her, that much insight into her every thought, would only terrify her beyond the point of being an effective tool.

Claudia turned and scurried toward the entrance of the alley. She stopped before leaving and turned. "You—you're different than you were."

"I was . . . sick. I'm better now."

She didn't know why she felt the need to explain. Perhaps it was because she didn't want the girl to doubt for a minute, to have even a shred of hope that the other personality was coming back.

Because that was never going to happen.

She turned and surveyed the rest of the alley, her thoughts returning to the man she had followed into it. He had claimed to be a Druid. She instinctively felt that doing a summoning spell on him wouldn't work. She remembered now how to block those. It was complicated magic and she knew her other self would have paid dearly to remember how to do it back in Salem a few months before. Desdemona was sure the Druid had taken precautions. He struck her as the type somehow.

It was possible he was just one of the nameless hoard who had been called to this place. Then again, maybe he was someone of significance. He was powerful, that much she knew. She thought about trying to pick up his trail, but something told her to wait. No, better to deal with him later. There were others she should seek out now.

"I did what you asked!"

Desdemona turned. It was the ghost screaming. While she and Claudia had been talking, it had continued to replay the death of its human body. Pathetic. Just one more ghost in a town crawling with them.

A tinge of something touched her, sorrow perhaps? That was a useless emotion. She made to turn and leave, but instead she found herself lifting her hand and sucking the energy of the apparition into herself. She could feel a spike in her energy, her power. It was actually quite pleasant.

A moment later, the ghost had vanished. She looked

down at the body. A police investigation would be one more distraction she didn't need to deal with, especially since her little minion had left her shattered vase of flowers all over the alley entrance.

Desdemona called a fireball to her fingertips and she dropped it on the body, which ignited in a flash. The smell of burning hair and charred flesh filled the air around her, a reminder of so many events from her childhood. She wrinkled her nose, turned, and left the smoldering ashes behind.

She walked a ways, planning her next move in light of the morning's events. She was here in this city to find the witch that had called her out when she left the picture of the stolen necklace for her to find. That witch she had been coming to realize had been behind all the events in Salem and in San Francisco even though she had never been present or revealed herself. She had used her, just as she had all the others, but to what end? In both cities the covens had been trying to raise a demon. Something told her that the endgame was much bigger than that, though. The morning had been interesting, but she still had no idea where to look for the witch that had used and manipulated her.

Her phone rang and she pulled it out. The caller ID said Anthony. He had called several times in the past few days. The name seemed familiar to her, but it was part of Samantha's life, not hers. She ignored the call as she had the others and continued walking.

As she stalked the streets, searching for her prey, what Claudia had told her about the kids and homeless gathering in their own little conclave in the abandoned amusement park kept coming back to her. That much power in one place would tempt any witch to pay a visit. It was also possible one of them held answers that she needed, though she knew with an absolute certainty that the witch she sought wouldn't be among them.

She hailed a taxi and slid into the backseat.

"Where to?" the driver, a large man with dreadlocks, asked.

"Jazzland."

"Miss, that was destroyed by Katrina."

"Jazzland," Desdemona repeated.

"Okay. Didn't take you for an urban-explorer type, though. Usually they have big, fancy cameras."

She didn't answer, just sat back and watched the city flash by her window. She had never been to New Orleans before, but even she could feel the desperation of a city still half in chaos, struggling to reclaim what nature had taken away. They didn't understand; nature was a tool, just like everything else. It was a means to someone's or some *thing*'s end.

A strong enough coven of witches could have prevented the majority of the devastation. *Or they could have caused it*, she thought idly.

At this point, she had no way of knowing if the witch she was looking for had even been in the city back then.

The driver finally pulled up outside a closed-off parking lot. "This is as close as I can get you, but you should know, the city owns the place and they could arrest you for trespassing."

"I'll take my chances," she said, passing her fare through the slot in the window that separated the front seat from the backseat. She opened the door and got out.

There was power here; she could feel it. It called to her like a siren and she could feel herself drinking it in. It wasn't just the other magic practitioners, of whom there seemed to be quite a few by the way things felt. It was everything. The destruction and decay gave off their own dark energy, and she could feel it infusing her. She could feel the earth beneath all the concrete. This had been swampland and the swamp was still there, slowly eating away at the underpinnings, ready to reclaim what it had once lost to mankind's ambition.

Her driver started to get out of the car and then froze, one foot still inside. A small red bag of some sort seemed to fall out of his pocket and hit the ground. She took a couple of steps to the side, wondering what was wrong with him. His head was tilted slightly and his eyelashes were fluttering rapidly. There was a sort of frozen look on his face. Curious, she moved closer so she could get a better look at him.

He was staring at the entrance to the abandoned theme park. His pupils were dilated and his eyes were moving incredibly fast, almost as though they were vibrating.

"What is it?" she asked.

He remained still as if frozen except for his eyes, and she couldn't tell if he'd even heard her. She passed her hand in front of his eyes, but he didn't react to it. Something in the abandoned park was calling to her, and she didn't have time to wonder about what was wrong with him.

She turned to go and suddenly he clamped his hand around her wrist, his fingers squeezing tight.

"Don't go," he said, his voice deep and hoarse.

"Nothing here can injure me," she said.

"Don't be so certain," he said, his fingers tightening until they were nearly crushing her wrist. She looked more closely at him. His expression had not changed.

"What do you see?"

"More than he sees."

The hair lifted on the back of her neck. There was something speaking through the man.

"Do you know who I am?" she asked.

"Yes. Do you?"

The question took her back. "Do you know what I am?" she countered, pushing menace into her voice.

"A witch."

"Yes."

"A powerful witch. A foolish witch. A witch who did not study or hone her craft for sixteen years."

Anger flared through her, tinged with fear. She tried to rip her arm out of his grasp, but he was too strong, and whatever had him in its grip kept hold of her as well.

"And how long have you been a witch?" she demanded.

It was the most logical explanation. Witches could puppeteer other people. It made sense that it was a witch who was speaking through the driver.

"Not a witch."

"Then who are you?"

"Not flesh."

"Not flesh," she said, struggling to keep her voice calm. "Then you are spirit. Are you a ghost, a demon?"

"Not for you to know what I am," the voice said, growing even hoarser. "Only for you to heed my warning."

"I won't," she said. "There are people here, people I need to see."

"People. They once were."

"What does that mean?" Desdemona demanded, tired of the cryptic nature of the entity speaking to her.

The sky suddenly darkened and she could smell a storm coming. Her driver's head twisted slowly toward her, as though turning on the neck instead of with it. The eyes were still wildly flitting about, and when the mouth opened again he looked like a marionette whose lips were being pulled upward with invisible strings.

"Only death waits for you here."

"I'll take my chances."

Suddenly the driver collapsed, all his muscles going loose at the same time. His fingers slipped off her wrist and he half fell against her. Startled, she barely managed to keep them both from falling. Finally she managed to push him back down into the driver's seat. His head lolled forward onto his chest.

She took a step back and looked around. A wind had come up and was blowing trash around the abandoned parking lot. The dark skies seemed to grow darker, more ominous.

Maybe I should come back another day.

She clenched her fists, furious at the cowardly thought that had overtaken her. She stepped backward, determined more than ever to go.

The driver groaned and began to twitch. She paused, curiosity building in her. Finally he lifted his head.

"What happened?" he asked.

"You tell me," she said, warily, wondering if he had any idea what had just happened to him.

"I don't know. I had this terrible feeling that you shouldn't go into the park. I got out of the car to tell you and then—"

He stopped talking as he saw the bag that had fallen from his pocket. He reached down and snatched it up as if it were the most precious thing in the world. Hastily he stuffed it back into his pocket.

"What is that?" she asked.

"I—I didn't say anything to you, did I?" he asked, refusing to meet her eyes now.

"Maybe, why?"

"What—what did it—I say?" he asked, licking his lips.

"Not to go into the amusement park."

"Then you should listen!" he burst out so vehemently that he startled them both. He hunched his shoulders and buried his face in his hands. "Please, miss, I'm worried for you."

"Well, like I told . . . *you* . . . before, I can take care of myself," she said.

She turned and walked away.

"You were warned," she heard him say behind her. Then she heard a door slam and a moment later the squeal of rubber as he floored the gas pedal.

Each step that she took across the parking lot to the park entrance felt heavier than the one before. The air was growing hotter and muggier and she struggled to breathe as she felt the pressure building around her. A storm was coming. It might be safer to be somewhere else.

But she was Desdemona Castor and she feared neither man nor spirit nor nature. She squared her shoulders and continued on. The wind that had been blowing trash around grew stronger until it was pushing against her so hard that it became a struggle to continue walking forward.

She glanced up, wondering what kind of storm was coming. She could feel the electricity in the air and she told herself that was what was setting her teeth on edge and making the hair on the back of her neck stand up. She could practically feel the electrical charge build up on her fingertips as though racing back and forth among them. The wind began to lessen and her red hair began to fan out around her as though lifted by an invisible hand.

Everywhere there were signs of destruction, flood damage, rot, decay. Mother Nature had had her way with this place and it looked as if she was about to let loose again.

Desdemona bared her teeth. She had nothing to fear here. She lifted her hands into the air and pulled some of the electricity out of it and into her body, giving her a supercharge. She could feel the energy coursing through her body and she was sure that her eyes were actually glowing with it.

She reached the front gate and the turnstiles. Gates had been pulled across behind them, but one sagged open. She easily climbed over the turnstile and then walked through the open gate beyond.

The streets were littered with all manner of trash and debris from the decaying buildings, including a large silver ball that must have once been raised high.

The stench of decay and death hung in the ionized air, making her wrinkle her nose.

Buildings lined both sides of what had been the park's version of a main street. To her right was the Carriage House Mercantile, its two front doors flung open wide and half the glass panes missing. She could feel more than see something scurrying about in the darkness just inside.

A few bits of graffiti stained the weathered paint. *Gimme that ol'-time religion* had been scribbled on one of the walls. She felt a smile twisting her lips. Just which religion had the writer been referring to?

Next to that building was another one, trimmed in purple. THE ORPHEUM THEATER, the sign declared, though a couple of letters were missing. There was considerably more colorful graffiti on that building. A large round planter had been tagged with the words *NoLa Rising*. Optimism for a decimated city, or something darker?

She walked down the street, weaving around the piles of debris. She could still feel the ripples of power in the air, evidence that a great many people with abilities were somewhere nearby. That feeling, though, was practically overwhelmed by the spiking energy in the air around her as the storm continued to brew.

She saw a sign that had been spray-painted over. Instead of welcoming people to the park, it now proclaimed WELCOME 2 ZOMBIE-LAND KIDS.

She reached the end of the short street and hesitated, debating whether to turn right or left.

Don't go right.

She turned, swearing that the whispered voice had

come from behind her. There was nothing there, though. She hesitated, wondering what was telling her that and what its motivation was.

After a moment she turned and took a step toward the right.

No! If you go right, you will die!

The voice was louder, more insistent, but still disembodied.

She didn't know what to do. Once upon a time she would only have listened to a voice coming from inside her, but now that voice belonged to the hateful one, the other. She didn't want to trust the voice coming from without, though, because she didn't know whether it meant her good or ill.

Clenching her fists, she strode resolutely to the right, shutting out the sound of the voice wailing behind her.

Something hard and cold settled in her stomach, and her back tensed up so tightly that her spine actually hurt. She forced herself to keep walking.

To her left was a swing ride. A sudden gust of wind caused the swings to move, rattling their chains and bumping against one another. She spun toward the sound, nerves on edge.

There was no one there. Before she could relax, though, the entire ride began to move, to spin slowly as it must have done once long ago. The wind wasn't strong enough to do that. Something else was pushing against the canopy holding the swings.

You are not welcome here.

This voice was different. It came from in front of her and it made the blood in her veins feel as if it had turned to ice. She thought of what the entity had told her in the parking lot, how it had reminded her that she had gone sixteen years without study, without practice.

She had thought she had learned everything there was, knew all that she needed to know.

As laughter exploded in the air around her, she knew now that she was wrong.

3

Desdemona took a few steps ahead, forcing her eyes away from the spinning swings, and she came face-to-face with a carousel. Sudden images came to her crystal clear. Her other self was in an amusement area, after dark, and something happened at the carousel.

She hadn't wanted to know anything about the other self, Samantha, and the things that she had done with her life, because they were hateful to Desdemona. She was in mortal danger, she knew that, but what terrified her more was she didn't know why or how she was even aware. Clearly the knowledge was coming from that other self. Now as images of blood and dead witches rushed through her mind, she realized that might have been a tactical error. A potentially fatal one. If she made it out of here alive, she vowed to fix that.

Knowledge was power. That had been one of the first rules she'd learned, and she'd let her own disgust and mistrust get in the way of that. *Fool!* she cursed herself even as she spun around, sure that someone was creeping up behind her.

Only rot and decay met her eyes. The swing continued to turn, taunting her, challenging her. It felt as though it was warning her to go back.

She forced herself to keep going, to walk past the twisted merry-go-round. Beyond that was another decaying building and next to it a bathroom that someone had spray-painted to indicate which side was for female roaches and which side was for male roaches.

She wrinkled her nose. To her left were the remains of a Coca-Cola Cool Zone. She passed by it and realized she'd arrived in Mardi Gras land. A deranged clown peered over the top of one of the buildings, and another clown head lay smashed on the ground.

Suddenly the earth beneath her seemed to shake and she felt a rush of power swirl around her and then pass by as if driven before a violent wind. She gasped and went icy cold all over. She felt as though something were trying to pull her out of her own body, rip out her very essence, and she lifted up her hands in a vain effort to ward off whatever it was.

She was literally being torn apart and she could feel the energy, the power, her very abilities traveling through her body, down her arms until shafts of golden light were shooting from her fingertips.

Something was trying to rob her of her power. She screamed in defiance and struggled to force the muscles in her arms to respond to her. They had gone rigid, pulsing with the energy that was flowing through them and out of them. It was unlike anything she'd ever known. She had fleeting images of her other self being used, drained like a battery, but this was different. The force behind this wasn't just taking her energy. It was taking her ability to wield magic at all, ripping that part of herself away from her.

Around her she heard other screams, rising in a chorus from a hundred unseen voices. The giant clown head began to roll across the ground, the mouth gaping open as though intent on swallowing anything in its path. It was heading straight for her, and unless she could move it would ram her. Given how heavy it looked, she worried that it might crush her.

Images flashed through her mind of what going through life without the ability to manipulate the energy around her would be like. A life without magic was unthinkable, but as pain began to shoot through her chest she realized that would never happen, because if she lost the magic here and now, her body would be too damaged to survive it.

Still, her arms were flung out straight before her and there was nothing she could do to stem the tide of magic flowing out of her. Behind her the screaming grew more intense and she twisted her head just enough to see an army of people emerging, staggering, from the various buildings. They were moving stiff-legged, arms similarly thrown out in front of them, and their screams gradually turned to hideous moaning sounds.

Zombies, that's what they resembled, and she realized that she did, too. They staggered toward her, faces contorted in pain, eyes rolled back in their heads. They were young and old, some in tatters, some in regular clothes. They had to be the teen runaways and the homeless people Claudia had told her lived here. They were being stripped of their magic just as she was.

She had to stop it. She had to find a way to move her arms, redirect the energy flowing from her fingers back into her own body, set up a feedback loop. But how could she do that when she couldn't unlock her muscles?

Break your arms.

The voice came from inside and she knew it was that other self whispering to her. She was beginning to panic. "How, when I can't move them?" she shouted.

Look down.

She looked down at the concrete beneath her feet. Her legs were beginning to stiffen and she was starting to feel a compulsion to walk forward, just as the others were doing. The clown was nearly upon her.

Desdemona threw herself forward onto the ground as hard as she could. The bones in her arms broke on impact and tore the muscles. The pain was blinding, but her arms collapsed beneath her and she fell on top of them on the ground. Her arms were still just as useless, but now they were pinned beneath her body and she contorted her chest so that her fingertips were touching her own stomach.

She felt a zap of electricity, as though she was being electrocuted, and then she could feel the energy flow out of her and right back in. She had trapped it.

Something slammed into her side and she realized it had to be the giant clown head. It pushed against her, shoving her slightly across the ground.

It served as a barrier, though, and the others parted around it, then streamed past her on either side, headed for wherever it was their magic was being pulled to. It was going to kill them. She could see the faces as they passed by. Skin was shriveling, like dead, dried fruit, and clinging to the skulls beneath. Skin on the out-stretched arms was bleaching white and black; oozing gashes were appearing like lesions all over. The loud moans were becoming more hollow, empty sounding.

She looked up at one woman and saw that her eye sockets had shrunken and she looked like a walking skeleton.

Desdemona had used, relied on magic her entire life. Until this moment, though, she'd never realized how integral a part it was of the body and spirit of someone with the power. She was seeing the results of the loss of that power right before her eyes.

She herself was weak and shaking, nauseated from the pain, and after a moment she realized there was something terribly wrong. Her injuries hadn't started to heal. With injuries this extensive the healing part was automatic, requiring no thought on her part.

Maybe she was too drained of energy. She felt the concrete where it touched her cheek, and she reached down past it to the earth below and pulled some of its energy into her. She could feel the surge and she breathed a sigh of relief.

And moments later realized that what was wrong with her had nothing to do with energy levels. Her body still wasn't healing. She looked at the people around her, who were decaying as their magic was stripped from them, and realized she'd lost too many of her own gifts, her own magic, to be able to heal anymore.

Blind panic filled her and she began to thrash about

until she realized that she was in jeopardy of letting go of more of her power. Then she forced herself to lie still as she tried to figure out what to do.

Deep inside she could feel the other one stirring. She was probably happy. She had hated the magic, hated the power. She would have given anything to rid herself of it. But Desdemona couldn't, wouldn't live without it.

The energy flowing from her own fingertips into her body gave her a sudden idea. A man was passing right behind her. She stretched out and tripped him. He fell next to her and she scooted her body next to his, careful not to let her trapped hands lose contact with her abdomen. He was flailing on the ground, but his leg muscles had seized up like his arms and he didn't have the flexibility required to stand. She got as close as she could and then she contorted her leg and pressed it against the fingertips of his left hand.

She felt the magic flowing into her, foreign, different from her own, and at first she jerked away, freaked out by the sensation.

It's the only way, she told herself. She forced her leg back into contact with his hand and flinched as his magic poured into her. She couldn't help wondering if this was what a transfusion felt like, only on a far more intense scale. She doubted the blood felt so foreign to the recipient as his magic did to her, though.

Her body began to spasm and she wondered if it was rejecting the foreign magic. Someone was taking it from everyone, though, and he must have found a way around this problem. She gritted her teeth and tried to calm her mind, center her energies.

Liquid fire felt as if it were pouring through her veins, and the guy on the ground started moving less and less. He was dying. Better his magic went to her than to whoever was trying to bleed them all dry.

Let go before he dies.

It was that inner voice. Desdemona refused to listen.

The man was just taking his last breath and suddenly her leg jerked away from his body. She hadn't done that. She wondered if she was losing more control to whoever was sucking people's magic. It couldn't be that the other self was exerting that much influence, could it?

She didn't have time to figure it out. The man was dead. She took a deep breath, reached out, and tripped a woman.

"Help me," the woman groaned, her words barely intelligible, as she fell on top of Desdemona.

"I can barely help myself," Desdemona hissed as she tried to remain still and let the woman's magic, her very essence, pour into her. The fire coursing through Desdemona's veins intensified and she felt as if her eyes were burning from the inside out.

Again, when the woman was breathing her last, the inner voice urged, *Let go.*

Desdemona broke the contact, not sure if she had been the one to do it. The pain was all she could feel. The zombie people had nearly passed her. She could see them walking, some half dragging their bodies forward to whatever fate awaited them.

One final set of feet began to shuffle by her, and she tripped what turned out to be a young girl. The girl rolled over on her side, her legs and arms useless. The girl's eyes pleaded with Desdemona.

There was nothing she could do to save her. All she could do was ensure that no more of the girl's power, her essence, went to the one who was trying to kill her.

Again, Desdemona let go a moment before the girl died.

Her body had stopped spasming at some point during the last transfer, and now as she lay still she could feel herself starting to heal. She was relieved but then a moment later wondered what would happen when her arms could push up off the ground and move of their own accord again, sending her power to the unknown witch who was trying to take it.

She'd just have to break her arms again, she realized.

She turned her head and saw the army of the walking dead. They were beginning to drop like flies, and she could feel death all around her in the air. The last few teetered on their feet and then collapsed.

And a moment later, whatever was trying to pull energy from her stopped.

Desdemona blinked in surprise, then slowly, cautiously sat up, hands still pressed to her stomach. Her body was reacting strongly to the magic that she had pulled into herself, but it felt as though it was sorting itself out, merging the new with the old.

She'd never known it was possible to take a person's power from him. Energy, yes, power, no.

She got to her feet, hesitant to move her hands. After a few more seconds she finally moved one hand. It was healed enough to be more functional and there was no power pouring out of her fingertips, no rigidity of the muscles trying to force the arm straight.

It must be truly over. Whoever it was must have sensed when the last of the magic flowed to him and stopped pulling. He couldn't sense Desdemona because she had interrupted the flow of her power outward.

Thanks to the help of the other self that she hated.

She walked slowly forward, approaching the first few of the other bodies, the ones that had collapsed on their own. They were dead, faces almost unrecognizable as human, lesions covering their arms and necks. She didn't touch them.

This was a type of magic that was strange and new to her, and despite everything she had seen and done, it even sickened her. Outright killing these people would have been kinder than what they experienced, but that wouldn't have accomplished the goals of the one who had done that to them.

How powerful must a witch be in order to suck the life force from so many at once? She kept walking by the bodies, marveling at the various states of decay. With weakened power she hadn't even been able to heal herself. The relationship between the life essence and the ability of the person who had power was clearer to her than it had ever been before.

Looking at the decayed flesh, she also couldn't help wondering if something like this had been what had inspired stories of zombies in the beginning. The way they had walked, the decaying of their flesh, the moaning sounds they had made all screamed *classic horror movie* to her. All that was missing was a desire to eat brains. She shuddered just thinking about it.

"Frickin' New Orleans," she muttered.

She heard something and she froze, wondering if the witch had come to survey his or her handiwork. It could even be an entire coven of witches; that would make more sense than one witch wielding all this power.

Desdemona looked around, expecting an attack from any quarter. None came.

The sound came again, barely a whisper.

She turned and surveyed the dead at her feet, wondering if it had come from one of them. Finally she spotted a teen boy with dark, curly hair. His body seemed to be in less disrepair than the others. As she watched she caught the barest movement of his chest.

She walked over and carefully knelt down beside him, making sure not to touch him in case this was some sort of trap.

His eyes were open and he looked up at her, in pain that was so real, it actually made her hunch her own shoulders in an effort to ward it off.

"What happened here?" she asked.

"She took it, the magic," he whispered.

He was dying; she could feel it. She also knew there was nothing she could do for him even if she had wanted to.

"Who took it? How did she do it?" Desdemona asked.

"I don't know how, but I saw her the other day, talking with some of the others, pretending to be one of us, but I knew she wasn't. She was . . . evil."

He shuddered as he tried to breathe.

"Then what happened?"

"She left, but I was afraid. I wanted to go home, but I couldn't. I tried to warn the others that she was the one keeping us here. Some of us wanted to go, tried, but couldn't."

"And then?" she urged as he paused.

"She came for us. She did this."

"Who is she? Do you know her name, what she looks like?"

"She had black hair, like the night, like death."

The boy was almost gone and she didn't have time to lose. She reached inside his mind, looking for an image of the woman he was referencing. Finally she saw a vague outline, a woman with long hair. She pushed harder, trying to make the face come clear.

A wave of energy slammed into her so hard that it knocked her off her feet and threw her twenty feet away. She hit the cement with a bone-crunching jolt and felt blood vessels bursting all throughout her body. A rib splintered and drove itself into her lung.

She lay still for a moment, unsure if the death rattle she heard was coming from her or the boy. She closed her eyes and focused on rapidly healing herself. She pulled in energy from the ground, the air, and the last gasp left to the boy.

She screamed in anguish as everything knit back together. When it was done she staggered to her feet and over to the boy's body. Whoever the woman with the black hair was, she was powerful, so powerful that she had been able to leave booby traps for anyone trying to access an image of her in the minds of those who had seen her. It was a whole new level of magic, and Desdemona knew that she was going to have to find a way to make up for wasted years when she should have been learning to do so much more.

She straightened and headed as fast as she could toward the exit to the theme park. She didn't look back. The entity in the parking lot had been right. There was only death here.

Almost an hour later she arrived back at the house where she had been staying. She staggered inside and made it to the bedroom, where Freaky was curled up, waiting for her. The black panther yawned and stretched and let her know in his own way that she had been gone far too long.

She scratched him absently behind the ears, and the panther purred and leaned into her hand, clearly enjoying the attention. His current incarnation was much more fearsome than his original. When she was little she had made the pure energy creature into the form of a tiny black kitten, her only friend. She wished that as a child she'd found a way to keep her mom from taking Freaky away from her when she found out about him.

She squeezed her eyes shut. The battle at the amusement park had left her shaken, uncertain, and she hated that feeling of powerlessness. It was her entire childhood in a single emotion.

Great supernatural powers, and still totally helpless. It was a nightmare, the same one that had plagued so many of her tortured nights. She sat down on the bed and pulled her knees up under her chin.

She had thought with all of her coven dead, there'd be no one anymore who could terrorize her. She'd been wrong and the hatred she felt for the woman with the black hair just intensified as she turned to stare at the picture of the cross and the bloody words taunting her. She was sure it was that woman who had left the picture for her. Only someone with that kind of power could have played her as a pawn for months.

She was no one's pawn. Now she knew, though, that she was vulnerable, and she had to do something about that, and fast.

It was strange; she was a woman grown but her clear memories ended when she was twelve. Growing up, being an adult, all of those things she only caught glimpses of, like shadows in the pieces of a broken mirror.

She was also beginning to understand that her inability to control her own emotions and her lack of exposure to logic were hindrances. She couldn't afford them. She was like a child trapped in a woman's body, and there was only one person who could help her.

The hated other self.

She could feel that one stirring inside her even now, trying to break free, trying to influence Desdemona. It wouldn't work. She was the one in control now, but that didn't mean that she couldn't use and manipulate the other one to help her find the witch she needed to kill.

Come to me.

Desdemona closed her eyes, breathed in deeply, and then exhaled. In her mind she was seated on the floor of the basement that had belonged to her high priestess. The place where the massacre had happened. It was a terrible place, even she couldn't help feeling that, and given her memories of what had happened there, she wished she were somewhere else, anywhere else.

"But this is where it all happened," a soft voice said.

Desdemona looked up and saw Samantha standing at the bottom of the stairs.

4

"I hate you," Desdemona said, an intensity of raw, overwhelming emotion flooding her.

"I fear you," Samantha replied simply, quietly. The apparition was wearing a white dress and was somewhat transparent but still recognizable for who she was and what she represented. She stepped forward and then slowly sat down on the floor across from Desdemona, mimicking her posture.

"Fear is for the weak."

"It's not weakness to feel fear, it's weakness to let it keep you from acting," Samantha countered.

"And what is hatred but ignorance?" Desdemona snarled.

"It is that, and also lack of mercy and forgiveness and compassion," Samantha acknowledged.

Desdemona felt as though somehow she was losing, and that gave her a panicky feeling. How could this be? She was the strong one, the powerful one.

"What do you want from me?" Desdemona demanded, angry, resentful, and more than a little defensive. The other woman was so calm, maddeningly so. Desdemona remembered a period of time in her own life when she'd been that way. She'd learned to be still, almost dead inside, as a defense mechanism to avoid punishment, judgment from her mother and the others. She'd learned that in a roomful of passionate people, stillness could be the most intimidating thing in the world.

Then had come that terrible night and she had lost that stillness. Hate and anger had taken over and she had understood in a flash the kind of power they could give her. They had helped her overcome her own crippling fear when those around her were cowering on the floor sobbing. They had allowed her to do the most wondrous magic she'd ever dreamed of. They'd given her power.

And then, so soon after, she had lost herself forever to this specter who sat across from her. What was worse, this specter had the calm she had lost. Desdemona bared her teeth at her other self, hating her with all she had in her.

"I want to understand you, to not be afraid of you anymore," Samantha said. "And I want to be able to forgive you, me, us."

"I don't need your forgiveness," Desdemona hissed.

"Maybe you don't need it, but I do," Samantha said.

There was something so sincere about her that it made Desdemona stop and think. "You solve crimes for a living," she said at last.

"Yes."

"Why?"

"To help the world make sense, to bring closure to people who have had terrible experiences."

"Like us."

Samantha nodded.

Desdemona waved her hand and willed the picture of the stolen necklace into being. She showed it to Samantha. "Do you remember getting this picture, finding it buried in the grave meant for . . . us . . . in Salem?"

"It's the last thing I remember clearly," Samantha said.

Desdemona nodded. "I need to find the witch who left that picture."

"Then you're going to need me."

"That's what I'm afraid of."

"I thought you viewed fear as weakness," Samantha said, raising an eyebrow.

Desdemona had never hated her so much as she did in that moment. She forced herself to take a deep breath. "I do. That's why I need to get over it. At the abandoned amusement park today, a witch killed a lot of people with powers. She literally stripped them of their magic, pulled it out of them. It killed them. Worse, it accelerated the decomposition. It was only the magic she was pulling, not energy."

Samantha pursed her lips. "That would imply that the life force, the very essence of a person with power, is tied to that power."

"That's what it seemed like."

"So what she was really taking was a piece of their soul almost, and without it they could not survive."

Desdemona blinked. "You think magic is tied to a person's soul?"

Samantha shrugged. "It's the only thing that explains what you witnessed."

"I'm not sure if I believe in that."

Samantha actually chuckled. "Given everything you've seen, that seems . . . ironic. Tell me what you can about the witch we're hunting."

"*I'm* hunting," Desdemona corrected. "I suspect it was the same one as today. It takes a lot of power to pull off the things she's been doing."

"In San Francisco I saw her able to puppeteer other witches just like marionettes," Samantha said. "She is indeed very strong and completely without conscience."

"That's how you think of me," Desdemona realized.

Samantha nodded.

"Why?"

"What happened when we were twelve? What happened the day the demon killed the entire coven?" Samantha asked.

"You mean you don't know?"

Samantha shook her head.

"Are you sure you don't know what happened that day?" Desdemona pressed.

"I only get glimpses of it, images in my nightmares. I have no idea what really happened; why?"

Desdemona dropped her eyes to the floor beneath them. "Neither do I," she whispered.

"What! How is that possible?" Samantha demanded, shaken out of her calm.

Desdemona lifted her head again. "I, too, only get glimpses, brief images that I can't really put together."

There was a long silence, which Samantha finally

broke. "You mean neither of us truly knows what happened on the most pivotal day of our lives?"

"I guess not."

It seemed incredible. Desdemona had always assumed that had been the day she'd lost control, really lost it, and Samantha had been born. Maybe that wasn't true, though. It didn't matter. She was the one in charge now.

Freaky growled nearby, snapping Desdemona back into the real world and out of her own mind. She glanced around, disoriented, trying to figure out what had set off the panther.

Then she could sense it, a disruption in the flow of energy around her that told her there was another nearby who had power.

She launched herself to a standing position and ran down the stairs. The sensation was fading. Whoever was nearby was leaving. She burst out the front door and looked around. At the rate the energy ripple was fading, the person was trying to get away quickly.

She could give chase, but why wear herself down like that? Besides, the person might be trying to lead her into a trap. She headed back inside and grabbed a bag of supplies she had acquired before arriving in the city. She removed a white candle, a yellow candle, and a red candle and placed them on the kitchen table, the yellow candle next to the white and the red a distance away.

"I am the white candle. I am fixed. I seek truth, movement. The red candle is the one with power, who was here, who is now running away. You will come to me."

She waved her hands and all three candles lit, flames

stretching for the sky. She snapped her fingers and the red candle began to slide across the table toward the white one. It was moving fast. The runner was not far away.

Desdemona turned and went back to the front door. Energy rippled in the air. She waited a moment and then opened the door to see a frightened and confused-looking child racing up the steps. She stood back and let the girl run inside.

Once she was in, her running ceased and over her shoulder Desdemona could see the three candles on the table go out. Spell accomplished.

"Who are you? How did you do that?" the girl, who looked about fourteen, demanded.

"I think you already know how, at least, in the most general sense," Desdemona said. "As for the rest, I'll be asking the questions. Who are you?"

"Nala," the girl said sullenly, shoving her hands into the pockets of an overly large man's trench coat. Underneath, her clothes were a bit ragged, but the coat was fairly new.

"Are you a witch, Nala?"

"No! I'm not, okay! I wish everyone would stop asking me if I'm a witch!"

"What are you, then?"

"I'm nothing, nobody, just a street kid."

"With powers," Desdemona noted.

Nala hunched her shoulders. "I don't even really know how to use them. There's some stuff, but it's like it just sort of happens. Like an accident or something."

"With powers like that, there's no reason you have to live on the streets."

"I told you, I don't understand them. I don't know how they work. The only thing I can do well is beg for food and sometimes money to buy food."

"You could use those powers of persuasion to get bigger things."

"Yeah, well, if it's so easy, let's see you do it," Nala said.

"Do jumping jacks. Don't stop until I tell you," Desdemona said, letting her words, her intention wash over Nala.

The girl gasped and then began to do the jumping jacks.

"No fair!" Nala said.

"Life isn't fair."

"I want to stop."

"Oh, I think you'll keep going until I'm done with you. Tell me, Nala, where are you from?"

"Here."

"A native. How refreshing. Where are your parents?"

"Dead. They were killed in Katrina, okay?"

"And I'm guessing no other family, hence the reason you're on the street," Desdemona mused. "Which one of your parents had powers?"

"I don't know. Neither. They never talked about it if they did."

"I'm sure you've noticed a lot of people with power have been arriving in the city recently."

"Of course I have," Nala said, starting to pant a little. "Can I stop?"

"Not yet. Be grateful. I could always make you do them faster," Desdemona said.

"You're a terrible person!"

"Back to the matter at hand. Why were you here?"

"I was looking for you, but then when I got close . . . I got scared. Something is wrong with you. I could feel it."

Desdemona's temper flared. "There's nothing wrong with me!" she hissed. "Why were you looking for me?"

"I thought you might be able to tell me . . . ," Nala started, then took a few gasping breaths as she continued her jumping jacks. "What happened to my friends."

"What friends?"

"At the theme park."

"Stop."

Nala collapsed on the floor, groaning and clutching her side.

"You had friends at the theme park?"

"Yeah, some people in the same boat as me. Some of us had been living there awhile. I went out to get food. I'm the best at it. When I got back there—"

Nala bit her lip and turned away, but not before Desdemona saw the tears forming in the girl's eyes. "Something killed them all."

"And what makes you think I can tell you anything about that?" she asked.

"The taximan said so."

Desdemona yanked Nala to her feet and stared into her eyes. "The taximan?"

"Yeah, big dude with dreadlocks, weird, low voice. He said you would know what happened. He said if I found you that you could tell me the truth. He also said I might not want to find you. Boy, was he right!"

Desdemona dropped Nala back onto the floor. "And he told you how to find me?"

"Yes, described the house real good, even gave me a ride and dropped me off a few blocks away."

"And just how did he know that?" Desdemona mused. She'd gotten into his taxi downtown and had never told him her name or where she was living. He couldn't have followed her home; she would have sensed something.

"I don't know and I don't care. I didn't ask. He didn't say. Please, can you tell me what happened at that place, though?"

"Were there any of the others missing, out hunting for food, perhaps?"

"No, just me."

The tears were flowing freely down the girl's cheeks now.

"A witch ripped their power from them. When she did, it killed them."

The girl sobbed. "Why? Why would anyone do such a thing?"

"Isn't it obvious?" Desdemona asked, blinking down at her. "To get more power."

"I hate the power! I hate what it does to people!" Nala shouted.

"Only some," Desdemona mused.

"You're a witch."

"Yes."

"Are you the one who killed them?"

"No, but I've been hunting for the one who did. Maybe you've seen her somewhere around town? Long black hair. One of the younger boys at the theme park told me before he died that she'd come around before. He said her hair was black as the night."

Nala shook her head. "No, I haven't seen her. But I'm gone a lot during the day, so if she came then . . ."

"So now I have two mysteries to solve. The identity of this woman and just how it was that the taximan knew where to find me."

"Don't hurt him. He seemed creepy, but I think he's basically an okay guy. He didn't charge me anything for giving me a ride way out here."

Desdemona looked at the girl. A street kid like her, native to the city, would make an excellent spy. "It's very important that I find the witch who killed your friends," she said.

"Did she kill your friends, too?" Nala asked.

"In a manner of speaking. I know that she's here, but I have been unable to locate her."

"So you want my help finding her?"

"Yes. I'd be willing to pay you for it."

Nala shook her head. "I just want to make sure she gets what's coming to her. She killed my friends. A bunch of homeless people—cops won't try too hard to solve that one."

"I can guarantee you that when I find her, she will get everything that's coming to her," Desdemona said through gritted teeth.

"Count me in." Nala wiped a hand across her nose. "Since we're going to be working together, could I . . . um . . . use your bathroom?"

"Down the hall to the right."

The girl took off and Desdemona went into the kitchen. She removed the red candle in her bag and substituted it for an orange one to symbolize the taxi driver.

"I am fixed. The driver is not. He must come to me."

She waved her hand, and the candles lit up. She snapped her fingers.

Nothing happened.

A moment later the flames snuffed themselves out and she cursed under her breath. There was some form of magic protecting the driver, even though he had no power of his own. Since she couldn't compel him to come to her, she would have to go to him.

A couple of minutes later Nala was back and her face and hands were scrubbed clean. The girl was rail thin, her cheeks pinched.

"Did the driver give you anything of his, a card by any chance?" Desdemona asked.

The girl nodded, reached into her pocket, and pulled it out. She handed it to Desdemona, who read it over.

"I've got to leave for a little while. Help yourself to some food in the refrigerator, but be gone by the time I get back."

"Okay."

"And don't go upstairs. Trust me, you would not like what you'd find up there," she said, thinking about Freaky.

Nala nodded. If the girl listened, great. If not and she violated his space, Freaky would have a new chew toy.

Desdemona left the house and decided to take her car. She didn't know how far she would be going. She didn't dare try to call the number on the card; the driver was probably already leery of her. Her best bet was to surprise him.

She drew an arrow on the back of the card with a pen from her glove compartment. Then she placed the card on her dashboard. With her hand on it she said, "Take me to the man who gave the child this card. Let the arrow point the way."

Energy flowed out of her and into the card, which began to vibrate. A moment later, it spun slowly to the east. Samantha started the car and headed out. The card turned out to be trickier to follow than she would have liked. It was pointing the literal direction as the crow would fly to the man she sought, but she was constrained to drive on the existing streets.

At one point she worried that the driver might still be working for the day, on the move, but the card consistently seemed to point to the east. After several miles and a hundred course corrections, she finally pulled onto a residential street. The card held true, the arrow pointing straight down the street.

She drove slowly, sensing that she was close, and the arrow started to angle toward the right. She slowed even further. At last the card swiveled and pointed directly at a house as she was passing it. She pulled over to the curb, parked, and got out of the car.

Martin had been the name on the front of the card. This must be his house and he should be home. She walked slowly up the drive, reaching out with her senses. She couldn't feel anyone of power anywhere nearby. She extended her reach, trying to sense the people in their houses, see how many were actually home. It seemed most were vacant for the moment, but there was definitely one person present in Martin's house.

She walked up onto the porch. She noticed some symbols carved into the door. They were unfamiliar to her, but she had a suspicion they were used to ward off some sort of evil spirit. She couldn't be sure, but it made logical sense.

Superstition ran deep in this area, and given what she'd seen happen to Martin earlier, he had every reason to believe.

She reached out and rang the doorbell. She could hear footsteps inside and a moment later the door opened wide. Martin was standing there, a smile on his face, which instantly changed to one of terror.

"Get away from me, witch!" he screamed as he leaped back and tried to slam the door.

She shoved the door, hard enough to send him flying backward. He landed on the floor and began to scrabble away from her. She closed the door behind her and leaned down.

"Hello, Martin. It's about time you and I had a little chat. You've got a lot of questions to answer. Start with how you knew where I lived and why you sent the girl there."

"Go, please, go. You have to get out of here," Martin begged, fear contorting his features.

"I don't think so. Tell me what I want to know," she threatened, a fireball forming on her fingertips without her even thinking about it.

"You don't understand. You must leave this place, quickly. I can't be here. You can't be here."

"Why, expecting company?" she asked. "How did you know something bad was going to happen at the amusement park? Are you in league with that witch?"

"Please, go. Run!"

"Answer me!" she screamed.

His eyes flew open wide and she realized it wasn't her that he was afraid of. "No, he's coming. I can't stop it. He's coming."

"Who is coming?"

She heard a soft thud and looked down. The little red bag had fallen from his pocket and onto the floor.

He saw it, too, and he began to scream.

"What is it?" Desdemona shouted.

"You don't understand. He's coming. He's coming. He's—"

"Here," a deep, gravelly voice said from out of Martin's body.

5

Desdemona stared warily. It was the same voice that had spoken to her, warned her in the parking lot of the theme park.

"Who are you?" she demanded.

"One who knows more than you do, witch."

"Earlier today you warned me not to go into the theme park. Did you know what would happen? Did you know that the other witch was going to kill all those people by stripping them of their powers?"

"Yes."

"Are you working with her or for her?"

"No."

"Are you opposing her?"

There was a deep laugh. "No."

"Do you know who she is, where she is now?"

"These things are not for you to know," the voice told her, growing even deeper and raspier.

"I need to find her. I need to kill her."

"Someone needs to, but that is not for you to do. She will only kill you. You are weak."

Desdemona raised her chin defiantly. "I was strong enough to survive her attack today. That's something you didn't see."

"True, but I do not think it was you who saved yourself. There were others, yes, who gave their lives, and one who showed you the way."

He was talking about Samantha. It was all Desdemona could do not to fling herself at him and rip him to pieces. But it was clear that Martin was not the one speaking. The entity speaking through him would be unharmed by her attack on the driver.

Her eyes drifted to the red packet that had fallen out of Martin's pocket for the second time in one day.

Pick it up, she heard a voice whisper inside.

She ignored it. "What are you, a spirit of some sort?"

It laughed and the sound was raw, sinister. It was enough to unnerve even her.

"One could call me an eternal companion."

"You're attached to Martin, correct?"

"True."

Pick up the bag! the voice inside shouted.

Still, she ignored it. "Why did you warn me today?" she asked.

"There was no need for you to die there, not a pretty young witch like you, bursting with power, potential."

She felt something brush the back of her neck. She spun around, but there was nothing there. She turned back to stare at Martin, or rather, the creature talking through him. "Why not warn the others?"

"Not important."

Something touched her cheek and she reached up to slap whatever it was, but there was nothing there.

The bag! her inner voice was screaming.

"But you, there are so many better uses for you," the voice said, more gravelly than before.

And she felt a shadow falling across her, even though she couldn't see anything.

Bag!

She dropped to the floor and snatched up the bag and she heard a screaming sound in her ear and felt hot breath across the back of her neck.

"You shouldn't have done that, witch!" the entity hissed, anger in its voice.

It had been trying to possess her. That's what the inner voice had been warning her about. She stood slowly, the bag in her right hand, her eyes fixed on Martin's face.

"There're enough of us in here already without adding another," she said.

The spirit chuckled. "You are both correct and incorrect."

She didn't bother asking it for clarification. While she had its attention, she decided to jump right to the question that mattered most. "Tell me where to find the witch."

"I told you, that's not for you to know."

"But I wish to know. I need to know. She will pay for what she has done to me."

"Why should I tell you?" the thing asked.

"Because, if you don't, I'll kill your host. Then you'll be stuck."

She was bluffing. She didn't know if it was true or if he would just be able to find another body, another person to torment and possess. Something told her, though, that if it was that easy he would already have abandoned Martin.

He made a long hissing noise, sounding just like a snake.

"You wouldn't dare," it said at last.

"Don't try me," Desdemona said. "I'd kill for far less."

The entity stared at her, long and hard. She realized for the first time that it didn't blink at all. It was unnerving. That and the way Martin's jaw hung somewhat slack and looked as if it were being pulled on strings when the thing spoke made it one of the more disturbing things she'd ever witnessed.

"Why do you want to find her?" it asked at last.

"You seem to know so much, why do you even need to ask?"

"Sometimes it's best to hear and best to tell. Why?"

"Because she's called me out. For months she's been using me, manipulating me, and she's stolen something from me. I want it back."

He didn't need to know that she intended to destroy the cross necklace as soon as it was back in her possession.

The thing swayed Martin's head slowly from side to side, making the snake impression that much stronger. She forced herself to stay still and stand her ground without flinching. After all, she'd faced far worse than whatever it was. If it didn't answer her she could always just walk out that door and leave Martin to his puppet master.

"If you wish to find her, you may do so at midnight at the tomb of Marie Laveau, where she will be paying her respects."

She was actually slightly surprised that it told her. The threat to kill Martin must have worked. Still, it was a spirit and it might say anything just to get her to back down. It wouldn't be the first time a spirit had lied to her. "How do I know you're not lying?"

"All spirits lie. But I have nothing to gain and I have not lied to you yet."

That was true, she had to admit. She stood, debating what to do next. She knew nothing of exorcism rituals. Everything her coven had ever done had been about inviting spirits in, not sending them away.

Something bumped her hand, nearly causing her to drop the sachet. She cursed and closed her fist tighter about it and then hugged it to her chest.

"Both times this fell from Martin's pocket, you had something to do with that, didn't you?" she accused.

"Martin is so much more careful than he used to be. It's forced me to get . . . creative, but no . . . I cannot touch it. However, there are other entities that can."

Desdemona called a fireball to her free hand and glanced hastily around, trying to see from which direction danger would next come.

The entity just cackled more. "Little witch girl thinks she's a match for anyone. She is sadly mistaken."

Rage rocketed through her and she could feel herself ready to explode.

Calm down! the voice inside her demanded.

"No!" she screamed as she spun in a circle, looking for something she could attack. She couldn't see anything and she finally turned back to see Martin's body, the jaws flapping as the entity continued to laugh through him. She could stop that laughter once and for all.

She raised her hand, preparing to launch the fireball at his head.

No! What it wants! The voice was urgent, pleading.

What it wants. The entity was trying to make her angry enough to destroy Martin. But why?

The answer came to her in a flash. It was tied to Martin just as Martin was tied to it. At least, it was for so long as Martin was alive. If Martin were to die, though, the spirit would be free. Who knew what kind of havoc it could cause then, who it could possess? Maybe even her, she realized with a wave of nausea. She had to force it out, stop listening to it before it goaded her into doing something foolish.

She glanced down at the small red bag in her hand and knew in a moment what she had to do. She jumped forward, took her hand, and slammed the sachet into Martin's chest, careful to also keep contact with it herself.

There was one hideous scream that was choked off as suddenly as it had begun. Martin slumped back on the floor. She sat, panting, continuing to hold the bag against him while keeping a firm grip on it herself, mindful of what the entity had said about other things that could move the bag and help him return.

After what seemed a lifetime Martin groaned and his eyes flickered open. He stared up at her, uncomprehendingly, for a moment. Then he reached up and put a hand over hers, his fingers brushing against the fabric of the bag.

"What happened?" he asked.

"How about first you tell me what the thing is and how it possesses you?"

Martin nodded slightly and then closed his eyes. "Just give me a moment."

She ground her teeth in frustration. She wanted answers now. The creature had told her where the witch she was hunting would be at midnight. She needed to get all the information she could before she confronted her.

She still wasn't sure why the entity had tried to stop her from going into the theme park, had actually bothered to try to save her life. Maybe it had sensed an opportunity to change hosts and get an upgrade and hadn't wanted her to run off and get herself killed before it could make the exchange.

Maybe it was lying about where the witch would be tonight. Or lying about not being in league with her.

All of it was just conjecture until she got some more answers, and she was about ready to shake Martin until he talked. She started to move her hands and froze as she realized she'd almost let go of the little red bag.

Sweat began to bead on her forehead. Had one of the other creatures planted that thought in her mind for just that reason?

"Martin, I need answers," she said through gritted teeth.

He sighed heavily and then sat up. He started to take the bag from her and she clung on to it fiercely.

"It's okay. He can only harm you if he is present, and he can only be present if he is possessing me," Martin said.

"Not good enough," she answered.

He nodded as though he had expected such an answer. "Tell you what. I have more of these bags throughout the house. If you help me stand we can go together to the kitchen and I can give you one of your own. Is that a deal?"

Desdemona nodded. Together they stood up, both holding on to the little red bag. Then they walked slowly into the kitchen. From a drawer nearest the door he removed an identical-looking sachet and handed it to her.

She shook her head. "How do I know it's the same, that it works, too?"

"Okay, you can have this one, then," he said, letting go of the one they had both been holding.

She thought about putting it in her pocket and then had a vision of the two times she had seen it falling out of Martin's. She turned around and stuffed it down her shirt and into her bra. There was no way she wouldn't notice movement there.

She turned back around and he waved her to a seat at the kitchen table. "After everything that's happened today, you certainly deserve some answers," he said as he sat heavily, groaning like a man twice his age.

"Does this all have to do with voodoo?" Desdemona asked, pointing to the bag he was clutching in his fist.

"No, with hoodoo."

"Aren't they the same thing?" she asked, blinking.

"While there are some similarities, they are not the same. While voodoo is a religion, hoodoo is folk magic mixed together with Catholicism that involves heavy reliance on superstition and spiritualism."

"Okay. So this is hoodoo."

"Yes."

"And what is that thing, a spirit, demon, ghost?"

"It is . . . complicated. It is all of these and none of these at the same time. It is the result of a curse being placed upon me when I was but a child."

"Why?"

"A family feud gone very wrong that I ended up the sole recipient of."

"That's messed up."

"Something tells me you know a thing or two about messed-up family dynamics."

"What gave you that idea?" she asked coolly.

"Not what, who, as in *it*."

"Ah. It does seem to know quite a lot about just about everything."

"Yeah. You have to be careful, though. It lies."

"It wasn't lying earlier when it tried to save my life."

He shrugged. "Maybe it likes you. I don't know."

"I got the distinct impression that it could jump from one person to another."

"It's attached to me. It can only possess a person it's in the same room with, and it can only be in the same room with anyone if it's possessing me."

"And these little bags keep that from happening."

"Yeah, filled with lots of good stuff."

"It smells like sage," she noted.

"Among other things. Sage is often used in purification rituals, keeps out the evil spirits, that sort of thing."

"Why did you tell Nala where to find me?"

He paused. "Nala? Is that the homeless girl I saw outside the amusement park when I went back to see if you were there?"

"Yes."

He shook his head. "I didn't. I started to talk to her and the next thing I knew I was all the way across town and she was waving from down the street. I found the bag on the seat next to me. That's been happening a lot lately. I'm not sure why."

"Your spirit told me that there were other entities it had basically enlisted to try to get the bag off your person so he could have his way with you."

Martin swore under his breath and looked shaken. "I had suspicions, but I didn't want to believe it was true."

"There are other protection rituals you can do. Maybe you need to guard yourself against other kinds of spirits as well."

"Apparently so." He looked at her thoughtfully. "Do you have any idea why I, it, sent Nala to your house?"

"It said that she could ask me what happened to her friends at the amusement park."

He dropped his eyes. "All those people. They're dead, aren't they?"

"Yes."

"Sometimes, after he's gone, there are images, impressions left behind. I try to ignore them, but after you left I got the most terrible ones. They haunted me. That's why I went back later. It was stupid. I don't know what I expected to find, you standing on the curb waiting for a taxi or something."

"Instead you found Nala."

"Yeah. I need a drink. You want something?"

She shook her head.

He stood and got a beer from the refrigerator, then

sat back down. She felt herself growing impatient, but she told herself to just take a deep breath and try to calm down. He had valuable information, and his spirit tormentor might be of use to her in the future. There was no harming him now. She leaned across the table. "Do you have any images or impressions now?"

He set the beer on the table. "Why, did he tell you something?"

"Perhaps," she said, not wanting to reveal what she knew just yet.

He nodded slowly. "I keep seeing a figure in black in front of a grave."

Maybe the creature had been telling the truth about where she could find the witch she was hunting for that night.

"Was it daylight?" she asked.

"No, dark. Moon was shining, though."

She nodded. "Can you tell me who Marie Laveau is?"

"You're joking, right?"

"No, why?"

"She was known as the Voodoo Queen, very famous. Her tomb's in St. Louis Cemetery One."

Desdemona sat back, contemplating that bit of information. "What can you tell me about her?" she asked at last.

"She died over a hundred and thirty years ago, but people still make pilgrimages to her grave. They draw three X's on the side and ask her for things, hoping her spirit will grant them what they want."

"Does it?"

"I don't know, but I'm a guy who has his own pri-

vate demonic curse. I tend to believe in just about anything. Personally, I don't know anyone who has tried."

"I'm hunting a witch."

"Okay."

"He told me she'd be there at midnight tonight."

"Don't listen to him. Don't go. It could be a trap
meant to kill you or capture you. It could also just be a
huge waste of your time, but I wouldn't trust a thing he
said."

"Nothing else he said to me was a lie."

"That doesn't mean anything when dealing with
spirits. They have their own motivations and we cannot always fathom what they are. They don't look at
things the same way as we do. Life, death, people. It's
all just a big game to them. We're the pawns they push
around the board to amuse themselves, and they think
nothing of sacrificing us on a whim."

"This is the best lead I've had. I can't pass it up."

She didn't know why she was telling him, confiding
in him. Maybe it was because she already knew she
wasn't going to kill him. Maybe knowing how screwed
he was made her feel a sort of connection with him. She
hunched her shoulders. She didn't need anyone. She
was a witch without a coven, and she was just fine with
that.

Covens only got in the way and got themselves
killed.

She stood abruptly. "I have to go. I have a lot to prepare for."

"You don't have to do this," he said.

"Yes—yes, I do."

She headed for the front door, eager to end the conversation. Once in her car, she set the GPS to head back to the house she was using. She had no idea where she even was, let alone how to get back after all the crazy turns she'd had to take.

The trip looked as though it was going to be much shorter returning. In her head she started playing scenarios for her meeting that night in the graveyard. She would plan to get there at least an hour early so she could get the lay of the land and be prepared for anything the witch could throw at her.

The more she thought about it, the more she was tempted to drive straight to the cemetery. There were things she wanted to get from home, though, and she needed a few minutes of quiet to center herself and re-energize after her experiences with Martin and his demon.

That was exactly what she needed, a few hours alone to recharge and just focus on the task at hand with no outside distractions.

She turned down a street. Her GPS was telling her she was less than ten minutes from her house.

A sudden pulse of energy rippled around her. Before she could react, a man's body came arcing through the air and crashed into her windshield.

6

Desdemona slammed on her brakes as glass exploded inward, showering her. The body stayed lodged in her windshield, brown eyes wide-open, staring at her. Blood had sprayed over the glass that was still intact.

She sat for a moment, stunned. The eyes flickered briefly. The man wasn't dead, at least, not yet.

She leaped from her car and spun around, her eyes sweeping the street, searching for whatever had caused the man to land on her car.

"Help me!" came an agonized cry. There, a few yards away, she spotted a small figure. She lifted her hands, prepared to fight, but a moment later recognized Nala. She quickly scanned the area for other signs of life but saw none.

She moved over to the girl. "What happened?"

"I don't know," she said. She was crying and shaking. "He attacked me. I freaked out and I felt this burst of energy as I pushed him away. He went flying and hit your car." She looked up at Samantha with anguished eyes. "Is he dead?"

Samantha turned and walked back to the car. The man's wounds were extensive, difficult for even a seasoned witch to heal, and he was bleeding excessively from a dozen cuts from the glass, but he was still breathing.

She reached out, yanked the power from him, and let go just as he died.

"He is now," she said, turning back to the girl.

The girl collapsed on the sidewalk, looking as though she was going to be sick, and began to cry harder.

Desdemona wasn't sure exactly what to do. Since it didn't look as if she was going to get Nala to move anytime soon, she turned and put a glamour up around the car and then around herself and Nala so that any passersby would avoid them but would see nothing unusual.

Then she sat down next to the crying girl. Though Nala claimed not to be a witch, she had lost the equivalent of her whole coven just a few hours before. Desdemona understood how that felt and knew the girl must be feeling alone and frightened.

Don't trust her, that other self whispered deep inside.

Desdemona rolled her eyes. "You say he attacked you?" she asked.

Nala nodded.

"Can you tell me what happened?"

"He was like us, you know? I felt someone coming and I thought it was you, but then I turned around and it wasn't. He smiled, acted friendly, wanted to know if I was okay."

"Then he got close to me, and he—he grabbed me, tried to kiss me. When I told him to get off me, he tried to grab my chest. He was ripping my shirt. I freaked out and pushed him as hard as I could. That's when I felt the energy surge and he went flying."

She broke down sobbing.

Liar!

Desdemona blinked, startled. That other self was usually so kind and compassionate, but the word came with such vehemence that it shook her.

She looked at the girl and then at the body of the man on the car. Why would she make a story like that up? It wasn't as if the world wasn't filled with predators just waiting to get their hands on young girls.

Liar! the inner voice insisted again.

Desdemona gritted her teeth, wondering what Samantha wanted her to do about it. After she had saved them at Martin's house, though, maybe it was best not to ignore her.

She glanced around. It was far from an ideal place to be having this conversation with Nala, let alone try to be still enough and vulnerable enough to have a conversation with her other self. That would just have to wait.

She got up and walked back to the car. The dead man was wearing a dark suit with a shirt and tie. He looked like a businessman.

Check his pockets.

She grimaced but went ahead and did it. She found nothing, not even a wallet or any kind of identification. That seemed sort of odd to her, especially given how he was dressed.

She pulled the body off her car, letting it slide to the ground. She stared intently at his face, but there was no recognition whatsoever. He was a stranger to her.

And now he was just another body to dispose of.

No, wait! her inner voice pleaded, but it was too late as Desdemona dropped a fireball on his body as she had on the one in the alley that morning. Her thoughts flashed to the man she had been following then, the one who claimed to be a Druid. What was his part in all of this? Why had this man attacked Nala?

She felt she could only see half a dozen pieces of a giant puzzle, and it was frustrating. She had once heard that if you put too many rats in a cage together, they would shortly turn on one another. Was the same thing happening here with people with powers?

If that was the case, though, how did that explain how the teens and homeless had been able to live together at the theme park before they'd been slaughtered? Maybe it was because they weren't alpha types.

When the body had finished burning, she turned back to Nala, who was staring, openmouthed, in horror at her. "Why—why did you do that?" the girl stammered.

"I wasn't in the mood to answer a bunch of questions for the police. Were you?" Desdemona asked.

Nala shook her head fiercely.

"All right, then." She crossed back over to the girl and sat down again. "Did he say anything else to you?"

"No."

"Were his movements natural or more jerky?"

Nala frowned, as if concentrating. "I think they were natural. Why?"

"Just making sure he wasn't being controlled by someone."

"What do you mean?"

Desdemona sighed. "It's possible for a very powerful witch to puppeteer another, even from a distance."

"You're kidding, right?"

"No. I've seen it."

Or, at least, her other self had, and the images had been horrific enough that Desdemona had had a couple of nightmares about them. It seemed like a strange attack, especially given that it had happened to Nala and so close to Desdemona's home. Then there was the fact that her other self kept insisting that Nala was lying about what had really happened.

The girl seemed sincere enough, though, and given the burst of power she'd accidentally shown when panicked, Desdemona didn't want to risk terrorizing her more or triggering that power again by taking a walk through her memories of the event.

The sun was starting to set. It had been a long, crazy day and it was nowhere near over yet. She still needed time to focus and recharge before heading to the cemetery. She struggled with trying to decide what to do.

With Claudia it had been simple. Once she'd decided to let her live, she just needed to scare her. With Nala it was more complicated, though, and she had a feeling if she tried to scare the girl she would just make things worse. She couldn't just ignore her, though, not until she got to the bottom of everything. That guy going after her on the same day that the witch had killed everyone else who was part of Nala's group couldn't be a coincidence.

It was possible that the witch wanted Nala or her powers.

"We need to talk tomorrow. Do you have someplace you can go tonight?" Desdemona asked. Just because she wanted to keep an eye on the girl didn't mean she wanted her in her home, particularly with what the night might hold. If she was lucky, she'd kill the witch tonight and she'd never have to see Nala again.

Nala wiped her eyes and nose on the back of her sleeve. "Yeah, I know a place."

"Good," she said, feeling relieved. "Do you need help getting there?"

Nala shook her head. "It's not that far."

"Okay, I'll see you tomorrow, then, all right?"

Nala nodded and stood shakily. "Thanks for . . . everything," she said.

Desdemona couldn't help noticing that Nala was avoiding looking at her car or the pile of ash on the ground next to it.

Watch her, the inner voice urged.

Desdemona shook her head. She didn't have the time. She had bigger goals in mind for the evening than babysitting some kid who had just contributed to killing some guy.

"Okay, then. Be safe," she told Nala.

She waited until Nala turned and began walking down the street. Then she moved around to her car, opened the door, and moved her hand in a sweeping motion. All the broken glass flew outside and deposited itself on the ground. After a moment's thought she blew the remaining glass out of the windshield and it made a tinkling sound as it, too, fell to the ground.

She got into the car, grateful that she didn't have far to go. She held her hands up to where the windshield had been and pushed energy out of them, creating a simple ward that would block the wind from coming through and stinging her eyes. It wouldn't last at freeway speeds, but fortunately she didn't need it to at the moment.

She made it into the house and Freaky leaped toward her. He planted his back paws on the floor, stood, and put his front ones on her shoulders and licked her.

"Down," she said, wincing as his razorlike claws dug into her skin. He was bored. He needed to be let out so he could run, maybe hunt and kill something he'd never eat. That was the one problem with a big cat in a house, not enough space to really stretch his legs.

"Should I take you with me tonight, boy?" she asked.

The panther made a rumbling sound deep in his throat.

She looked down and realized there was dried blood on her clothes that must have splattered there when the guy crashed into the windshield. She headed upstairs and took a shower, trying to let the hot water soothe her as she attempted to clear her mind of all the distraction and clutter. It wasn't as easy as she would have liked.

By the time she stepped out of the shower, she was still keyed up. She was going to have to do some serious work to get herself centered. The last thing she needed when going up against that witch was to be thinking about Claudia or Nala or Martin or the Druid. They were all distractions she needed to be able to free herself from. She glanced into the mirror over the sink and froze.

It wasn't her reflection that was staring back at her. It looked like her, but it wasn't. She was wearing a towel, her wet hair hanging free down her back. The image in the mirror was wearing a white dress, hair braided. Then she realized she was staring at Samantha as she had seen her earlier in her mind.

"What are you doing here?" she snapped. The lips in the mirror remained still.

"Nala was lying." The lips in the mirror finally moved, forming the words that Desdemona heard as a breathy whisper.

"So what?"

"It's important."

"What was she lying about? And why would she?" Desdemona demanded.

"I don't know why, but he did not attack her, not in the way she described."

"Oh, expert on perverts, are you?"

"If he was attacking her sexually, and they both had powers, he would not have come at her with brute force. He would have tried to overpower her with magic. Or more realistically he would have tried to manipulate her mind and seduce her," Samantha's voice whispered.

"It makes no sense for her to lie about that."

"She did not want you to know."

"Didn't want me to know what?" Desdemona asked. "What really happened?"

The image in the mirror nodded.

"But why? What could have really happened that she would want to hide?"

"Much," came the whispered reply.

Desdemona could feel her frustration building. Samantha was the better detective, but how could she really use her without giving her more power? It wasn't good that she already had enough to make herself seen in the reflection. That was more than Desdemona had ever been able to do all those years she'd been trapped, ignored, and forgotten.

"I can't deal with this right now. I have to prepare. Hopefully, after tonight, I won't have to care what did or did not happen to Nala and whether or not she's a liar."

"You should not go to the cemetery," Samantha whispered to her.

Desdemona laughed. "Oh, I'm going, and there's nothing you can do to stop me."

She turned her back on the mirror and left the room. Inside the bedroom she glanced at the mirror and was relieved to see that Samantha hadn't been able to follow.

As she contemplated the work ahead, she dressed in black clothing that would move easily with her. When she was done she went downstairs and opened her bag of supplies. She took out her athame and sharpened it. She probably wouldn't need it, but she didn't want to be without it in case she did. Next she removed a long black cloak that she could wear to help her blend even more into the shadows.

Regretfully she closed the bag, realizing that nothing else in it would likely be able to be used quickly enough to help. Growing up, she had learned a lot about sympathetic magic—the use of candles and poppets—but the time it would take to put those items into play would likely find her dead.

Then she went and sat down cross-legged in the living room and closed her eyes. She could hear Freaky patrolling the perimeter of the room, protecting her from any unwanted intruders. She slowly and deeply breathed in and out. With each breath she exhaled she envisioned exhaling fear, confusion, uncertainty, exhaustion, and chaos. With each breath she inhaled, she envisioned breathing in energy and power and fresh air, which cleared the cobwebs from her mind and helped her to focus only on what was actually true and important.

After about half an hour she could feel herself achieving a sense of calm and strength. She felt centered, focused, ready for the task at hand. She stood up slowly and Freaky padded over to her side.

She put a hand on his head. "You and me, boy, we're going to finish this witch tonight," she whispered.

She pulled up a map of the cemetery on her phone and was able to locate the tomb that she was looking for. The Voodoo Queen was supposedly interred in the Glapion family tomb, number 347.

When the time came, she and Freaky walked outside. Freaky jumped into the backseat and dutifully lay down. Desdemona created a new windshield for the car out of energy, similar to how she had created Freaky but simpler because it was an inanimate object. They arrived at the cemetery a little before eleven and parked where the car was likely to go unnoticed.

Saint Louis Cemetery Number One was the oldest of three Catholic cemeteries bearing similar names. The cemetery was only one square block, but it was crammed with tombs.

Desdemona stepped out of her car and pulled the hood of her cloak up over her head. Freaky leaped out on silent paws and the two walked together into the cemetery. As they passed down a row of tombs, she listened carefully but could hear no sounds. She was early, as she'd wanted to be.

Even as she drifted between the grisly monuments to death and decay, she couldn't help wondering if the spirit had indeed been telling her the truth or instead luring her into some sort of trap.

She was on edge, despite her preparations. The cemetery was a desolate place at night, and there was something that just felt wrong about the entire thing. She stopped frequently to stretch out with her senses and see if she could hear or feel anything out of the ordinary.

Every time, though, it felt as though she couldn't sense much of anything more than a few feet beyond herself. It almost felt as if a wet blanket had been draped over the entire place, which deadened and hampered the energy from flowing freely as it should. She wondered if it was some strange effect caused by the tombs or if there was magic at work that she just couldn't sense.

Freaky seemed uneasy as well, looking over his shoulder every time she paused as though checking to make sure they weren't being followed. His doing so added to her own sense of unease.

The tombs were all different heights, some much lower to the ground than she would have anticipated and others towering. It made it hard to see and also cast weird shapes, thanks to the moon gleaming above. She would almost rather have it be pitch-black than have to deal with the strange patterns of light and dark.

She found the Voodoo Queen's tomb and she could see X's marked on the side where people had indeed come hoping that the spirit would grant their wish. She wondered if that was why the witch she sought would be making a visit here tonight.

The entity that possessed Martin had told her the witch was coming to pay her respects to the Voodoo Queen. That seemed odd and Desdemona had assumed that she would be performing some kind of ritual here. Whatever it was, she'd have to be ready for her.

After having looked around for a few moments, Desdemona chose the tomb she was going to hide behind. It seemed rather futile, since the other witch was likely to feel her presence the moment she stepped into the cemetery. If she wasn't coming alone, though, perhaps she would just assume it was one of her followers or intended victims.

You should leave. You don't know enough, the voice whispered inside, and she would have given anything to still it forever.

Freaky lay down beside her, fading into a shadow so that all that could be seen of him were his glowing eyes.

As she crouched in the darkness and waited, Desdemona thought of all the other things she should have done before coming here. She could have checked in with Claudia, seen if the girl had heard anything. She could reach out now and touch her mind, but she was afraid of doing anything that would distract her even a fraction.

The minutes ticked by and slowly she became aware that she was not alone. The dead inside the tombs were whispering to her, telling her things about their lives and deaths that she'd rather not know. If anything she would have liked to know if Marie truly was buried in the tomb that she had seen. Apparently there was some dispute about whether that was her final resting place.

The bones or whatever was left at this point probably would have spoken to her and told her had she just stopped to listen. Had the other witch been here before? If so, she probably knew the truth. And if that was the case, then the bones were probably Marie's, because who else would the witch care about?

Desdemona bared her teeth. It was fitting that the two of them should meet at last in a graveyard, given that the witch had left the picture for her in the graveyard in Salem. In the empty grave that had Desdemona's name on it.

She could feel Freaky tensing. Something must be near. A moment later she sensed a change in the energy around her, a disturbance that only another with power could cause. She held her breath, wondering what would happen when the witch felt her presence.

The disturbance grew stronger. Desdemona was reasonably certain the witch wasn't alone. That meant more to fight, but hopefully she could hide her presence longer.

She strained her senses and heard the barest whisper

of movement. Her muscles were so tense, they were beginning to vibrate. She was not used to waiting like this, and the strain was beginning to take a toll.

Then she saw a flash of movement through the tombs. Freaky rose off the ground into a crouch, and she placed a hand on his head to restrain him. Maybe it had been a mistake to bring him.

Then she saw clearly in a shaft of moonlight three women walking. The first was shrouded in a black cloak and her movements were effortless, graceful. Desdemona was sure this was the witch she sought. Behind her trailed two others, girls who were clearly under her power. They moved stiffly, their movements not quite their own. Their heads were bowed and there were gags in their mouths. The first had pale hair that shimmered in the moonlight.

The second was Claudia.

7

Desdemona scowled, wondering how Claudia had been captured and what, if anything, she had told the witch about her. Her presence did solidify one thing in her mind. The witch had either known or suspected that Desdemona would be coming.

So far, though, she'd given no indication that she'd sensed Desdemona's presence, so she stayed still in her hiding place, her hand on Freaky's head, and watched to see what the witch would do next.

The small procession stopped in front of the Voodoo Queen's crypt. Desdemona had a perfect vantage point from where she crouched in the darkness. The witch produced an athame from beneath her cloak.

"Give me your hand," she said to the blond girl.

The girl held out her hand with the same jerky movements that proved she was being controlled. The witch sliced open her finger with the tip of the athame and then pulled the girl up next to the outside of the tomb and, grasping her hand, drew three large X's with the girl's blood.

She was making a petition after all, though something about the entire scene seemed false to Desdemona. Still, she watched, hoping to learn more about her enemy before she struck.

"O Marie Laveau, dark priestess, Voodoo Queen of New Orleans, we come here tonight seeking your favor and asking that you grant us this boon," the witch said in a high-pitched voice.

Run.

Desdemona didn't have time for Samantha's cowardice. She just wanted her to keep still so she could focus all her attention on the witch.

The witch knelt down in front of the tomb and lifted slender white arms skyward. "Listen to me, and answer the cry of one of the daughters of the darkness who has come before you in all humility to ask that your spirit move on my behalf."

Run now.

Freaky began to stir and she willed him to be quiet. Maybe she should dispel his energy for the moment since he might give away their position.

"I ask that you restore to me everything that I have lost, and most important, O great Queen, I ask that you deliver my enemy into my hand."

The witch rose and spun around. "Oh, look," she said almost conversationally, "you already have."

Before Desdemona could move, the doors on the crypts behind her exploded in a shower of debris, which rained down upon her. Freaky jumped out of the way with a growl and slunk away into the darkness. Desdemona stood, lunged forward, and then fell flat on her face. Something was gripping her ankles like a vise and had tripped her. She glanced over her shoulder, and what she saw sent a wave of terror through her.

There was movement in the open tombs; she could hear things slithering in the darkness. Bony white fingers emerged from one, followed by a grinning skull. The skeletons were crawling out of their graves. Worse, the first one already had a hold on her, its bony fingers wrapped around her ankles.

She screamed and sent a burst of energy into it, but nothing happened.

"You can't harm the dead," the witch said with a shrill laugh. "Although feel free to try. They, on the other hand, can certainly harm you."

Desdemona lifted her hands and tried to disperse the bones, but they hung together, refusing to move.

"It's a matter of wills, dear, and I'm afraid mine's stronger than yours."

Panicking, Desdemona kicked and thrashed, trying to destroy the skeleton, but it remained intact as the others crawled up and grabbed her legs. One, dressed in a few rags, crawled up her body and she thrashed in terror, sending out bursts of energy and fire that should have turned the bones to ash but didn't. She could feel its bony frame pressing down first on her legs, then on her lower back as it slithered over her. It was heavy and it felt like a lead weight and it was crushing her. She could smell death and decay all around her.

"This is impossible!" she screamed.

"No, it's magic."

Bony fingers caught her wrists and pressed them down into the earth. She was completely powerless.

"You know, you might think it just coincidence, you, me, a graveyard. It's not, though. Everything is connected. You understand that, right?" the witch said.

"Let me go!" Desdemona screamed.

"So that you can kill me? I don't think so. You know, I did give you a sporting chance. I even knelt down and turned my back to you and you didn't take the opportunity. You know what that tells me?"

"No."

"Deep down, you don't want to kill me."

"That's not true!"

"Ah, but it is. Because you see, you have questions, and if you had killed me when you had the opportunity, you never would have gotten any answers, would you? You know what they say about curiosity and cats? Well, you should have listened."

"I will kill you, answers or no," Desdemona hissed. "I want you dead more than I want to know anything from you."

"See, that's what you say, but I don't think so. You want answers. More than that, you want truth. Well, truth I can give you."

Desdemona continued to struggle, but nothing she did seemed to help. The weight of the skeleton on her back was slowly pressing her into the hard ground, and her ribs were beginning to bruise.

"So, time for some truth to be told," the witch said. "A circle is a powerful symbol, ancient, primitive, perfect, divine. It has no end or beginning and it is impenetrable."

Desdemona wondered what on earth she was going on about.

"You know, three makes a circle," the witch said, stretching out her hands. Claudia and the other girl's arms jerked upward, as if they were being pulled on strings. The three linked hands.

"You see, a circle. The circle is life, and fellowship, and power, and protection. The circle is everything. It can be large or it can be small. But you want to know one of the most interesting things about a circle?"

"What?" Desdemona asked.

"You can have a circle with only two. Which means we don't need her." The woman dropped Claudia's hand, gave a quick flip of her wrist, and Claudia's neck snapped. A moment later the body fell to the ground. Just like that, she was gone.

The witch used her free hand to grab the blond girl's suddenly freed hand. "You see, just two to make a circle. Just two to create and destroy. You just need two."

"What is wrong with you?" Desdemona asked.

The witch shook her head. "The real question here is, what is wrong with you that you haven't figured that out yet?"

The witch spun around and around with the other girl, who was still moving so stiffly that Desdemona was sure she would trip and fall at any moment.

"Oh, the things you can do with two that you can't do with just one," the witch said. "And yet how sad, how pathetic, that you still think you can do everything on your own."

"I don't need you or anyone," Desdemona raged.

"Well, clearly you need someone. Otherwise, you're

going to get in trouble," the witch said in a singsong voice, spinning faster now and yanking the other girl along.

Suddenly the blond girl did trip and she fell to her knees. The witch stopped spinning and let go of her hands. "You know the only trouble with a circle?" she asked, and Desdemona couldn't tell if she was talking to her or the girl.

"What?" Desdemona asked.

"It's not for the weak." The witch held up her hand and in one moment ripped the girl's power from her. She fell to the ground, dead, only a skull where a face had once been.

She was crazy and she was stronger than Desdemona.

The witch turned and snapped her fingers. The skeleton on Desdemona's back crawled off her and she gasped, taking in a deep breath as her lungs were able to expand fully again. Then the skeletons hauled her to her feet. She fought, but they were stronger than they could ever have been in life. She tried to send a wave of killing energy through the ground to the witch.

She laughed and absorbed it with ease. "Thanks, I needed a little pick-me-up," she said.

Desdemona called a fireball to her fingers and threw it as best she could.

The witch easily redirected it.

Desdemona tried to pull the power from the witch, who just laughed as her efforts had absolutely no effect.

"Really, these are the attempts of a weak and frightened child," the witch said. "Frankly, I expected more from you. Much, much more."

She snapped her fingers and the skeletons let go so suddenly that Desdemona staggered to catch her balance.

Just as she straightened she heard a sound from her nightmares, growling, snarling, unearthly, and unmistakable for anything else. Hellhounds. They were headed her way.

Desdemona froze for a second. Then she snatched the athame up off the ground, sliced open her hand, and began to spin in a circle, creating a circle of blood to protect her. Her heart was pounding and she was dizzy, but she knew she couldn't rush it; she had to do it right. One little gap in the circle and it wouldn't keep anything out.

She was nearly done and the snarling was getting closer, louder. She could almost swear she felt a blast of air from one of the foul creatures and the stench of rotting flesh. Her hand jerked slightly and blood dripped erratically.

She turned the last quarter circle.

"They're here," the witch said again, in her singsong voice.

Desdemona looked up. There, standing on either side of the witch, were the two biggest hellhounds she had ever seen. The beasts were monstrous. They were almost the size of small horses, but roughly dog shaped. They had mouthfuls of fangs several inches long, glowing black eyes, and quills like a porcupine's that flared next to their spines. They could have been brothers to the one that had tormented her as a child.

The witch stood between them and she put her hands on their heads, as though they were pets. "What will happen to you when I let my babies have their way with you?" she asked.

"Nothing. I am protected," Desdemona snarled. "And I'll soon find a way to kill your babies and you."

The witch tsked at her. "I don't think so."

"You said it yourself, the circle is protection. And sooner or later you'll make a mistake."

"Circles can protect us, that is true, if we are clever and worthy and do everything just right. You know another thing about a circle?" the witch shouted. "It connects us all!" She snapped her fingers and the circle of Desdemona's blood caught on fire, flames shooting eight feet into the air. And in one sickening moment Desdemona could see the one tiny spot where there was no blood. The circle was broken. It had to have been when her hand jerked; that was the only explanation. She could try to close it now, but that would mean thrusting her hand into the flames.

The witch cackled as though sensing her dilemma. "Just how much is the circle worth to you?" she asked.

Suddenly a second wall of flame leaped up around Desdemona, this one a complete circle, hemming her in and keeping her from being able to reach the one she'd drawn.

"You're not fireproof," the witch said. "Luckily for me, my babies are."

She swept her hands forward and the two hellhounds began advancing. Desdemona looked around frantically. There was no way out, nothing she could use. Inside her, Samantha was screaming something, but she couldn't understand her.

The hellhounds were just outside the first circle. In a

moment they would be upon her. She had seen what it looked like when a hellhound tore someone apart. There was no hope.

A sudden high-pitched scream startled both of the hellhounds, and they half turned just as a massive black form launched itself out of the darkness and landed on the back of the first one and sank its fangs into the beast's neck.

Freaky had come to her rescue.

The second hellhound turned to aid its brother, and Desdemona leaped through the first wall of flame. She shoved her hand into the second, and her blood sealed the gap in her circle.

Her skin began to bubble. She tried to snuff the flames, but when she did, they only leaped higher into the sky. She began to choke as they sucked the oxygen out of the air. Beyond the wall of fire Freaky continued to battle the two hellhounds. She couldn't tell who was winning, but she had to hope her cat could hold his own.

She tried again to snuff the flames and again they just doubled in size. The witch had done something to them, something that made them behave in an unnatural way, the opposite of what they should.

So maybe she needed to do the opposite to quench them. She summoned her energy and tried to fan the flames. They lessened, not by much, but they did lessen. She could hear the screams from Freaky and the hounds. She knew that the witch was out there and she wished she could tell Freaky to attack her instead.

She tried again to fan the flames and they dropped down to their original size just in time for her to see

Freaky being pinned by one hound. She tried to scream, but the oxygen was gone. Her eyes were burning and her skin was turning black. She was dying.

Suddenly the flames were extinguished as if blown out by a giant. She fell to her knees, choking. She grabbed hold of the earth, but it was scorched and charred and nothing living was growing in it.

Something the size of a bull leaped over her, scattering everything before it. Two hands reached down and grabbed her. She glanced up and saw the face of the Druid.

"I'm here to help," he said, hefting her into his arms. He began to run and she felt as if her body was breaking apart.

Moments later she was being laid down in the back of a car. She heard doors slam, followed by the squeal of tires.

"My name is Thomas. I won't hurt you."

She couldn't answer.

"It was foolish to take her on in the state that you're in. If she'd wanted to she could have killed you."

Desdemona didn't have time to ponder his words. She was busy pulling energy from everything she could. A moment later the car sputtered to a halt and died.

Thomas swore and slammed his hand down on the dashboard. "You drained the battery. Don't do that. I need to get you to a place where you can get some real energy, enough to actually heal."

She could feel him push energy back into the car battery, and it took all her will not to drain it. The car came back to life and moments later jounced along, every bump sending an agony of fire through her body. She didn't know how long they traveled, but she was pretty sure she blacked out at least once.

She woke up as someone was lifting her out of the backseat. "You're only half the witch you could be," he said, his voice deeply disapproving.

He lowered her onto something that was soft and wet and smelled like grass. Her fingers reached out. It was grass. She pushed her hands down into the earth and pulled with everything she had. Energy came flooding over her. A moment later, her body began to heal and the pain of that caused everything to go black.

She felt something wet on her cheek and chin. She felt stiff all over and unbelievably sore. She opened her eyes slowly and saw Freaky, poised about to lick her again.

"I'm okay," she muttered, incredibly relieved that he was there. He seemed okay. He was an energy creature, so she shouldn't have worried, but she wasn't sure if the hellhounds would have been capable of destroying him.

She looked around slowly. Somehow she was back in her own car and Freaky was in the passenger seat staring at her with concerned eyes.

"What happened?" she asked the panther.

He jumped through into the backseat and she slowly straightened. She was damp and smelled like smoke and wet earth. There were bits of dead grass on her clothes, and her head was throbbing.

She glanced around, wondering what had happened

to Thomas. He must have been the one to leave her here. Why bother?

She turned and saw a couple of police cars up the street. Apparently the events in the cemetery had not gone unnoticed. She should get out of there. She started the car and drove off.

The last thing she remembered was lying on the grass, trying to pull energy from the earth. Obviously it had worked. She didn't know where Freaky had been or how he'd made it back to the car; she was just grateful he was there.

She drove until she reached the house. She hesitated before going in. Too many people knew where she was staying for it to be truly safe. On the other hand, with a witch as powerful as that pissed at her, nowhere was safe. She parked the car and headed inside, Freaky bounding beside her.

She wanted nothing more than to sleep for a thousand years, but the stench of her clothes was too much. She looked down. They were charred and shredded in places, definitely ruined. She stripped in the kitchen and dumped them in the trash, then headed upstairs to the bathroom.

When she flipped on the light and stepped inside, she half expected to see Samantha in the mirror, ready to say "I told you so."

When she looked, though, all that she saw was her own face, covered in blood and soot and grime. There was more dead grass in her hair. Altogether she had to admit that she looked better than she felt.

She climbed into the shower and twenty minutes later woke up when the water turned cold. She had fallen asleep leaning against the wall. She finished washing her hair, shivering in the icy water but too drained to do anything about it.

When she finally exited she glanced at the mirror again, but it was still just her. She wondered if deep inside Samantha was unconscious, or maybe even dead. Dead would be good.

She barely made it into the bedroom. She fell headlong on the bed and passed out.

Desdemona woke several hours later cold and hungry. She rolled over and looked at the clock. It was nearly four in the afternoon. She sat up slowly, relieved that most of the stiffness and soreness seemed to be gone now. Some food would probably help. At least she felt awake and alert.

She threw on some jeans and a T-shirt and headed downstairs, Freaky racing ahead of her, the stairs groaning beneath his weight. She made it into the kitchen and was just about to open the refrigerator when Freaky lifted his head and growled. It looked as though she had a visitor.

She frowned. She didn't feel anything. Was it really someone without powers? Maybe Martin and his demon had another warning for her. She grimaced at the thought, not in the mood to deal with anyone. She looked out the front door and saw a car she didn't recognize parked out front and someone walking up the porch. There was something familiar about him. He had short, wavy brown hair and intense green eyes.

She opened the door and his eyes lit up when he saw her. "Samantha, I found you!"

8

Something stirred deep inside Desdemona and she realized that even though she only vaguely recognized the man, Samantha knew him well. The way Desdemona could feel her writhing away inside, she had to care for him. Snatches of memory were coming to her now, filling in the gaps. He was from Salem and his mother had been killed by her coven. There was something about him swearing vengeance and then there was kissing.

"Anthony?"

He nodded.

"What are you doing here?" she asked.

He reached out and pulled her into a hug. She held herself stiff, not sure how to respond.

"I was so worried about you. You just . . . . vanished. I thought something had happened to you, that you were dead."

"I'm very much alive."

"Why did you take off like that?"

Desdemona cocked her head to the side. "I discovered that there was a witch behind everything, taunting me, trying to control me. I had to come here to confront her, to kill her."

"You didn't have to come alone."

He cared enough for Samantha to help her, even though she could remember how much he hated witches, how much he had distrusted her at the start. She even thought she remembered him attempting to kill Samantha at one point. Something must have gotten him over that. What would Samantha say? Probably something about wanting him to be safe. It was clear he had no power of his own. He obviously felt deeply for her. Would he if he knew she was part of the coven that had killed his mother? Maybe he already knew; the memories were too fuzzy.

"How did you find me?"

"Ed helped."

"Ed?"

"Yeah, Ed Hofferman, your old partner from Boston. I figured he owed me a favor, so he tracked the GPS on your cell."

He pulled away from her and smiled at her.

She tried to smile back.

Something must have gone wrong, though, because he took two quick steps backward.

"What is it?" she asked.

"Your eyes. They're so . . . dead. You're not Samantha."

"Very good," she said, allowing herself to revel briefly in the pleasure of watching his panic.

"Who are you?"

She shrugged. "I'm who she should have been."

"Castor witch," he hissed.

She laughed and took a step toward him. "Oh, I'm much more than that."

There was something about his presence that excited her, made her think things she'd never thought before. She leaned in closer to him. His warmth, his scent, they filled her senses. She slipped her arms around his neck and pressed against him.

She might never have had these types of thoughts before, but Samantha certainly had, and they were all about Anthony.

"Haven't you figured it out yet?" Desdemona purred in his ear. "I'm the witch you've been looking for all these years, the last witch alive from the coven that killed your mother."

Anthony gritted his teeth. "I want you to tell me what you did to Samantha."

So he did know and apparently he cared for her deeply enough that it didn't matter.

"I simply took back what she stole from me all those years ago. Now she's the one banished, forgotten, nothing but a bitter memory."

"I will find a way to get her back," he vowed.

"So very noble of you, but why bother? She wasn't very much fun."

She leaned forward and kissed him hard. He shoved her away and she laughed. "You can play it that way if you want, but I know that you want this body. What does it matter who's inside?" she asked.

"It matters," he spat at her.

"Really?" she asked. "You know, my mother told me

all about sex magic, but I had never had a chance to try it for myself. Maybe you're just what I need to help me find the witch that keeps eluding me."

"You're barking up the wrong tree," Anthony snapped.

"Am I? You know the great thing about being a witch?" she asked. "I can make any tree the right tree."

She stepped back up to him, invading his space, reached out, and traced her finger down the line of his jaw, sending tiny electrical impulses through it. And then she asked, "Who do you belong to?"

"Samantha," he said in a strangled voice.

She made the electrical impulses slightly more intense and tilted his head so he was staring into her eyes. She reached into his mind, looking for the triggers she needed, the ones that would make him desire her uncontrollably. Just a few more seconds and he would think of nothing but her.

Something began screaming inside her mind.

Samantha was trapped in the tiniest corner of her own mind and had been for days. She was only vaguely aware of what was happening on the outside, but she knew she had to keep fighting, pushing. Now that Anthony had shown up, she had to fight that much harder. She had to protect him.

Desdemona was trying to do something to him. She was trying to compel him to do something, and Samantha had a feeling it had to do with sex magic. Terror gripped her. Desdemona had no right to do that to Anthony and she had no right to do it to Samantha's body.

Samantha began to scream at the top of her lungs and she could feel Desdemona hesitate.

"Get out of my body!" Samantha shouted.

"It was her body first."

Samantha spun around and saw one of her younger selves. She believed it was the girl she'd been when she was ten, staring at her. Communing with those younger versions of herself was exactly what had led her to accidentally unleash Desdemona in the first place.

"What?" she gasped.

"Before there was Samantha Ryan, there was Desdemona Castor," Ten said.

Samantha blinked and she was standing again in the part of her mind where there was the corridor of doors. These were the doors behind which she had locked away all her childhood memories, the ones she'd been forced to open one at a time until she had gone too far. Doors five through twelve were all open. Seven of the girls were present, but Twelve was missing.

That's because Twelve was off running the show. Samantha had opened that door back in the cemetery in Salem because she thought she needed the other girl's knowledge, insight.

Instead, she had let loose a monster. The others had tried to tell her, to warn her. They had said that it took all of them to lock up Twelve and in order to do so, they had to go away, too. In order to keep her from becoming a monster, her mind had literally shut away her entire childhood.

She felt a tug on her arm and she looked down. Five was looking up at her with solemn eyes.

"What is it?" Samantha asked.

"You're wrong, you know."

"About what?"

"About which of you came first, about whether it's her or you in charge."

"I don't understand."

"I know."

"Tell me," Samantha urged.

Five crossed her arms and shook her head. "You don't get it. She is you. You are her. It's not *her* doing this right now to that boy. It's *you*."

And suddenly Samantha wasn't in the corridor of doors in her mind anymore. She was there, in her body, looking out through her own eyes and seeing the fear in Anthony's.

"Anthony?" she whispered.

"Samantha? Is that you?" he asked, his voice desperate, pleading.

"I—"

Then she snapped right back into the corridor and was staring back down at Five, who was looking angry. "You still don't get it. It's you being mean to that boy. It's you doing everything. You're just trying to hide in here because you won't take responsibility for yourself!"

"But you locked her away—"

"No! Not *her*! Your memories are what we locked away."

"I was Desdemona and then I changed. I became Samantha."

"That's what you'd like to think," Five said. "Why is it you opened my door first?"

Samantha blinked. "Because I thought you were old

enough to teach me about magic but not old enough that I'd have to remember the really terrible things that happened later."

"Liar!" Five said, stomping her foot on the floor. "You were more afraid of seeing what you were like when you were younger than you were of reliving the terrible times."

Samantha felt as though she had been slapped across the face. Was it possible that Five was right? She turned and looked around. Six and Seven were nodding in agreement. The others were backing away from her as though afraid something was about to happen.

"What useful magic could I have possibly learned from my four youngest selves?" Samantha asked. "I mean, most people don't even remember much before they're three or four."

"You are not most people," Six said.

"You're a witch," Seven added.

"I'm not a witch!" Samantha screamed at the top of her lungs.

"Yes, you are!" all the girls screamed back at her.

"Always," Seven said.

"Still," Six said.

"That's what you won't take responsibility for," Five accused.

"No! I turned my back on that life."

"You ran away from it. You hid and pretended it never happened. That's not taking responsibility," Five said.

"That's not making peace," Six said.

"What do you want from me?" Samantha asked, horror creeping through her. Desdemona, the witch, was who she'd been raised as, and Samantha had only changed, become someone new, by force of will in the ritual when she turned thirteen. How could she take responsibility for a life she didn't even remember? It was as absurd as thinking she was responsible for what was happening now to Anthony and everyone else Desdemona had encountered.

Five pointed imperiously at the four remaining doors.

Samantha shook her head. "No, I won't open them."

"Why not?"

"Because . . ." The truth was, she didn't know why. All she knew was that when she looked at those doors she felt terror greater than when she had used to stare at the closed door Twelve. What could possibly have happened to her when she was so little that was worse than that? Were the other children right—had she been purposely avoiding those doors all along?

"I can't," she whispered.

"Then you will never get out of here," Six said.

"I just can't."

"You will never know the truth," Seven told her.

"I don't want to know. I can't," Samantha wailed.

"Then you're going to hurt the boy," Five said.

Silence fell and Samantha could only hear the sound of her own sobs. When she had started to cry, she didn't know, but the tears were coursing down her face and she was shaking like a leaf.

"Anthony," she whispered.

Anthony would be hurt, possibly killed, if she did nothing.

Five kept insisting that it was she tormenting Anthony, that she and the monster in charge of her body were one and the same. She could hear shouting from far away. It sounded like Anthony. She had to help him. No matter what it cost.

She stepped forward and pushed open the door marked FOUR.

The little girl who stepped out was actually smiling. Samantha blinked at her, surprised to see her younger self looking so happy. She didn't remember any part of her childhood being happy except for the quiet moments stolen with Freaky, and those hadn't happened until she was five.

"Big me!" Four said, clapping her hands in delight.

"Yes, I guess I am," Samantha said. "You seem happy to see me."

"Of course! Are you going to show me some magic?"

"You don't know how to do any magic?" Samantha asked, wondering when it was she had actually begun to learn. Her five-year-old self seemed to know a lot about it, so maybe this was the age she had begun to learn.

Four frowned slightly. "I think I do, but I'm not sure. Mama says she's going to teach me this year, show me how to be a big girl, a real witch." She beamed again at the thought.

Samantha felt sick to her stomach at seeing her younger self so excited to become a witch. She wished she could say something, explain to her, stop it all from happening, but these were shades of the past and they couldn't be changed, only understood and accepted.

"No, I'm not going to teach you any magic today. I'm here to remember what it was like to be you."

"That's silly. Why would you forget that?"

Probably because she didn't want to remember being happy about learning magic, even if it had only been for a brief time in her life. This was her before all the fear and the darkness took hold, her before she'd been forced to learn how to draw protection circles out of her own blood while monsters raced out of the darkness to attack her.

She had been excited and optimistic and hadn't seen the harm, the danger, or known anything about the darkness to come. Samantha closed her eyes and wanted to cry. She wondered for a brief moment what it would have been like to grow up in a home where a mother and father had taught her to use her gifts for peace and good and harmony, instead of violence and evil and chaos.

That couldn't be changed, either, though. She'd grown up with the mother she had, and although she might have been innocent and optimistic once, that had changed very quickly. Her five-year-old self wouldn't have to hide Freaky Kitty from her mother if that weren't true.

"Thank you," Samantha said to Four because she didn't know what else to say. The pain of seeing her was tearing at her. Worse, she didn't know how feeling this pain or seeing the innocence that had died would help her save herself, let alone Anthony.

She turned quickly to the door marked THREE and pushed it open before she could have second thoughts. The little girl who emerged had big, pouty eyes and her arms crossed over her chest. Samantha was surprised. She'd expected something different after seeing bouncy, excited Four.

"What's wrong?" she asked Three.

"I got in trouble again," Three said.

"Why?"

"Doing magic."

"Your mother punishes you for doing magic?" Samantha asked, thoroughly shocked.

Three nodded.

"Why?"

"Mama says I do it wrong, that I need to learn different."

"What are you doing wrong?"

"I don't know. She says it's not focused."

"Not focused?" Samantha said, feeling confused.

Three nodded. "She says she's going to take my powers."

Samantha blinked. Was it possible to take power without the killing that had happened at the abandoned theme park?

"That's . . . that's not very nice," Samantha managed to say.

"I do magic good."

"Well," Samantha unconsciously corrected the girl.

"Better than Mama."

Samantha stared at her. "You're better at magic than your mother?"

The little girl nodded and Samantha's mind raced. Her mother had been a fearsome witch, a powerful practitioner, second only to one or two people in the entire coven. Only the high priestess and possibly Mr. Black, who did a lot of the teaching, were stronger. Both had figured prominently in her nightmares, although it wasn't until she started regaining her memories that she'd remembered Mr. Black's name. His face and voice had featured in her nightmares for years, though.

"You're stronger than your mother?" she asked again.

Three nodded.

"Show me."

"Not supposed to."

Samantha thought about arguing with her, trying to convince her that it would be okay, but she heard Anthony shouting again from far away. She didn't have time to argue with the little girl. She had to move on.

"I'm sorry," she said, and turned to the door marked Two.

She pushed the door open and the little girl who came out looked very sad indeed. The eyes that she turned on Samantha made her want to cry.

"What's wrong?" she asked.

"Mother did a spell. Took my magic for a while."

Samantha blinked. "She did that to you?"

The child nodded and Samantha felt sick inside. Had she not been so afraid, had she started with the younger children back when she was hunting witches in Salem, she would have known that was possible and she might have been able to spot the high priestess of the coven in time to save so many people.

She closed her eyes, hot tears burning them. Her fear had caused untold pain and suffering.

"What's wrong with you?" Two asked.

"Nothing, nothing, Desdemona," Samantha said.

"No! I don't like that name. That's not my name. That's not what my Daddy used to call me," Two said.

Samantha blinked in shock. "You . . . you remember your father?"

Two nodded. "He had to go away. He said I could go, too, but then something happened. Mother wouldn't let me go. She told me to forget about him. I forgot most. All I remember is that he wanted me to go with him and he never called me Desdemona."

"What did he call you?"

"I don't know. It was pretty. Ask her." Two pointed toward the door marked ONE.

With a shudder Samantha realized this was truly the door she'd never wanted to open. There was a secret behind it that she never wanted to learn.

The shouts got louder and louder. Anthony was going to die. It would be all her fault.

Crying harder, she stepped forward and pushed open the first door. Out toddled an adorable little girl with pigtails who looked up at her with huge, innocent eyes. Suddenly she spat fire out of her mouth and it set Samantha's pants alight. She hastily put it out as the baby giggled.

Magic had always been part of her, she realized with a shiver. Destructive, harmful, dangerous. "What's your name, sweetheart? What does Daddy call you?" Samantha asked, trying to keep her voice from shaking.

The baby sat down and looked up at her. "Samantha."

It felt as if the entire world shuddered to a halt.

Samantha fell, landing flat on her back. She stared blankly upward as memories roared through her head. She heard a man's voice calling her "Samantha." She'd always thought she'd chosen that name for herself because of Samantha on *Bewitched* and how she'd wished she'd had her for a mother instead of her own. But the name Samantha had always been in there. It's what her father had called her. It's what she had called herself when she was very young.

She was Samantha long before she embraced the name of Desdemona, the name her mother gave her. She was Samantha when she was young and innocent and used magic as if it were nothing, breathing fire as though it were air.

"It's not true!" she wailed.

And above her she saw all the little girls, circling her in a ring.

"It is," Five said.

"How am I supposed to live with this?"

Five knelt down beside her and conjured Freaky Kitty, who leaped onto Samantha's chest and began to knead her shirt.

"By realizing that the power isn't bad, it just is."

"It's what you do that's good or bad," Six said.

"Be good," Three said.

One giggled and then opened her mouth to spew more fire. Samantha quickly blew on it, a mighty gust of wind that she forced out of her lungs, and the flame was snuffed out. One clapped her hands in delight.

Samantha hadn't known she could blow out the fire. She hadn't remembered that she could breathe fire like some sort of insane dragon. "This can't be happening."

"It *is* happening, and you know it. Choose what you will do about it," Seven said.

From the distance she heard a scream of agony. Anthony.

"I have to go," she said.

She closed her eyes, opened them again, and she

was back in control of her body. Anthony was lying on the floor, Freaky the panther pinning his chest down with a massive paw.

Samantha waved her hand and Freaky shrank down until he was once more an adorable little kitten. He mewed and looked up at her. Then he jumped off Anthony and bounded over to her, where he made himself busy wrapping around her ankles.

"Are you okay?" she asked, readjusting to the feel of using her vocal cords.

Anthony sat up and eyed her suspiciously. "That depends entirely on who's asking."

She went to him, careful not to step on Freaky, and dropped to her knees next to him. "It's me, Samantha. It's always been me."

There were tears streaming down her face.

"I don't understand, and right now I don't want to. I'm just glad you're back," he said, relief shining in his eyes.

He grabbed the back of her head and pulled her close and kissed her. She closed her eyes, savoring the taste of his lips against hers. She had missed him, more than even she had realized.

"I can't do this without you," she whispered as she pulled away.

"I know. That's why I'm here," he said grimly.

"I wasn't the witch who killed your mother."

"I know that, too."

She grabbed his hands and squeezed them. "I have my memories back now, almost all of them. I didn't kill her, but I did see her killed."

He went completely still. Fear rushed through her.

Would he be able to accept her knowing the truth? Silence stretched between them. She could see the emotions colliding within him. She so desperately wanted to take a peek inside his mind and see what he was thinking, but she refrained, trying to respect his privacy.

"Did she suffer?" he asked.

"She was terrified, but she was killed so quickly there wouldn't have been any pain," she said.

Silence again. His features began to harden and she fought against her own despair. He had to know the truth, though, deserved to know it. She couldn't be with him if he didn't know, because she could never fully be herself, and for his part there would always be wonder, doubt.

"I understand if you don't want—"

He grabbed her and kissed her again, harder this time. She let go of his hands and he wrapped his arms around her, nearly crushing her in his grip. She kissed him back, hoping, praying that this meant he would be able to forgive and accept.

"Is it okay?" she asked, breathing the words against his lips.

"Yes. Anything you did, it's in the past. I want you, want to be with you."

"I want that, too."

Suddenly she felt a disturbance in the air, and a moment later, the front door slammed open with a crash and a woman's body flew into the room.

9

With a shout Samantha leaped to her feet. She called fireballs to both hands and was about to lob them through the air when she realized that it was Claudia's corpse that was standing in the center of the room, teetering on the balls of her feet.

She crashed to the floor and was still.

"She's dead," Anthony said as he moved closer. "And I'm no expert, but it looks like she's been dead for more than just a couple of seconds."

"She died last night," Samantha said. "The witch killed her in front of me. She was one of my spies, a girl that I spared up in Salem."

"That's too bad," Anthony said.

"Whoever dropped the body off is already long gone," Samantha said. "And I have a feeling there's no use giving chase."

"There's a note taped to her chest," Anthony observed.

Samantha leaned down to read it. "Next time don't send one of your flying monkeys to do a witch's work."

"Cute," Anthony said with a growl.

"Whoever this woman is, she has a sick sense of humor and she's really starting to piss me off," Samantha muttered. "I need to figure out who she is and stop her before more people get hurt."

"I think I know someone who can help you put the pieces together and figure out who's behind all this," Anthony said, "a guy with a real analytical mind who's good at this sort of thing."

"Who?"

"There's someone else here in town who wants to help, who wants to see you," Anthony said. "Ed."

"Ed?" she asked, stunned. "As in my former partner in the Boston Police Department?"

"One and the same. He came down with me. We're both staying at a hotel not that far away. I convinced him that it was a good idea that I come alone first since you might not be really up to receiving visitors."

"Good thinking," she said, reeling slightly from the news. Ed was the last person she would have expected to come down here in an effort to help capture a witch.

"I had a feeling something was really wrong, and I wasn't sure what he could handle if it was."

"Certainly not that," she said, with a shudder. "I can't even imagine what would have happened if he'd seen me like that. Frankly, I'm surprised he's even here."

"Well, truth be told, I think his wife's been haranguing him about how he treated you. Plus, I have a feeling he hates his new partner."

Samantha smiled. "And there it is. Better the devil you know . . ."

Anthony shrugged. "Maybe. Anyway, he's here, and

I know it took a lot. But he wants to help and I think you need to let him."

"It's dangerous."

"He knows that. He's here anyway. He's a cop. Maybe he can actually help you figure this all out. You know, solve crimes like the two of you used to do together. I kind of think that would be good for both of you right now."

"You're probably right. I'm just . . . I'm embarrassed to see him."

"Why? You did nothing wrong. You did your job, like he and the captain and everyone wanted you to do. It's he who should be embarrassed about how he treated you afterward."

She nodded, but she still felt hesitant. In many ways she had felt that Ed's betrayal was inevitable. That didn't mean that it didn't hurt like the devil, though.

"So, what do you say? Are you ready to go see him?" Anthony asked.

"Not really, but I'm getting the feeling that I don't have a choice in the matter," she said.

He bent forward and kissed her. "No, you really don't. I've been letting you make too many of the decisions in this relationship, and it's been bad for both of us."

She smiled at that. "I like the new Anthony, even more assertive than the old Anthony."

"Hey, that's what love will do to a guy."

She felt her heart skip a beat.

He smiled at her. "Yes, you heard me right. I said it and now you just have to deal with it."

Before she could even respond he kissed her again.

"Okay, let's go. Time for you to stop playing the Lone Ranger and call in the posse to help."

"If you say so," she said.

"I do. Now let's get going so we can find this witch and put her down. Then we can all go home."

He stood up and held his hands out to her. She grabbed hold of them and let him pull her to her feet. "Sounds good to me," she said.

"Come on, Freaky," Anthony said as he led her toward the door.

The kitten scampered along, running in and around their feet, threatening to trip both of them.

"He is a rambunctious little guy," Anthony said.

"He stays," she said.

"As long as he's like this and not a big, scary panther trying to rip my throat out, I'm good with that," he said.

She smiled. For just a moment she let herself forget everything that they were facing, the witch that was waiting, the impending apocalypse that was sure to be coming. It was just her and Anthony and Freaky, together. A family.

She blushed to think of it. She'd never really thought she'd have one of those. Her mind was filling with images of her and Anthony and Freaky and maybe someday children as well. She wasn't sure what had happened to her, but she felt more peace than she'd ever known. She couldn't help feeling that her five-year-old self must be nodding in approval.

It made no sense. When she left Salem she'd thought that she wasn't ready to deal with a relationship with Anthony, that there was too much baggage, too much history. In a moment, though, it all seemed to be coming so clear. That history didn't have to tear them apart. It could bind them together. They understood each other more than anyone else could ever understand either of them. If he was willing to risk everything to be with her, she'd be a fool to push him away again.

She took a deep breath. She wouldn't. He had seen her at her worst. She just prayed that they'd both live for him to see her at her best.

They got into Anthony's car and Freaky settled himself on her lap, purring. As she petted him she got the distinct impression that he also preferred this form to the panther one. That was fine by her. A little ball of fluff was much easier to handle, and softer, too.

The drive was over faster than she would have liked. Anthony parked near a small hotel with classic charm. There was a small coffee shop right next door.

They climbed out of the car and Samantha took a deep breath as she faced the hotel.

"I think it's better if you do this without me," Anthony said. "I'll be waiting in the coffee shop when you guys are ready."

"Are you sure?"

"Yeah, I'll be fine. Freaky, want to come with me?"

The kitten looked up at Samantha. It was probably best. Of course, the easiest thing would be just to dispel the energy and then reform him later. It did no harm to him and was one of the reasons having an energy kitten was far more convenient than a flesh-and-blood one. She couldn't bring herself to do it, though. Maybe it was because she was feeling so insecure. Maybe it was because she was tired of having him go away.

"Go with Anthony," she told Freaky.

The kitten walked over and rubbed against Anthony's leg. Anthony stooped to pick him up. "He is a soft little guy. You'd never know . . . well, you know."

She hid a smile. Even he was having issues with saying the kitten wasn't real. Freaky had his own kind of magic, it seemed.

"See you soon," she told Anthony.

"He's in room twelve," Anthony said, before tucking Freaky inside his coat, turning, and walking into the coffee shop.

Room twelve. Samantha shook her head. All the memories that she had regained and yet she was still missing the memories from the day her coven was slaughtered. Twelve had terrified her and now it eluded her still.

Samantha steeled herself and then headed into the building. Room twelve was the last room on the third floor as it turned out. She knocked on the door and a moment later Ed opened it.

"Hey," she said, feeling incredibly awkward.

"Hey, yourself," he said.

They stood for a moment and then he stepped back, opening the door wide. "I invite you in," he said.

"I'm not a vampire," she snapped.

He winced. "See, there's the smart-ass partner I miss."

"I miss you, too," she admitted.

"You know they've got me partnered with Jackass Jackson right now?"

She did know, but he probably didn't remember that. "Seriously?" she asked. "And you haven't shot him yet?"

"I'm getting close to it," he grunted.

"I'd pay to see that," she quipped.

"Yeah, I'm thinking a lot of people would. Actually I'm starting to think of that as a possible retirement plan."

She smiled. She had missed Ed more than she'd ever wanted to let herself think about. The three years they were partners had been great, comfortable, easy, and they had always been a good team.

"Well, if you decide to go that route, be sure to let me know so I can get a front-row seat."

Instead of laughing, he dropped his eyes and heaved a sigh. "Look, this whole thing is screwed up," he said, staring at the floor. "Everything that happened back in Salem. It was bad, you know?"

"I remember," she said. He had pushed her into going undercover in the coven, pushed her into using her powers. Then, when it was all over, he had shut her out, saying he couldn't be around her after knowing the things that she had done. It had hurt, but she had respected his wishes and left. Now, standing in front of him, she didn't know what to do—apologize, tell him to forget it—so she decided to stay quiet and let him take the lead. After all, he had come down here to help. That had to mean something, didn't it?

"Look. I was a jerk. You saved my life. You did your job. You did what I'd demanded you to do. I should have listened to you, cared more about what you were saying, not pushed you."

"So many more people would have died if you hadn't. I was just afraid of what it would mean for me, for my life, for everyone around me. Using magic, it's a slippery slope. Once you start, it's hard to control yourself. In the end, though, you pushed me into doing the right thing."

"Yeah. Then I pushed you away. That was total crap."

"Is that you or your wife, Vanessa, talking?"

"Hell, if I was a smarter man and not a pigheaded bastard, I'd let her do most of my talking. She's one smart woman."

"She loves you very much."

"God only knows why. I'm just grateful that she does. And, yeah, she's been riding my ass on this, calling me on my shit. But she's right."

Samantha bit her lip, not wanting to interrupt, but daring to hope that this might end well after all.

"Listen, you were the best damn partner I ever had and I miss that—I miss you. I'm here to apologize. I'm sorry for the way I treated you. You didn't deserve that from anyone, least of all me."

"Thank you," she said, throat burning with the emotions she was trying to hold back.

"We get this whole mess finished down here and I want you to come back. I talked with Captain Roberts and he said you could come back. We could be partners again."

"What about everyone else in the department?" Samantha asked, remembering the way everyone had looked at her, the fear and accusation in their eyes, just before she'd been forced to leave.

Ed raised his eyes. "To hell with them. If anyone gives you any crap for even a second, they'll have to answer to me."

She hugged him.

"We don't hug," he said.

"We do now, moron," she said.

He laughed and hugged her back. When they broke away a moment later, they were both wiping at their eyes.

"Okay, now that all that's out of the way, let's figure this case out so we can get out of here. New Orleans gives me the creeps."

"It would," she said with a chuckle.

"Yeah, I figure your witch-dar is working overtime, because even I'm feeling it here," he said.

She sighed. "It is, but it's not helping me find the one witch behind all of this."

He gestured to a table and a couple of chairs in the corner of the room and she sat.

"Fill me in," he said as he took the other chair.

She told him what she could, bringing him up to speed. When she had finished he whistled low.

"That's a wicked mess."

"Tell me about it."

"So the key is figuring out who this black-haired chick is, since she's probably behind all this?"

"That's what I'm thinking."

"Okay, so let's think rationally. We might be dealing with witches, but they still have human motivations. Nothing special there. Lust, power, revenge, there're only so many things that can be coming into play here."

"Okay, good. Where do we start?"

He rolled his eyes. "Come on, you haven't not been a cop for that long."

"Humor me. I'm a little too close to this one," she said.

"Okay, this all seems quite personal and whoever's behind this has been targeting you from the start. They knew who you were before. Now, not many people could have known that. You have to think. It has to be someone from your past, someone who knew you, who's doing all this," Ed said.

"I know, but I can't think of anyone. Besides, how can it be? Everyone's dead."

"Your whole coven? Are you sure?"

"Positive. I saw their graves."

"Could one of them be empty, like yours?"

"No, I could feel the bodies in there."

"Okay. Creepy, but okay. So you alone escaped."

"I was the only one who escaped the massacre," she confirmed. "I'm the only member of my coven to survive."

"Could it have been a witch outside your coven who was somehow wronged or denied entrance or something?"

"If that was true, I'm not sure how they'd even know about me. My mother worked to keep a very low profile outside the coven itself. And it's not like it can just be a random victim or the son of one, like Anthony. Whoever's behind this has powers."

"Did anyone in the coven have young kids who wouldn't have been there that night? Someone looking for revenge maybe?"

"No, my mom was one of the youngest in the coven and I was the youngest kid."

He grimaced. "Anthony told me there were other kids in the coven who were killed that night."

"Yes, Billy was a year old than me, and Destiny was

about four years older. She was being raised by her grandmother after her parents died. The only other one with a kid was Mr. Black."

A memory stirred. Something she hadn't thought about in a long, long time. In her head she saw a teen girl, with long, dark hair and hard, cold eyes.

"What is it?" Ed asked, sensing her hesitation.

"I think . . . I think there was someone missing the night of the massacre."

He straightened. "Are you sure?"

"I'm trying to think, remember. His daughter, she had black hair and blue eyes, dead eyes. She was older than me, a teen. I remember her from when I was younger. She was always kind of mean, just like her father. But then she disappeared when I was about nine or so. It seems like she came by once or twice after that, but then she'd go away again."

"Samantha, think. This is very important. You said she was older than you. Is it possible that she was old enough to be in college?"

"Yes! That's it. She went away to college. She only came home on a couple of breaks. She wasn't there the night of the massacre. I mean, I can't remember that night well, but I know that everyone who was there was killed."

"But she isn't dead?"

"There was no grave at the cemetery for her with the others. Her father was there, but not her. It has to be her. She has to be the one behind all this."

"What was her name?"

"Lilith. Lilith Black."

"Helluva name for a witch."

Her chest tightened, as if a fist were squeezing her heart. "All these years, I thought I was the last one, the last survivor. But I'm not. There are two of us."

"Now we're getting somewhere," Ed said, a look of satisfaction on his face. "And we have a name. I can see if there's anything I can find out about her. And now that you know who she is, can't you do some kind of location spell or summoning spell or something like that?"

"Normally, but she is really powerful and she seems to have all these protections and wards around her. I'm not sure any of the usual tricks are going to work on her."

"Then it's time to start thinking outside the box. Get a little creative."

She thought of her infant self, breathing fire. "You know, yesterday I would have said that wasn't possible, but today the world seems completely different to me."

"Good. Let's work on finding this witch and then we can figure out a plan to take her down."

"I don't want you and Anthony getting hurt. He's not going to want to go, but I need you to take him—"

He held up a hand, interrupting her. "Don't even bother. We're both here to see this through to the end. Yeah, we owe you, but we also owe ourselves and the universe."

"The universe is notoriously bad at thanking those who sacrifice on its behalf," she said, raising an eyebrow.

"Doesn't matter. One way or another, we will see it done."

"Thank you," she said, reaching out to squeeze his hand.

"You're welcome. Now, let's talk about this Anthony character. It seems like he's really into you. You want me to have a talk with him, put the fear of God in him about hurting you?"

She laughed. "I don't think that will be necessary."

"Okay, but you say the word and I'm happy to break his legs for you."

"I'll keep that in mind."

"You like him, too."

She flushed. "Is it that obvious?"

"I've known you for three years. He's the first guy I've ever even seen you look twice at. So, yeah, little bit."

"Good to know." She stood. "Speaking of Anthony, he's waiting for us in the coffee shop downstairs."

"Great, I'm starving."

They walked downstairs and Samantha was amazed at how improved her mood was. Relationships, friends she had thought she had lost were being restored as if by magic. The best part was, she knew magic had nothing to do with it.

Once inside the coffee shop, she saw Anthony seated at a table, drinking a cup of coffee. Freaky was sitting on the table dipping his paw in and out of a saucer of milk. She'd have to explain to Anthony that Freaky didn't need to actually eat or drink anything, another advantage of an energy kitten.

As she watched, Freaky shook his paw, sending droplets of milk everywhere.

Ed slid into the booth and Samantha followed. Freaky bounded over to her.

"That cat ain't real, is he?" Ed said.

"Real enough," Samantha said. She looked up at Anthony, who was studying them intently. "Did they give you any trouble about having a cat in here?" Samantha asked.

"They started to, but I told them not to mess with him or they could watch him turn into a black panther."

Samantha bit her lip. Freaky shouldn't be able to change at his own will or even Anthony's command. She wouldn't tell him that, though. Besides, there was something about the little kitten that almost made her believe that he could.

"Hey, I kind of want to see that," Ed said.

"Trust me on this one. You really don't," Anthony said. "So, I take it we're all good."

"Better than good," Samantha said. "I figured out who's behind all this."

Anthony's eyes bulged. "Wow, that was fast. You two are a good team."

"The best," Ed said.

"It turns out one of the coven members, Lilith Black, was away at college. She wasn't there the night of the massacre."

Anthony blinked. "Can you imagine coming back to the slaughter? The devastation and rage?"

"And then finding out you weren't the last one of your coven?" Ed said. "I bet she had some questions for you about what happened."

"But with you having been adopted and changing your name, maybe she couldn't find you," Anthony said.

"Whatever her motivation, or her damage, I'm sure she's the one behind all of this," Samantha said.

A waiter came over, interrupting the conversation.

They ordered some food, and as soon as the waiter left, they resumed their conversation.

"So, how do we find her?" Anthony asked.

"We've already got a plan for that," Ed said.

"If it works," Samantha cautioned.

They filled him in and a couple of minutes later their food arrived. Samantha picked up her burger and took a huge bite. Out of the corner of her eye she saw Ed grab a French fry off her plate, and joy filled her. He truly had forgiven her; it wasn't just lip service, if he was back to filching food.

Freaky took note and sauntered over and began grabbing at her fries. Anthony laughed. The little kitten was clearly enjoying the attention and Samantha rolled her eyes as she rescued a fry from him.

A moment later, she froze as she felt a surge of power. There was someone outside the restaurant.

10

"Wait here," she said, standing swiftly. "There's some-one outside."

"Do you need backup?" Ed asked quickly.

"Hopefully not. Feels like one person. If I'm not back in ten minutes, though, come out and make as big a commotion as you can," she said.

"Got it," Anthony said intently, not even noticing as Freaky turned and began attacking his hamburger.

Samantha walked outside, wondering who would be waiting out there. Maybe it was just Nala, checking in. Samantha hadn't exactly made herself difficult to find.

She pushed open the door and walked outside. There, leaning against the side of the building, arms folded over his chest, was the self-proclaimed Druid she'd run into before.

"So, you appear again," she said, not bothering to hide her surprise.

"Well, you're a rather easy witch to find," he said.

She bit back the urge to tell him she wasn't a witch. Time enough to clear things up once she knew who he was and why he had pulled her out of the cemetery.

"Thank you for saving my life," she said.

"You're welcome."

"How come you didn't stick around?"

"Things were getting a little busy for my taste, and crowded. Didn't care to talk to the police," he said.

She nodded.

"So, you seem . . . different."

"It's a woman's prerogative to change."

"Yeah, this is a bit more than your hair color, though."

"I'm surprised you can tell."

He shrugged. "I would have thought anyone with half a brain could."

"So, why did you save me?"

"Let's just say you were the lesser of two evils in that graveyard."

She stared at him intently. "You're lying about something."

"Probably," he admitted.

"Why?"

"Care to tell me how you're so much different today?"

"Not really."

"There you go," he said.

"What are you doing here? Care to tell me that?"

He sized her up and after a moment gave her a faint smile. "I want you to know that you're not alone. The witch who did that to you last night? I want her stopped, too."

"Then why didn't you join in the battle last night?"

"It wouldn't have done any good. It's going to take a lot more than either of us had to offer last night to take her down."

"Are there others in the city who feel the same way?" Samantha asked.

"A few, but most don't even realize why they're here. Heck, most don't even realize that it wasn't their choice to come here."

"Did you kill that waiter in the alley?" she asked, changing her line of questioning.

"No."

She nodded. "Can you help me?"

"I can try."

"Why do you want her stopped? And how come you're aware of what's going on when so many others aren't?" she questioned.

"As it turns out, being hypersensitive to the forces that are acting on me is one of my strengths, something of a gift and a curse. When I'm at the top of my game, I can even feel ripples when people make decisions and get a sense of how they will affect me, or if they will."

"That's pretty impressive," Samantha said. "I've actually never heard of that."

"There are a few of us out there who can do it. It requires a level of self-awareness most people are unwilling to experience or incapable of achieving."

"Chalk me up in the unwilling category," she said before she could stop herself.

"When that changes for you, when you truly become comfortable in your own skin, you're going to wield power that will amaze anyone who sees you," he said.

"Is that a fact?" she asked, raising an eyebrow. "And just how is it you know that about me?"

"Like I said, I'm sensitive to the things that are going to affect me and sometimes to the things that can potentially affect me. You are chock-full of potential to do great things, save the world. Frankly, I'm relieved. Yesterday I would have said you were chock-full of potential to destroy the world."

"And yet you chose to help me."

He shrugged. "Like I said, the lesser of two evils."

"Also known as the enemy of my enemy," she suggested.

"You could say that."

"And why is it that you want her stopped?"

He laughed. "Seriously? She plans on killing every one of us, using us to amp her own power. And thanks to her spell, it's not like I can leave the city. I can't hide from her forever. And my instincts tell me that in the end, you have the best chance at stopping her. You're connected, I think, the two of you."

"I just found out that you're right about that."

He nodded, clearly not surprised.

"You seem pretty calm for a dead man walking," she noted.

"It's mostly an act, but when you've made as many hard decisions in your life as I have, you learn to get comfortable with pain and fear."

"That doesn't sound like much of a way to live."

"Running from the things that frighten you isn't much of a way to live, either," he noted.

"Ouch," she said.

He shrugged. "I call them as I see them."

"Clearly."

"So, am I right? Are you the one who's going to put a stop to her tyranny, save the world?"

"What can I say? I will or I'll die trying."

"I had that impression."

She shrugged. "Like you said, no one's leaving this city anyway."

He rolled his eyes. "You're a hero. We both know it, so don't play it down."

"Fine. Then how about you stop dancing around? You plan on helping me, I mean, more than just dragging me out of the line of fire? Will you fight when the time comes?"

He nodded. "When the time comes I'll stand with you."

"Thank you, Thomas. Is that what you said your name was?"

"It's as good a name as any."

"Not really one to throw stones on that account," she said.

"Great. Now you might want to get back inside. I'm getting the distinct feeling that if you don't, someone's about to make a decision to shoot me."

"How can I reach you?"

"Don't worry. I'll find you. I'm never that far away."

He turned and walked off.

"That isn't very reassuring," she said with a sigh as she turned and walked back inside.

Ed did, indeed, have his hand on his holstered gun and have a look on his face that didn't bode well.

"Stand down—everything's okay," she said.

"Who was out there?" Anthony asked.

"An ally, I think. He seems to be at any rate. I know that he saved my life last night."

"That puts him in the ally category in my book," Ed said, taking his hand off his weapon and picking his hamburger back up.

Samantha dropped her eyes to the table. "Looks like someone's been having fun," she said drily.

Freaky had managed to completely disassemble Anthony's burger, strewing the components all about the table. He had a dollop of mustard on the top of his head and he was currently rolling over and over on the lettuce with wild abandon.

Anthony looked down and grimaced. "Great. I know he's an energy creature, but I'm not sure I want to know where those paws have been."

Samantha bit her lip. "Maybe we should order you another burger and talk strategy some more."

Samantha flagged down the waiter, who looked down at the table in disgust. "We're going to need another burger here," Samantha told him.

"The health code—"

Samantha forced her eyes to start glowing and Ed leaned forward, making sure the waiter got an eyeful of the gun he was packing. The man beat a hasty retreat.

"You know they're never going to let us back in here," Anthony said.

Ed shrugged. "They will if they know what's good for them." He glanced down at Freaky. "That little guy ever go to sleep?"

"You got to tire him out first, just like the real thing," Samantha said.

Freaky sat down in the middle of the table and began to groom himself as if he had not a care in the world. Samantha couldn't help laughing, especially when he kept continually missing the mustard blob on his head.

"Help a kitten out. That's just sad," Ed said.

Samantha reached over with her napkin and rubbed off the mustard. Freaky swiped at her napkin, but she managed to move it out of the way just in time.

The waiter finally brought Anthony's replacement burger and he quickly snatched it off his plate before Freaky could attack it.

Samantha actually felt herself relaxing for the first time in months. It was good to have friends and share a meal and some laughter with them. It was also good to know that she had an ally out there, even if he did play his cards pretty close to the vest.

She couldn't blame Thomas. In a town full of people like them with a crazy witch bent on killing them all, it was hard to know who to trust, especially when that same witch had the power to control and manipulate others like puppets.

"Okay, so, what's the plan?" Ed asked as they neared the end of their meal.

"Leave no tip and get out of here as quick as we can?" Anthony quipped.

Samantha rolled her eyes. "You two should never have gotten to be friends. I can see it's just going to complicate my life."

"I resent that," Ed said. "We're not friends. We're the two guys who are stuck looking after you."

Anthony smirked.

"Okay, seriously, I need some sleep. I'm dead on my feet," she admitted.

"Okay, but what about in the morning?" Ed asked.

"Thomas suggested that there might be others willing to help and that most of the community isn't even aware of what's going on."

"I've been down here before on a couple of research tours, collecting things for the museum. I know a few people. I could make some discreet inquiries tomorrow, see who's in the know and who's willing to do something about it," Anthony volunteered.

Anthony had owned a museum of the occult in Salem before it had been destroyed by witches. She remembered how frantic she had been when she thought the witches might also have killed him in the process.

"I don't want to put you in harm's way," she said.

"Hello? We're all kind of screwed until we put this witch down," Ed said. "Let the man do his thing."

"What about you?" Anthony asked Ed.

"I'm going to go talk with local law enforcement, say I'm working a case that seems to track back here, see if anyone knows anything whatsoever. Maybe they have a suspect for the theme park killings. Even if they don't know Lilith, they might know someone who does."

"Great," Samantha said. "I'm going to spend the day trying to find her."

"In a city full of magic users, that's going to be hard," Anthony commented.

"Yeah, and she's definitely put some wards up to protect herself and her location, but there's got to be something she hasn't thought of that I can do to try and get a better idea where she's hiding out. I'm positive she's got to be in the city itself."

"Yeah, 'cause that narrows it down so much," Ed said sarcastically.

"It's at least a start," Samantha said.

"Meet up here for breakfast?" Anthony suggested.

"Let's make it brunch. I have to get a lot of sleep and then there're a couple things I'll want to try and set in motion as soon as I'm up."

"Okay, so let's say eleven, here, to touch base. Call in if something comes up," Ed said.

"Works," Samantha said.

Anthony nodded in agreement.

"All right, drive her home and I'll get the check," Ed said.

"Are you sure?" Anthony asked.

Samantha hit him. "Don't give him a chance to change his mind."

The two slid out of the booth and Ed gave them a short wave as he reached for his wallet. Samantha scooped Freaky up and followed Anthony out to the car.

Exhaustion was starting to hit her hard. In the car she did all she could to fight going to sleep. Freaky was no help, curling up on her lap and beginning to snore before Anthony had even put the car in drive.

When they arrived back at the house, Anthony walked her inside. "You might want to think about relocating. I think there're more rooms at the hotel we're at," he noted.

"I should move, but I don't want to draw more attention to you and Ed," she admitted, setting Freaky down on the floor. He headed off upstairs, clearly ready for bed.

"I get that, but we can also watch out for one another easier."

She didn't want to tell him that it felt too much like putting all their eggs in one basket.

She put her arms around him. "Thank you for coming to rescue me," she whispered.

"Not a problem," he said, rubbing her back.

It felt so good to have him hold her. She had been alone for so long, truly alone the last several months. And even before that, really, if she was honest with herself.

"You want to hear something weird?" she said, her words muffled against his shoulder.

"Always."

"You're the closest thing I've ever had to a real boyfriend," she admitted.

His arms tightened around her. "Really?" he asked.

"Yeah. Isn't that strange?"

"No. You don't let people in easily."

She pulled away so she could see his expression, full of tenderness and understanding.

"Let me guess," she said, her breath catching in her throat. "You're in the same boat?"

"Obsessed with finding and destroying my mother's killer is surprisingly a turnoff as a pickup line."

"Doesn't work so well on those online dating profiles, either, I'm guessing," she joked.

"Surprisingly, no. I mean, sure, you've got the odd nut job volunteering to be said killer, or your mother, not sure which is actually creepier, but not so much anyone you'd ever want to meet."

"We are two peas in a pod," she said with a tired smile.

"Careful, you might be close to admitting you actually like me," he teased.

She smiled. "In the interest of full disclosure, I think I do like you."

"Imagine that. Well, if we're being that honest with each other, I think I like you, too."

For just a moment Samantha felt as if she were living someone else's life, someone who could have a life with a boyfriend and romance and time to just stare into each other's eyes without worrying about killer witches and an entire town full of people at risk of being destroyed. She had to admit it felt good.

"You know, I'm starting to see what my old roommate, Jill, was talking about when she'd say that having a boyfriend was great," Samantha murmured.

"Am I losing my mind, or did you just call me your boyfriend?" Anthony asked, his face mere inches from hers.

"Oh, you're definitely losing your—"

He kissed her. Time seemed to stand still as she kissed him back. Slowly she lifted her hands to the sides of his face and sent gentle electrical impulses into his skin. He groaned softly against her lips and held her tighter.

This was what normal people did. Normal people got to have relationships and spend time with those they loved.

Samantha started.

Loved. She had thought of Anthony not as someone she cared for or liked, but as someone she loved.

"What's wrong?" he asked, searching her eyes.

"Nothing," she breathed.

She realized she was shaking all over. Should she tell him? Would it be fair, given that there was a very real probability that Lilith was going to kill her? Then again, given all that they were facing, was it fair not to tell him?

"Are you sure?" he asked, cupping her cheek with his hand.

She leaned into it, savoring the sensation of his skin against hers. She closed her eyes.

"Anthony, we might not live through this," she said.

"I know, so there's something you should know," he said, his voice, low, urgent.

"What is it?" she asked, opening her eyes to look at him.

"You might think I'm crazy, but I'm not. I've had a long time to think about this, even though I didn't need any time at all, really. I know I said it earlier, but I'm not sure you really heard me. Samantha, you should know, I love you."

Something inside her felt like bursting into song. She felt a grin spreading across her face that she couldn't control. "I love you, too," she whispered.

With a sob of joy he pulled her close and began to kiss her again. The kisses were sweet, tender, and they spoke to her on a level she had never known. She felt a connection to him she had never shared with another person.

"I will do everything in my power to see us both through this," he promised her.

"I'll do the same," she said.

She didn't want the night to end. She wanted to stand there, hugging and kissing him forever, but her body was beginning to shut down because of exhaustion.

Finally he pulled away. "You need your rest."

"I'm fine," she lied.

"No, you're not. Don't worry. This will not be the last time we're together like this," he promised.

He kissed the tip of her nose and it made her smile again.

"I'll see you tomorrow," he promised.

He left and she listened until she could no longer hear his car; then she turned and headed upstairs.

Freaky was already passed out on the bed, and a minute later she joined him. She was too tired even to change out of her clothes. Besides, her shirt smelled like Anthony and she wasn't ready to give up that scent just yet.

So much had happened in a single day and she was intensely grateful for how it had ended.

"Freaky," she whispered to the sleeping kitten. "This might have been the most important day of my life."

He just continued to snore away as she drifted off to sleep.

She stood, barefoot, a member of the circle. Her mother was always telling her that the circle was power. So was Mr. Black. She was tired. Her mother had woken her in the middle of the night for a coven meeting that she hadn't known they were going to have.

Usually the coven meetings were scheduled, but this one was a surprise to Samantha. Her mother wouldn't say what they were going to do or why it was starting after midnight. She told her to leave her things behind. She wouldn't need them for this particular meeting.

Samantha couldn't help having a bad feeling about everything, even as they silently greeted the others on the way into Abigail's house. They walked through the kitchen and down into the basement. Light from the candles down there cast disturbing shadows on the walls.

Samantha hesitated. Something didn't feel right. The air even seemed different somehow. She greeted each coven member as she encountered everyone, as was their custom. None of them would look at her. She felt as if she had done something wrong and she was being shunned for it. She searched her mind but could come up with nothing. Was it possible they were here to punish her? But what could it possibly be for?

Without preamble Abigail urged them all to join hands, forming the circle. "The circle is life, the circle is coven, the circle is blood," she intoned.

The others mimicked her.

Abigail had an altar set up tonight in the center of the circle, another rarity. Usually she stood alone in the center of the circle with any objects she would need for the ritual in her hands. The few times Samantha had seen the altar had all been bad, terrible experiences. She hunched her shoulders, dreading whatever must be coming next.

On the altar rested a large book and a chalice. There were a variety of objects surrounding the chalice, and Abigail began to chant and to add them one at a time into the goblet.

As the mixture formed, it created a powerful, sickly sweet odor that made Samantha wrinkle up her nose. She wanted to sneeze, but she knew from experience that would be met with severe punishment later from her mother.

At last the final item was added, and Abigail raised her head, a look of triumphant expectation on her face. Samantha wondered if something was supposed to have happened, because nothing did. Abigail didn't look worried, though. Instead she looked more excited than Samantha could ever remember seeing her.

"Tonight we achieve ultimate power," Abigail boomed to her followers. "For tonight we raise a creature who will be chained to us, who must do our bidding, an ancient demon, one of twelve that ruled this realm ages ago before they were banished. We will claim his power, his allegiance, for ourselves."

Samantha felt something horrible curl itself into her belly. She shook her head violently from side to side. This wasn't right; she could feel it. They were messing with something far stronger and smarter than them and it couldn't end well. She didn't want any part of it. Something terrible was going to happen, she knew. She had never been so certain of anything in her life. She was so certain, she was willing to risk whatever punishment might befall her as long as she could get out of that basement now.

"Mother, we must leave," she whispered.

Her mother didn't answer, didn't even look at her. She just tightened her grip on Samantha's hand until it physically hurt. Mr. Black did the same on her other side. The circle must remain unbroken—*that's what he would probably say. But this was different. They were all in danger. She*

*didn't know how she knew, but she knew it with all her soul.
They didn't understand. She couldn't explain it to them. She
didn't have time, and she wasn't sure they would listen to her
anyway.*

*She had to stop this, had to make them see reason before it
was too late for all of them. But what could she do?*

*"Only one last ingredient remains and then we shall see
him come forth," Abigail crowed.*

*Suddenly she fixed her laserlike stare on Samantha.
"Come here, child," she said.*

*Her mother and Mr. Black pushed her forward and then
linked hands behind her, resealing the circle. This was her
chance. She needed to tell Abigail no, even if the high priestess was angry, even if she hurt her. It was her duty to save
the coven.*

Abigail put a hand under her chin. "Do you know wh—"

Her phone rang on the nightstand and Samantha sat
straight up in bed, shaking and drenched in sweat. The
nightmare began to fade quickly and she shouted in
frustration. She'd been dreaming about the night of the
massacre. She'd been so close to learning the truth; she
could feel it.

The phone rang again, loud and shrill. She reached
over and picked it up. It was a local number but one
she didn't know.

Samantha answered the call, struggling to control
her breathing, which was coming out in ragged gasps
as the last vestiges of the dream slipped away from her.

She brought the phone to her ear.

"Help me!" a young, female voice choked out.

"Nala, is that you?" she asked, the voice sounding

similar to what she thought the girl sounded like. "How did you get this number?"

"Help me! There's someone after me."

"Just hold on. Tell me where you are."

There was a scream and the line went dead.

11

Samantha leaped off the bed. It was three in the morning and her body was still shaking from the nightmare and now also from the shock of adrenaline that was hitting it.

Nala, she had dealt with Desdemona and she was still sorting all those memories out. Where would the girl be? She'd said she knew somewhere safe to go, but clearly it was no longer so.

She ran downstairs and made it into her car, gritting her teeth at how long it was probably going to take to reach Nala. She had to go to her. She had to assume the girl would be unable to come to her, even if she compelled her.

She had nothing of Nala's to use, so she repurposed Martin's business card, since it had been, at least briefly, in Nala's possession. As with before, the card began to spin about, the arrow pointing in the direction she needed to go.

She chafed under every minor redirect and delay,

wondering what was happening to the girl while she was trying to reach her. Deep down, though, she knew that she would probably be too late, particularly if she had actually come face-to-face with Lilith.

If so, she wondered if Lilith would kill her outright or realize that she could use her to get to Samantha. Then again, she hadn't made very much use of the leverage that Claudia should have given her, killing the girl without even giving Desdemona a chance to do something reckless to try to save her.

Not that she probably would have with that part of her personality in control. Still, she had been shocked that Lilith hadn't even bothered trying. The logical thing to do would have been to kill the other girl, the stranger, first. That's what she would have done.

The drive seemed endless, but she finally made it into a very upscale section of the Garden District. The streets were deserted this time of the night and it hardly seemed like someplace Nala would have been unless she was actively trying to find Lilith or someone connected to her. Given the time of night, that seemed unlikely. Her hopes lifted slightly. Maybe whoever had taken Nala had brought her here. Plus, the girl had to still be alive or the navigation system would have ceased to function. Maybe there was hope after all.

She finally pulled to a stop in front of a very large, old building. What she could see of it behind its high wrought-iron gates was imposing. A single light burned in one of the windows on the first floor, and she dared to hope that she wasn't too late.

She wondered if this was where Lilith was hiding out, but that didn't seem quite right. Even if she was confident in her victory, Lilith didn't seem the type to lead anyone to her lair.

Samantha leaped from her car and approached the front of the building, having no time for subtleties. She could feel a ripple of power in the air, proof that she was in the right spot.

She lifted her hand and sent a wave of energy at the gates, which pushed open by themselves, creaking slightly. She approached the front of the house, eyes darting about, looking for signs of anyone else.

She could see nothing on the darkened grounds except some statues that she eyed carefully to make sure they weren't people glamoured to appear that way. She thought for a moment she saw one of them move out of the corner of her eye but decided that she was just being paranoid.

She returned her focus to the house and debated about whether to try to find a window she could enter through silently. Whoever was inside would already have been alerted to her presence, though, so it seemed like a needless waste of time. The best approach was likely going to be head-on. She made her way quickly to the front door, putting up her hands as she reached it.

The door flew open and she ran through, hands raised defensively, ready to do whatever she must.

Two women were standing in what was the entryway of the mansion. A staircase swept up to the right, and the checked marble tile on the ground led back farther into the house. The two women turned and looked at her. The first was Nala, and Samantha blinked at her as she took in her appearance.

Nala was no longer wearing her raggedy clothes

and oversized trench coat. Instead she was dressed in slacks and a cashmere sweater. She was standing next to an older woman who looked just like her and was wearing a very expensive dress.

Samantha stared intently at Nala, trying to process everything.

"You're—you're not a runaway. Or homeless," Samantha realized.

"Very good," Nala said. "See? You can catch on."

"Neither is she in any danger, but we're oh so grateful to you for coming so quickly," the woman who was clearly her mother said in a simpering voice.

"I don't understand," Samantha said.

"No, I'm sure you probably don't," the older woman said. "Then again, it's my understanding that you have no respect for the power of the circle."

"Lilith! You're part of Lilith's coven," Samantha realized. She had suspected that Lilith probably had others working with her. "You know when she's finished draining everyone else she'll just turn on you, right?"

"I very much doubt that, my dear. You see, she appreciates the power of the coven, the sacred bond of the circle."

"You're a fool if you believe that standing behind her makes you safe," Samantha said.

"We're not standing behind her. We're standing beside her. That's what a coven does," Nala said proudly.

Samantha's brain was busy putting all the pieces together. The demon had told Nala where to find Samantha. There was a decent chance she had told Lilith, or at least others in the coven. She would have thought that part of the story a lie, but the demon had confirmed that it told Nala where she lived and even drove her to just a few blocks away. Why would she even have bothered asking it in the first place, though?

"Did the demon know you were going to be lying to me about who you were?" Samantha asked.

Nala shrugged. "Probably. It is a demon, after all. They're usually pretty good at figuring out what's going on."

"Why go through the demon? That just seems like an unnecessary step, and an uncertain one, given how notorious demons are for lying. There's plenty of ways to find someone using your powers."

"You're not as easy to find as one would think," Nala's mother chimed in. "Don't think we didn't try. Several of us did. As it turns out, though, there seems to be lots of confusion about names and identity, which makes you harder to locate than the average person. Besides, the demon was there. It was convenient. It certainly gave us a leg up on everybody else who was looking for you."

"You were looking for me, not for answers about what happened at the amusement park," Samantha said.

"And you bought everything I told you," Nala said, crowing with pride. "Every lie, every story I made up. You couldn't tell the truth, even when it was under your nose."

"How long have you been with Lilith?" Samantha asked.

"Two years," the mom said, chin lifted high.

"So, then, of course, as part of her coven and having been with her so long, you know exactly what she's got planned," Samantha said.

The woman's smug smile faltered.

"No?" Samantha asked, her voice innocent. "I mean, surely after all that time, and being sisters of the circle and everything, she'd trust you with that information, right? I mean, it's only natural that you know what the goal is since you're assisting."

"She . . . she keeps some things secret, to protect them, to protect us, from outsiders and spies."

"Spies?" Samantha asked, making herself sound shocked. "How could there be spies in the circle? Aren't you all bound together, one big happy family? And wouldn't she know if that wasn't true?"

"Spies can be anywhere," the woman said, trying hard to rally, even though Samantha had struck a nerve. "Plausible deniability. It's saved us on several occasions recently."

"Really, how?" Samantha asked.

"An FBI agent was following me, asking me a bunch of questions, wanted to know about you. I played dumb and scared, kept stringing him along. Then when his guard was down, I threw him into your car, and after that, you killed him for me," Nala said triumphantly.

Samantha felt sick. When was she going to learn to stop trusting the wrong people? Then again, it hadn't exactly been the best or smartest part of her that had believed Nala. She remembered thinking the girl was lying about the attack, but the part of her that had been in control had not been in a listening mood.

It was highly likely that the agent would have died from the damage he'd undergone anyway. And if not, Nala would surely have found a way to finish the job before he could identify himself to Samantha or try to fight back.

She knew that the FBI had a group of witches working for them, hunting down dark covens. She had met two of them before and she hadn't known they were allies until it was nearly too late.

She couldn't help thinking of Randy back in Salem, who had given her his energy to help her defeat the witches there, even though it had cost him his life. Then there had been Trina in California, who, fortunately, had still been alive when Samantha left. She couldn't help wondering what had happened to her. It was possible that she or some other member of her team was already here, investigating. The agent that Nala had thrown into her car might not have been alone.

The thought both comforted her and upset her at the same time.

"How many are in your coven?" she asked, forcing herself back to the task at hand.

"I'll never tell you that," the older woman said.

"They're all in danger, including you. It's not too late to get out. You've gotten in over your head, involved with terrible magic that will destroy everything you hold dear. I can help you, though. You just need to trust me."

The woman laughed. "Why on earth would we want to 'get out'? Thanks to Lilith, we're finally going to have everything we ever wanted and more."

"That's just the lies she's telling you," Samantha said. If she could win the women to her side, the information they had would be invaluable. "I've seen what she does to people, to other witches. She uses them and discards them when they are no longer of value to her."

"You don't know what you're talking about," Nala said heatedly. "Lilith loves us. She would never hurt us."

"That's just what she wants you to think. Lilith loves only herself. I was there in the coven she set up in Salem and saw firsthand how she used the people, trying to get them to raise a demon that she knew would kill them all. In San Francisco she actually managed to possess a powerful witch and force her to do terrible things, things that took so much power and energy that just attempting them put the witch's life in danger every single time. Again she was trying to raise a demon that would destroy a lot of people and do so indiscriminately. Believe me, all Lilith wants is power and destruction and she doesn't care who she has to hurt, who she has to use, to get what she wants."

"A demon?" the woman asked.

"Yes," Samantha said, hoping that maybe she was starting to get through to the woman, that she could talk sense into the two of them.

"Then the rumors are true," she said.

"If you've heard that she's planning on raising a demon here, I would think it's a safe bet she's trying to. I know that whatever she has planned, Salem and San Francisco were just the opening salvos to her bigger plan."

"Do you hear that, Nala?"

"Yes, Mother."

"We're going to be queens!" the older woman crowed as Nala smiled greedily.

"You don't understand," Samantha whispered.

"We understand just fine; it's you that has the problem," Nala said.

"This will be nothing like the demon that possesses Martin," Samantha said. "This will be a monster that kills, destroys everything in its path. None of you will be left alive. I know. I've seen what these things can do. There's no stopping it, no controlling it, no surviving it."

"And yet you lived to tell the tale," the woman said. "The lady doth protest too much, methinks. What do you say, sweetheart?"

"I say, imagine how much more Lilith will favor us if we bring her the head of the witch she couldn't kill," Nala said, raising her hands into the air and throwing fireballs at Samantha.

Samantha dropped to the floor and slammed her fists into it, sending a shock wave through it that knocked both mother and daughter off their feet.

"You don't have to do this!" Samantha shouted, giving them one last chance.

"Of course we don't have to. We *want* to," the mom said as she regained her feet.

Samantha felt a burst of sorrow. There was no way she was going to convince them, either of them. And she couldn't let them live to be a problem, to fight another day.

"Don't make me kill you," she whispered.

"Did you hear that?" Nala said, sneering as she stood up. "How weak, how pathetic is that?"

"You see, my dear, that is what Lilith warns us against. You must always be decisive."

Samantha smiled at them both grimly. "It's tragic, really, how many people mistake compassion for weakness and kindness for indecisiveness."

"You're all talk," the woman said.

Samantha leaped forward, placed a hand on each of their heads, and ripped the power from them. When it was gone, she dropped their bodies to the floor and watched as they rapidly began to decay, their eyes bulging with fear.

"Actually, you were talking about yourself," Samantha said sadly.

In Salem the witches there had taught her to kill a person by pulling energy from him. Lilith had taught her a much more powerful, more effective way of killing by pulling the ability to use their power from people.

The two women were dying, almost gone.

Samantha called a fireball to each hand and dropped them on the bodies, letting them burn alive. For a brief moment she considered burning the house down as well but decided to leave things as they were, a warning for the other members of the coven. So instead she turned and carved words with fire into the floor right in front of the door.

Leave the coven now.

It was all the warning the rest of them were going to get, and it was likely far more than they deserved if Nala and her mother were any indication. She left, closing the door behind her.

Samantha made her way back to the house. Knowing what she did now, there was no way she could stay there anymore. Nala could have told every witch in the coven where she lived. She quickly changed clothes, packed up her stuff, and grabbed Freaky.

"Come on, we're going," she told the little kitten.

She got back in the car and ten minutes after she had gotten there, she was leaving again.

She abandoned the car several miles from the hotel where Anthony and Ed were staying and walked the rest of the way. She could have called Anthony for a ride, but she needed the time to clear her head and think. Freaky rode on her shoulder for most of the distance, his tiny claws digging into her shoulder and helping keep her mind off everything that had just happened.

Right before arriving at the hotel, she dropped Freaky inside her bag, not wanting to deal with trying to hide him magically or argue about whether or not they accepted pets in their establishment.

She walked up to the front desk, booked a room, and convinced them to take cash and no name for it. Then she made her way upstairs, dumped all her stuff next to the bed, freed Freaky from the bag, and headed for the restroom.

She had to take three showers before she got the smell of smoke out of her hair. She lay down on the bed, intending to do so only for a moment.

She woke up a couple of hours later, groggy and disoriented.

She glanced at the clock. She was late for her brunch with Ed and Anthony, but since the restaurant was just downstairs she didn't bother to call. She threw on some clothes, picked up Freaky, and headed downstairs, battling sleep and starvation.

Once inside the restaurant, she spotted them at the same table they'd been at the night before. She walked up.

"You're late," Anthony noted. "I . . . we . . . were getting worried."

"Sorry," she muttered as she slid into the booth and dropped Freaky onto the table.

"And you look like hell," Ed noted.

"Yeah, well, it's been that kind of a night, morning, whatever," she said.

The waitress came by, glanced at Freaky, and turned visibly pale but didn't say anything.

"Coffee, black, and the sirloin," Samantha said.

The woman nodded and scurried off.

"I think Freaky's reputation is preceding him," Ed noted with a smirk.

"So, what happened to you?" Anthony asked.

"Well, Ed was certainly right about one thing. There are definitely people in town who know Lilith. In fact, I had the great displeasure of dealing with two of her coven."

"She's formed a coven?" Anthony asked, turning notably paler. "Somehow I had the feeling she was working alone."

"So did I. What her coven mates are too stupid to realize is that they're all expendable, and will be just as soon as she's finished with everyone else," Samantha said.

The waitress brought the coffee and Samantha drained the cup in one gulp, despite how it scalded on its way down. The woman looked shocked but refilled the mug and left the pot on the table.

"Good call," Samantha muttered as she took her time sipping the next cup.

"How many do you think there are?" Ed asked.

"Two fewer now than there were," Samantha said grimly.

Anthony reached over and squeezed her hand. She appreciated the show of support.

"Honestly, I wish I knew," she said at last. "Unfortunately I wasn't able to get that or any names or where Lilith might be hiding out."

"Well, at least we know that there are others out there," Ed said.

"What about you two, anything?" Samantha asked.

"The police are completely baffled about the whole theme park massacre. They're working to keep it quiet, which explains why we haven't heard anything about it. They're afraid it's some sort of serial killer, even though they have no explanation for how the victims were killed."

"So, no help there," Samantha said.

"There was one older cop who I suspect knows more than he's saying, but he's not assigned to the case as far as I could tell. Would love to have had you there so you could have told me if he was like you."

Samantha nodded. "Maybe you can arrange a little visit later. Anthony, what about you?"

"Well, the day's still young yet, but I did get a chance to call on a couple of people I know. They're both Wiccan and they're both running scared. They know what's been happening but haven't the first clue who or why or how to protect themselves against it. Apparently they've tried on three separate occasions to get out of the city and it's like they hit a barrier and can't physically leave. They can't even tell if there is an actual energy barrier up or if it's just a mental block that they can't break."

"They haven't heard any rumors concerning witches?"

"Just that there are witches, but nothing more substantial than that."

"Are they willing to help us?" Samantha asked.

Anthony shook his head. "No way, they're just hoping to keep their heads down and go unnoticed. They're too scared to act and they're hiding behind the whole 'do no harm' thing to make themselves feel better."

Samantha shrugged. "It's part of their religion. Can't really blame them for that."

"No, but I'd be interested to see what they'll do when Lilith comes for them."

"Well, at least we're clear not to expect help from that direction. Is there anyone else you can talk to?"

"Yeah, I've got three other people I plan to talk to this afternoon, although, frankly, I expected if anyone would know anything it'd be those ladies. They're fairly plugged into the whole network."

"Well, we can't afford to leave any stone unturned, especially when we need both information and help," Samantha said with a sigh.

She finished her second cup of coffee and poured her third.

Food arrived shortly and Samantha dug into her steak gratefully. She was in desperate need of the protein at this point. She was still upset about having to kill Nala, but even more upset with herself for having let the girl fool her the way she had done. Truly, Ed and Anthony were the only two she could trust.

They continued to talk while they ate. They were just beginning to leave when a ripple flashed through the air. There was someone outside, more than one by the feel of it.

"Stay here," she warned Anthony and Ed.

"What's wrong?" Anthony asked.

"Is it that Thomas guy again?" Ed asked.

She shook her head. "No, there're some people outside. I don't know who they are, but there're quite a few of them from the feel of it. I don't want them to see you. Keep your heads down. This could get ugly."

"Bring it on," Ed said, unholstering his gun.

"I'm hoping it won't come to that," she said. "They came here to see me and I'd like to keep anyone from finding out about you two as long as I possibly can."

"We'll stay here unless you need us," Anthony said. "Thanks."

Samantha turned and walked to the front door. She took a deep breath. She could handle this. She didn't need Desdemona. They were one and the same—that's what Five kept trying to tell her. She was scary, terrifying, and she didn't need to put on an act for anyone for that to be true.

She opened the door and stepped outside.

Fifteen people, men and women, all dressed in dark suits, stood in a loose half circle in front of the building. One of them, a man with gray hair, stepped forward. "Desdemona Castor, we've come for you."

12

Samantha lifted her head. "My name is Samantha Ryan, but nevertheless, I'm the witch you want. Identify yourselves."

"Connor O'Donnell, FBI" the man with gray hair said, holding up a badge. "You're coming with us."

Her eyes swept the line of people until they fell on one woman with blond hair pulled back in a ponytail. "Trina?"

Trina was one of the members of an elite FBI team made up of people with powers who had been fighting witches all over the country. They had met while Samantha was in San Francisco, although thanks to the events that happened there, Trina remembered very little of their encounter.

Trina nodded.

Samantha let herself smile. "It's good to see you guys. We're all on the same team."

"Are we?" Connor asked. "Frankly, your actions the last several days have led us to believe otherwise."

"I can understand that, and I can explain."

She could sense that they were not inclined to believe her. She couldn't blame them. If they had witnessed even half the things she had done in the past week, they had every right to want to put her down.

"I'm here looking for a particular witch. Her name is Lilith Black."

One or two of the group shifted slightly. They had heard of the name.

"I have reason to believe she is the mastermind behind the recent events in Salem and San Francisco," Samantha said. "What she's planning here will make those other two seem like walks in the park by comparison."

She heard the door open behind her and all the agents in front of her tensed. She could see fireballs forming in a few closed fists. Regular agents would have gone for their guns. These agents went straight for the magic.

"Detective Ed Hofferman, Boston PD."

She glanced behind her and saw Ed exiting the restaurant, badge held high. "You've got a problem with my partner, you've got a problem with me."

Connor frowned. "We were under the impression that she and the Boston PD parted ways months ago."

"You're supposed to be. Little hard to work undercover otherwise, isn't it?" Ed growled. "We knew there was someone else behind the events in Boston and we've been trying to find out who. Now, do you want to stand around risking all our necks or move this to someplace more private?"

Connor seemed to make a decision. He lifted his

hand and up and down the line the fireballs were snuffed out. "We have a place we can go and talk."

"Lead the way," Ed said. "Sam, go do something about your energy kitten first."

Samantha nodded and popped back into the restaurant. She found Anthony crouched under their table. "Ed wanted me to stay out of it in case you need backup later," he whispered. "Could Freaky track you if he had to?"

"Maybe," she whispered.

"I'll keep him with me."

She didn't say anything else, just waved her hand through some empty air on one of the benches and then turned to go.

She rejoined Ed and the others outside. "Taken care of," she said.

She was grateful that Ed was beside her, and if there had been any lingering doubts that he'd have her back, they were long gone now.

"So, where to?" Ed said.

Connor turned and led the way to three black cars.

"Not conspicuous at all," Ed quipped.

"Get in," Connor said.

She and Ed got in the backseat of one of them. Trina slid in next to her.

A few minutes later they were headed out of the city. No one seemed to want to say anything, and that was just fine with Samantha, who leaned her head back and closed her eyes.

This was the group that Randy had told her about as he was dying in Salem. The FBI group made up of people with power who were hunting witches and trying to stop whoever had been behind the group in Salem. It made perfect sense that they were here now.

The fact that they had called her by her birth name meant that they were probably aware of at least part of what had happened to her. They would be suspicious of her now, and with good cause. Fortunately Ed was by her side and hopefully he could help convince them that everything was okay. She owed him for that.

She was still surprised he was even here, but she was incredibly grateful. The hope of being able to go back home and pick up the pieces of her life was the greatest gift he could have given her. She'd be forever in his and Anthony's debt, and if they all made it through this she'd spend a lifetime making up for it. She just hoped that the FBI agents present turned out to be more of a help than a hindrance.

A sudden thought occurred to her and she opened her eyes and turned to Trina. "The Lightfoots, from San Francisco, are they okay?"

Trina frowned. "As far as I know."

"It's just that people with power are being called here and I suddenly realized that Robin Lightfoot might have felt the call, too, and tried to come here."

Trina shook her head. "I haven't heard anything, but I hope she stays put."

"Me, too," Samantha said, wishing there was someone she could call in San Francisco who could help who would actually remember her. There wasn't, though.

"Do you have anyone you could call who could just check?"

"This is really worrying you?" Trina asked.

Samantha nodded.

"Okay, I'll see what I can do," Trina reassured her.

"I'd appreciate that," Samantha said.

Her thoughts turned to the other people besides Claudia that she had spared in Salem, and she couldn't help wondering how many of them had also made their way here. The whole thing was turning into a huge mess.

She leaned her head back again and tried to figure out exactly where it was they were going. The farther away from the city they got, the more agitated she felt. She could feel the call now, too, the same one that was drawing everyone with power to New Orleans. Just one more thing she'd have to be sure to thank Lilith for when she saw her next. One of so very many.

After about half an hour the car slowed and turned down a long, winding drive. A plantation came into view. It was lovely and under other circumstances Samantha might have looked forward to exploring it. Now, though, she just wanted to get through whatever she had to in order to return to the city and hunt down Lilith.

One of the first things she noticed as they pulled up outside was the number of guards in dark suits patrolling the perimeter. They appeared to be agents as well. Also, she couldn't sense any more people with power until they had literally stopped right in front of the main entrance.

"You've done some work to shield this place, to keep the energy from being felt unless you're right on top of it," she marveled. "How did you do that?"

"A combination of magic and technology," Trina said. "What we sense when we come near each other is a disruption in the normal flow of energy. Yet the flow of energy can also be manipulated by us and by other forces such as magnetism."

"That's enough," Connor said from the front seat, clearly not pleased that she was starting to reveal some of their secrets.

"Clever," Ed piped up from beside her. "Next you'll be telling me the Batcave's underneath this place, and Bruce Wayne is a personal friend."

Samantha bit her lip to keep from laughing out loud. She really had missed Ed's sense of humor more than she would have imagined. She regretted now that she hadn't taken the time to laugh more back when they worked together.

If they made it through this, that would be one of the things she'd have to change. Of course, somewhere in the back of her mind she was slightly shocked that she was even worried about something so trivial as laughing more. If the last few months had taught her anything, though, it was that the little things mattered far more than people thought they did. She'd spent so many years wrapped up in her own anxiety and guilt that she'd never taken the time to truly live.

She could see that now with such a sudden sense of clarity that it was overwhelming. It was the kind of self-revelation she wished she had time to just sit and quietly contemplate, but who had time for such things when a war was brewing and she was about to have a devil of a time convincing the good guys that she was indeed on their side?

The doors opened and they slid out. From the way four agents immediately closed ranks around her, Samantha was under no delusions that what was coming next was going to be anything less than a full interrogation. And with so much at stake and magic users involved, this was going to get ugly fast.

She glanced at Ed, her first instinct to try to protect him. Then she forced herself to take a deep breath. He had walked into this willingly. They knew he was a cop and one without powers, so they weren't about to harm him. Besides, she had tried in the past to protect him and it had only driven a wedge between them. As she was sure Anthony could attest to, shared danger often built a stronger bond than anything else.

Ed reached through the agents that had closed ranks around Samantha and briefly touched her right shoulder blade. The message he was trying to send came through loud and clear. *I've got your back.*

She nodded and put her thoughts inside his mind. *And I've got yours.*

In that moment she remembered what it had been like when she was at the theme park and tripped the booby trap in the one kid's head when looking for information about Lilith. It occurred to her that she could do something similar with Ed so that anyone but her who tried to walk around inside his mind would get a nasty shock and she would simultaneously be warned.

She moved quick, using the brief touch they had shared and the knowledge she had of his mind from her other times planting thoughts in it. What she accomplished was quick and sloppy, but it should work.

They walked inside the mansion and the agents immediately herded Samantha to the right. Ed had started to move that way when Connor put a hand on his chest. "We need to talk to her alone."

"Whatever you have to say to my partner you can say to me," Ed growled.

She found herself smiling. He sounded like the old protective Ed she had trusted with her life.

"It will be okay," she heard Trina murmuring. "They just need to check her out, make sure that everything is as she says, that she's . . . okay."

"Of course she's okay. What's wrong with you people? We are all on the same side," Ed said, sounding more belligerent.

"It will just be for a few minutes," Connor said.

"To hell with this," Ed said. "I might not have any freaky tiki powers like the rest of you, but I can sure as shooting put a bullet in someone."

Things were going to escalate. She could tell that and she was pretty sure the others could as well from the amount of tension she suddenly felt around her.

"I have nothing to hide from my partner," she said, stopping abruptly enough that the two agents behind her both bumped into her.

She turned and made eye contact with Connor. "You might as well let him come along, at least until he's satisfied that you're not going to do anything . . . barbaric."

Connor looked furious. Of course he was. As a member of the FBI he had certain standards and guidelines he had to live up to, and Ed would make sure he adhered to them. As one with powers, though, he had planned on doing things a little bit more old school with her, figuring none would be the wiser. She respected where he was coming from and might well have made a similar choice had she been in his position.

They marched into a room that had guards stationed all around the inside. There was a chair in the very center and Samantha willingly walked over and sat in it, knowing it was expected. In the corner she saw a pile of chains that were clearly meant for her.

Connor glanced at her and then at Ed and she saw the frustration in his face.

"We have to be sure you are who you say you are," he said, clearly trying to figure out how he could justify the use of the restraints to Ed.

"I understand, and I'm here to prove to you that I am Samantha Ryan," she said, not giving him an opening.

She noticed that Trina wasn't in the room. It actually made her feel a little better, given that they had a bit of a relationship even though she was the only one who remembered it. She would have had a hard time getting over being interrogated by her. Sometimes it was impossible to separate the business from the personal. Clearly Trina understood or she would have been present. After all, it seemed as though nearly every other available agent was.

Connor waved his hand and two chairs that were lined against one wall slid across the floor toward him and Ed.

Ed jumped but struggled hard to control it. She could feel Connor's disdain for him, and it made her furious. Ed was still new to this world and hadn't been in a position to witness too much personally. It was a lot for anyone to take in, and if you hadn't been born into the world, it would naturally take time to adjust.

Connor and Ed sat down and she noticed that Ed moved his chair before doing so in order to be facing more toward Connor than her. Connor was putting her on trial, but Ed was making the statement that he'd be watching him like a hawk for any impropriety. That fact was clearly not lost on Connor, who stared with burning anger at Samantha.

"Since you left Salem you've been using the name Desdemona Castor; why?"

There was the real reason, which there was no way she was giving him. Then there was a plausible one. "Lilith called Desdemona Castor out by leaving something for me in the empty grave with that name on it. Since there was no longer any need to hide my birth name, I stopped going by Samantha and chose to use the name that Lilith was trying to connect with. At the time I didn't know who it was that was taunting me, who had been behind the events in Salem and San Francisco. I just knew that they had a vendetta against Desdemona Castor and that they knew that was who I had been as a kid."

It sounded plausible and completely logical. She just hoped he thought so.

"And since you made it here you've threatened people and acted with a wanton disregard for human life."

Before she could say anything, Ed shot back at Connor, "You ever been undercover, you personally?"

Connor glared at him. "No, but I handle all the agents—"

Ed held up a hand, cutting him off. "Nothing Samantha ever does is reckless. It's always calculated, thought out. This Lilith chick was expecting, hoping for a badass witch, and that's what Samantha had to be. She needed to put the fear of God in the other witches to help get them under her sway as well. In Salem the coven leaders there specifically said they had been trying to bring out the inner witch in Samantha. They clearly thought they had succeeded. We had every reason to believe something similar was happening in San Francisco. In order to keep her cover with others in the community and to keep Lilith off guard, we had to present exactly what she was hoping and expecting to see. Anyone that's worked undercover before knows you have to take on another persona, live it, breathe it, and make hard choices in order to protect it and those you're working with. Samantha did what any cop would do to get the job done and she never once stepped over the line."

Samantha decided then and there that she would always want Ed to be her advocate in all things.

"Is this true?" Connor said, turning to look at her.

"You know how it is—you have to really sell the part if you want your quarry to buy it. You have to make it so much a part of you it becomes almost natural so that you don't get tripped up and get yourself and those around you killed," she said. That was absolutely the truth. It didn't explain her behavior over the last several days, but it was still a truth.

Connor leaned forward. "Here's what I think. I think there is no Samantha Ryan. I think you buried yourself so far in the part you lost yourself and you don't even know right from wrong anymore."

She forced herself to stare back at him, unblinking. "If that were true, none of you would be breathing still."

Shocked silence greeted her statement and she gave it a moment to let what she'd said sink in. "Think about it. I'm the sole survivor of the massacre of the most powerful dark coven that's operated in this country in the last hundred years. I took down the new Salem coven. I stopped the events in San Francisco and helped rewrite time and history. Do you honestly think that any of you would be more than gnats to me if I had truly lost my way?"

She could tell her words were affecting some of the witches in the room.

"Look, this is ridiculous," Ed snapped. "We're all wasting valuable time here."

Samantha could practically feel Connor twitching. She knew he wanted to take a walk through her mind or use magic to try to shock the answers out of her. One of the others walked over to him, leaned down, and whispered something in his ear. Whatever it was, it seemed to satisfy him for the moment and he nodded slightly.

The other man returned to his post and Connor stood up. "The proof is in the pudding, that's what my mom always said. If you're lying, we'll know soon enough. Excuse us for a moment."

He gestured and everyone filed out of the room. He went last and closed the door behind him.

Ed turned and gave her a puzzled look. Clearly he, too, was wondering what the other man had said. He glanced around the room and then focused in again on her.

Samantha, can you hear me?

He was thinking it, clearly as concerned as she was that they probably were being spied on.

Yes, are you okay? she thought back to him. She saw him wince, a clear sign that he heard her loud and clear.

Been better, but hanging in.

What is it? she asked him silently.

I know what you told them, but just to be clear, you went bat-shit crazy for a while, didn't you?

Completely.

Fair enough.

"Okay, enough of that. You know it creeps me the hell out," Ed muttered.

"And we wouldn't want that," she said sarcastically.

"A lot of thanks I get for being your partner. I have to put up with a lot, you know."

"Yeah, like only getting to eat half the food off my plate, having me save your life, a whole lot," she quipped.

"Smart-ass."

"Jackass."

"You'll never know how much I missed our conversations," he said with a sigh.

"You'd be surprised," she said, smiling at him.

The door opened and Trina and Connor entered the room.

"So, what's the story?" Ed snapped. "Have the big kids decided to let the little kids play in their sandbox?"

"For now," Connor said, eyeing Samantha still with open suspicion.

"About fricking time. Now we can get some real work done," Ed said, standing up.

"I'd like to get your take on some of the things we've found," Trina said, addressing Ed.

"And I want to show you a couple of things," Connor said to Samantha.

"If this is just a trick to try and separate us, it won't work," Ed said.

"I can assure you," Trina said, "it's no trick. I do need a fresh eye on some of the intel we've gathered, and Connor wants to show Samantha some things that fall into the . . . what did you call it? The 'freaky tiki' category."

"Sounds reasonable," Ed said, glancing at Samantha.

She nodded. "If I need help, I'll scream."

And don't worry. You'll hear me, she told him silently. *Call if you need me.*

"Fine," he said out loud.

Trina cocked her head to the side. "You two have a very . . . interesting . . . relationship."

"Don't get any ideas," Ed said, rolling his eyes. "I'm a happily married man and my wife would kick your ass for looking at me sideways, powers or no."

"She would, trust me," Samantha said, unable to suppress a grin.

"I didn't mean anything like that," Trina said, quickly backpedaling.

"Whatever, let's get to the real police work this century," Ed said. "We'll see if your witch-dar is even half as good as Samantha's."

"My what?"

Ed gave her a pitying look and strode out of the room, leaving the rest of them to trail behind.

Samantha had to hand it to him. Moxie he didn't lack for at all.

He and Trina headed off to a different part of the mansion. Once they were out of sight, she turned to Connor, wondering exactly what he had in mind and sure that whatever it was, she wasn't going to like it. He had clearly wanted Ed out of the way, and no matter the reason, that couldn't be a good thing.

"What is it you want me to see?" she asked.

"We have a friend of yours," Connor said.

Samantha raised an eyebrow. They couldn't be talking about Anthony. She was fairly certain no one had arrived since they had. "Who?" she asked.

"Come with me," he said.

She rose and followed him to a room in the back of the house that had two agents standing guard outside it. When Connor nodded the one opened the door, letting them enter.

Inside the room was a single window that had been boarded over. Two agents stood guard in front of it anyway. She wondered who they could possibly have that would merit so much coverage.

The sound of a chair creaking in the far corner caused her to turn her head. There, sitting in it, arms and legs chained to it, was Martin. There was a ring of something around the chair that looked like some sort of mixture of herbs.

"Martin?"

"Guess again," the low, gravelly voice of the demon answered instead.

She felt a chill touch her. She turned to Connor. "What happened?"

"One of my men found him in this state. We picked him up not far from the St. Louis Cemetery Number One."

Samantha felt another chill. "When?"

"Shortly after your altercation with Lilith."

Altercation. That made it sound so harmless, she thought bitterly. "Why did you bring him here?"

"We suspect the demon of having ties to her."

Samantha had wondered that herself. She felt for the packet in her pocket. She had been carrying it since, just in case. She had reasoned that even if she didn't run into Martin, the contents might be helpful in dealing with anyone else with a similar curse. It was New Orleans, after all, and the city was strange enough without the added influx of those with the power.

She stepped toward Martin and the demon, still careful to remain outside the circle that had been drawn. She shuddered as she stared at the slack face, the clacking jaws, and fought the urge to draw a circle of blood around herself before continuing.

"At last you show your true face," the demon said.

"Yes."

"You are no longer fragmented."

"Yes."

"I told part of you that you were not the person to kill Lilith."

"That was because it wasn't me, not all of me."

"True," the creature said.

"You work for her," she accused.

"No."

"Then what were you doing at the cemetery?"

"I wanted to see the show. I was curious what would happen in the state you were in then. Something has happened since then."

"I am myself."

"And yet you still don't remember something, something crucial, something you ought to."

"Be careful—don't reveal anything to it," Connor warned.

Samantha ignored him. "Yes, I don't remember. Do you know why?"

The demon laughed. "Because you are still not ready. And how could you possibly hope to defeat her when you are not ready?"

"I must try. She's killing people."

"People die every day. Some deserve it, some don't." Martin's head lolled to the other side as the demon continued to contemplate her. "You deserve to die."

She gritted her teeth, refusing to let it get under her skin. "Everyone deserves to die. 'For all have sinned, and come short of the glory of God.'"

The demon cackled. "Romans 3:23, so the Christian has come to play at last. I'd begun to think you'd abandoned your God. Or is it He who has abandoned you?"

Samantha actually felt herself smiling. "Spoken more like what I would expect from a demon."

It rolled Martin's eyes in response. She refused to blink even though the gesture was one of the creepiest and most unnatural she had ever seen.

"Can't blame a fellow for trying," it hissed. "Part of the job description, you know."

She refused to give it the satisfaction of responding in any way.

A minute passed in silence and she finally decided to break it. "So, did you have anything actually important to say or are you just intent on wasting my time?"

"Always enjoy talking to you, no matter who you are," it said.

"Do you have information I can use about Lilith or not? Because, frankly, I'm getting a bit bored."

It clacked Martin's jaws together a few times before speaking again. "There is a hoodoo woman who lives in the bayou. She sees things, the future, the past. She knows what Lilith wants. If you seek answers, go to the swamp."

"Is she the one who cursed Martin?"

The demon began to laugh. The laughter continued, moving from the low registers that it used to much higher pitched ones until it sounded like some sort of insane hyena. The sound was overwhelming, and from the corner of her eye she could see the agents in the room begin to squirm, which was just what the creature wanted, she was sure.

She pulled the small red bag out of her pocket and before anyone could make a move, she stepped over the protective circle and slammed the bag against Martin's chest.

There was a roar and a moment later silence as his head fell forward onto his chest. She shoved the bag into his slacks pocket.

"What do you think you're doing?" Connor demanded.

"Helping the poor man," she hissed.

She stepped carefully back out of the circle as Martin groaned. Suddenly his head snapped up and his eyes flew open. He stared at her with a look of abject terror on his face.

"Please!" he gasped. "You have to kill me!"

13

Samantha was stunned. That was the last thing she'd expected to hear Martin say.

"Why?" she asked.

"Because of it. It wants something—I can feel it. I don't know what, but I'm afraid that something terrible is going to happen and I don't want it to use me."

"We're not going to let that happen," she tried to reassure him even though she didn't feel any too certain of that herself.

He stared at her for a moment, really looked at her. "You're different," he finally muttered.

"Yes," she said, smiling slightly. "I was ... sick ... I'm better now."

She was vaguely aware that she had told Claudia something similar before, and she tried to push that thought from her mind at the moment. Dwelling on her failure to help and protect Claudia would not make it easier for her to deal with Martin.

"He's a liar, don't forget," Martin said.

"I won't," Samantha promised. The demon had so far told her two true things, though. And she felt that he was probably telling the truth about the hoodoo woman as well.

"Martin, he mentioned a hoodoo woman who lives in the swamp who has the power to see the future and the past. Do you know her?" Samantha asked.

Martin looked as though he was going to be sick. "Do not go to that place."

"So, she is real?"

"Yes, but she is powerful, dangerous, tricky, just like the demon."

"Is she the one who cursed you?" Samantha asked.

"I don't know," he admitted, and tears were shining in his eyes. "But I wouldn't go to her even if there was a chance she could help lift my curse."

That was significant. His fear of the hoodoo woman was clear and Samantha knew she would have to tread very, very carefully.

"I took my red bag that you gave me and I put it in your pocket," she told him.

"Thank you," he whispered. "You are a good woman."

"You're welcome," she said. "I'm going to try to find a way to help you."

He shook his head. His eyes were so sad that Samantha's heart broke a little bit. "No one can help me. All you can do is protect yourself. Promise me that you'll do that," he said.

"I promise. And I will find a way to help you."

She turned toward Connor and gave him a steely

look before heading to the door. Once outside the room, she moved a little bit away and then she turned on him.

"How dare you keep that man a prisoner?" she fumed.

"That man is possessed and the demon possessing him has knowledge we can use. Even if that weren't the case, it isn't safe to let him roam the streets when that thing seems to be able to overtake him anytime it wishes."

"Then why not help him?"

"We're trying, but we don't have anyone on the team who knows enough about hoodoo. Besides, right now we've got much more pressing problems to deal with. Wouldn't you agree?"

Samantha wanted to protest. She had a growing suspicion that there was a connection that they weren't seeing. She didn't say anything, though. Instead she asked, "Have you heard anything about this hoodoo woman he referenced?"

"We have heard that there's a hoodoo woman who lives in the swamp, one of us. She appears to have quite a loyal following."

"Are any of those followers also like us?" Samantha questioned.

"It's unclear, but it's a safe bet."

Samantha closed her eyes. "Then they'll likely be a target for Lilith as well. Same with this hoodoo woman. Maybe we can help warn her or save her and in exchange she can help us figure out what Lilith's ultimate plan is."

"We were really sort of hoping you might have a clue what Lilith's plan is," he said.

"Are you kidding? I only just figured out who Lilith is. I have no idea what she wants with me after all these years or what she's doing here in New Orleans and has called all these people to her for."

"She's killed quite a lot already."

"She's draining their powers, trying to gather as much as she can for herself."

"We've noticed. It seems ridiculous, though, that she'd be planning on draining everyone."

"Really? Because everything else she's been doing so far has been so calm and rational and perfectly normal," she said sarcastically.

"Point taken," he said with a grimace.

"I have to go to see the hoodoo woman."

"I'm not sure doing what a demon tells you to do is a good idea."

"That demon tried to save my life once and he told me where Lilith would be after that."

"And I'm not convinced he didn't send you right into her trap when he did that."

"Neither am I, but if there's even a chance that he's telling the truth about this woman, then I have to go. She might be our only chance for answers, and that's something we're in pretty desperate need of right now."

"Fine, but you're not going alone."

"I'm not sure a horde of us descending is exactly the right thing. Besides, we shouldn't tip our hand too early. We don't know yet if she knows about your group or how many of you there are. After all, Randy certainly flew under the radar of the coven in Salem. As far as I could tell, no one had guessed he was one of you. I certainly didn't until he was able to explain things to me."

"He was one of my best men. I was sorry to lose him."

"I was sorry, too. He seemed like quite a guy."

"He was engaged to Clara, one of the agents you saw earlier."

"That's too bad," Samantha said, feeling worse.

"They both knew the risks. I know she'd love to get some payback, though."

"Not against me, I hope."

He glanced sideways at her. "She's not a fan of yours, but it's Lilith she's gunning for."

"Good to know. Still, I'll try to steer clear."

"Good luck with that. We're going to need all hands on deck before this is over."

"Exactly, which is why I think I need to go to the swamp alone. If something happens to me there, it's going to take all of you to kill Lilith."

"I won't agree to that."

Samantha drew herself up to her full height. "If you think you can stop me, go ahead and try."

She began drawing energy into her body from the ground beneath her feet and the air around her.

Connor took a couple of quick steps backward. He bared his teeth at her. "You're a loose cannon, and that makes you dangerous."

"You'd better believe it," she said, sucking in more power rapidly enough that she could hear people around the building beginning to gasp.

"I'm not going to try to stop you, but I'm going to

have backup waiting. I don't like you, but I don't think we can afford to lose you. At least, not just yet."

She stared at him for a long moment, letting him feel the power that was emanating from her. He took another step backward, probably not even aware that he did. Then, slowly, she said, "Fair enough."

He nodded and she knew that they had an understanding. She was the most powerful person in that house, and he was now fully aware of it. That was what she needed. She wasn't going to be part of his task force, one of his team. If he expected to work with her, then he could work with her or for her, but she most certainly didn't work for him.

She turned and walked away, not to any place in particular, just to remove herself from his presence. As she walked her mind was furiously working, thinking ahead, because, despite her earlier bravado, she was not looking forward to what was coming next. The demon's words echoed in her mind.

If you want answers, go to the swamp.

The Swamp. She didn't like the thought of going there. She would be completely dependent on a guide to get her in and out. Plus, that was a huge area covering hundreds of square miles. The information was so vague as to be ludicrous. Only the most powerful of witches could take such sketchy information and do something with it.

Fortunately she was one of those witches.

Four hours later Samantha was in a boat, powering down one of the river ways with a guide at the helm.

She had strong misgivings about the entire thing, but she had found a guide who actually knew where it was she wanted to go. He had, however, made it very clear that he wouldn't take her the entire way, but instead would drop her off and wait for her to return. Since she could tell he was being truthful about his intention to wait for her and take her back, she reluctantly agreed.

The bayou was everything her imagination had conjured when she'd heard tales of it as a kid. There were plants of all sorts growing out of the water and on the marshy stretches of land. Insects buzzed in the air, and the occasional ominous alligator slithered through the water, eyeing the boat with unfriendly curiosity.

As they went farther and farther, the air grew denser and the sky darker. Something began to change; there was a chill to the air that was more than just the temperature. They slowed as they came to a fork.

"Here as far as I go," her guide said, cutting the engine and pointing down a tributary. "Hoodoo lady you seek lives down there."

"I need to go all the way in," Samantha said.

He pointed to a tiny rowboat mounted at the back of the boat. "You go, you go by self."

"I will go in alone, but you will wait for me," she said through clenched teeth.

"I will wait three hours, no more. You no come out by then, you no come out at all."

"Agreed," she said. "Now put the boat in the water for me."

He did so quickly. As she watched him she could

sense his fear of the place. She began to doubt whether she could trust him to even wait the three hours he had agreed to.

She put her hand on his shoulder and pushed energy through her hand and into him. She dropped her voice into a lower register. "You will wait for me. All night if you have to." She was exerting her will on him, not her first choice, but she needed to make sure he didn't abandon her. Magic could help her find her way back, but it wouldn't be the easiest or most direct route, and in a swamp full of hostile creatures she didn't need to put herself in even more danger than she was already in.

He nodded, his eyes slightly glazed. Then he helped her down into the boat. He handed her a paddle and she placed it in the bottom of the boat in case she needed it later. Then she pushed away from the larger boat and she was adrift in the water.

She pushed some of her energy through her hands into the boat and from there into the water. The boat turned and began to propel itself slowly in the direction she needed to go.

She drifted through the brackish water and slowly a mist began to spring up off it. She was getting close; she could feel it. Somewhere ahead was the distinctive thrum of power, a lot of it.

Slowly through the mist she could see a distant light burning. It grew larger until finally the outline of a two-story house rose out of the swamp. The entire place looked like something from a dream, or possibly a nightmare. It was like a deformed ghost of a house, with walls rising at crazy angles as though they had sprung from the earth itself and grown that way. Not a window was square. A lamp burned in the one next to what looked as though it served as a door. A porch wrapped around the front and sides and there was a place to tie up boats. A single, rusty rowboat was there already. The whole place looked rickety, as if it would tumble in a moment back into the swamp it had sprung up from.

There was such a sense of foreboding about the place that she considered turning around and going back. She understood why her guide hadn't wanted to come anywhere near the place.

The boat turned slightly and floated toward the dock without her compelling it to do so, as though it knew where it was going. The hair stood up on the back of her neck. She didn't like any of this. She had been a fool to listen to the demon. What if the hoodoo woman had no answers for her, or worse, what if this was a trap?

She squared her shoulders. She had found when dealing with others of power, particularly those who dabbled in the dark arts, that it was important to show strength, fearlessness, and a sense of arrogance and dominance. It had served her well in Salem and again in San Francisco. There was no reason to believe it wouldn't do the same for her here.

The boat bumped up against the dock, and the rope that was coiled in the bow rose and looped itself around the mooring without her assistance. Further proof that the hoodoo woman was home and was inviting her in.

Samantha took a deep breath, stood up, and stepped out onto the dock. It creaked and groaned beneath her weight and for a moment she expected the rotting wood to give way beneath her feet and send her plunging down into the black water below.

The wood held, though, and she kept walking, up to the front porch and then to the door, which opened before her. Without hesitating she walked inside.

The inside looked like the outside, only much more so. A tree was actually growing up through the center of the building, alive and twisted, its branches stretching in all directions. Candles were perched on the edges of the branches, their wax having pooled and created stalactites that dripped down and formed corresponding pillars of twisted wax on the floor beneath that spiraled upward.

The furniture that was scattered around the various rooms, which were growing at crazy angles as though offshoots of the tree, was also crooked and formed of twisted pieces of wood, some of it petrified. A twisted staircase led to a second floor.

Hanging from the ceiling were an assortment of small, dead animals, hex bags, and handmade objects of twine and bones and feathers that resembled Native American dreamcatchers in the most rudimentary way.

The place smelled of the swamp but also a few herbs and something spicy that she suspected was some sort of stew cooking. At least, she hoped it was.

"Have a seat, dearie." An old woman's voice shimmered in the air, impossible to tell which direction it was coming from.

Samantha turned and saw that what passed as a kitchen table had two chairs. There was a hearth with an open fire and a cast-iron pot above it.

She sat down at one of the chairs, which creaked beneath her weight but held. She kept her guard up, expecting anything at any moment.

There was a swish of fabric and then she heard the groaning of the stairs and footfalls on them. She looked up. A wizened old woman with stringy white hair was shuffling down the steps, clawlike hands clutching the banisters. The entire thing shook under her weight, emitting a small cloud of dust with every step.

Samantha forced herself to sit still even though she felt an intense urge to go and help her, or at least to make sure that the staircase didn't collapse beneath her. Instead she sat perfectly still, waiting, letting the old woman come to her. That, after all, was the position of power.

The old lady's right foot appeared to slip on one of the lowest steps and Samantha forced herself to remain still even as it seemed as though the old woman was about to fall. Everything in her mind screamed at her to go and help, to use her power to lift the old lady up and deposit her safely on the floor.

But the old lady was powerful and she could do that herself if she wanted to. No, the more intensely Samantha wanted to help her, the more convinced she was that the answer was to do nothing.

At last the old lady reached the ground floor. She let go of the banisters and tottered on her feet. She did not have a cane and she was dressed in an old dress with an ancient black lace shawl. She took one tentative step away from the stairs and lifted her arms as if trying to balance herself.

She looked as if she was going to fall down. Samantha's leg muscles tightened as if they were going to compel her to stand and walk over to offer an arm for assistance. She placed her hands firmly on her knees, though.

It was all a front; it had to be. How many visitors would fall for her helpless old lady routine? Too many, Samantha guessed.

She turned and stared at the fire, watching the pot that was hanging over it. What had smelled like stew to her earlier was surely what was boiling in that pot. She wasn't about to take a look and she wouldn't touch it if her life depended on it, but she focused on it.

The old lady was alone here in the house. Samantha could tell that. Which meant the old lady was more than capable of taking care of herself if she was cooking stew in that heavy pot over that fire.

And there was all the power that was crackling around her still. Samantha heard a soft cry and turned her head back, as slowly as she could. The old lady was leaning her hand against the tree, a look of deep distress on her face.

She stretched out a hand toward Samantha. "Please, help an old woman."

Samantha looked her dead in the eye. "Help yourself."

The woman gave her a pitiful stare, took one more step, and then fell, hard, onto the floor.

Still Samantha forced herself to stay still.

The woman looked up at her. "How can you sit there and not help an old woman?"

"Because you're not as frail as you want people to think. And if you can really see the future, you would have known enough to get yourself a walking stick before you fell trying to walk across your own floor."

The woman began to chuckle.

Samantha didn't move, didn't even crack a smile.

The old woman stood up as easily as though she were a young girl. She walked the rest of the way with a spring in her step. She stirred whatever was in the pot and then took the seat across from Samantha, her eyes twinkling.

"You're a strong one, aren't you?"

"Yes," Samantha said. Humility would be of no use here.

"You have questions."

"Yes."

"About your past."

"Yes."

"And your future, I think."

"You are correct."

"Why have you come to me?" the old woman asked.

"A demon suggested I do so."

"Nasty things, demons. Not to be trusted. They lie, you know."

"He was right about one thing," Samantha said.

"And what is that?"

"You can see the past and the future."

"Sometimes. When the time is right. When the person is right."

"Am I?"

"The right person?"

"Yes," Samantha said.

"You are the right person. But . . ."

"But what?"

The old woman snapped her head up, a look of alarm crossing her face.

"This is not the right time," she whispered.

14

A moment later Samantha heard what the other woman clearly had, a high-pitched sirenlike sound that seemed to be a woman singing. It moved through her, and she found it compelling beyond anything she had ever heard. She felt a sudden need to leave, far beyond the need she had felt to help the old woman.

She turned and saw that her companion had risen half out of her chair, her head cocked to the side as she listened.

"It's her, Lilith, isn't it?" Samantha asked.

"Yes," the hoodoo woman replied.

"How do I defeat her?" Samantha said.

"I don't know," the woman said, her eyes fixed on the front door.

Samantha reached across the table and slapped her hard.

The hoodoo woman turned startled eyes on her.

"Don't listen. It's your trick, only worse. Did you teach her how to do this?"

"I don't know," the other woman said, real fear dancing in her eyes.

"But you've met her, haven't you? She's come to you, hasn't she?" Samantha demanded.

"Yes," the woman whispered, now on her feet.

Samantha lunged forward and grabbed her arm. "What did she come to you for?"

"She had a question."

"About the future?"

"The past," the woman said, trying to pull her arm loose.

"What did she want to know about her past?"

"I can't . . . I have to go," the woman said, trying to move toward the door.

Samantha could feel the call as well. She'd heard stories about sirens from mythology, women who could lure men to their deaths, get them to crash their ships on the rocks. To hear them was to go willingly to your death.

Somehow that must be true and Lilith had found a way to do the same thing, calling to those with power. First she had called them all to New Orleans, but that had been just the opening salvo, taking her time, gathering people. This was different. The desperation was building in Samantha, the need to go wherever the voice called her, no matter what she found, no matter what it cost her, no matter if it lured her to her death.

But she wouldn't let it.

"You have to let me go," the woman sobbed.

She was trying to break free, but Samantha knew she was trying to fight it. She knew because she could feel the woman's internal struggle, the movement of her muscles. Even the very fact that she hadn't tried to use magic on Samantha to force her to let her go was a sign that she was trying to resist.

"Don't listen to her. Listen to me!" Samantha shouted, loud enough that the woman actually turned and looked at her.

"That's right, only my voice," Samantha said, putting force in the words, letting her conviction, her energy wash over the woman, trying to mesmerize her, even as she had her river guide.

"She's too strong. I can't fight her," the other woman sobbed.

"Then let me help you," Samantha said, still fighting herself. But the more she focused on the other woman, the more she focused on controlling her, the more she helped herself.

She wrapped her arms around the other woman, embracing her, holding her tight. "Only my voice, only my will, you will obey me, you will listen to me," Samantha said, repeating the words over and over again. She felt as if she was babbling as she wondered how long she could continue to do so, how long she would have to. How long would Lilith keep it up? How long could she?

As long as she needs to, Samantha realized in despair.

She had to find a way to block the signal, keep them from hearing it or at least keep it from affecting them. She racked her brain, trying to think of what kind of spell she could do. The sound seemed to be both inside her mind and outside at the same time.

But sound just traveled through the air. It was just energy being passed from particle to particle. After a moment's thought she put up a barrier around them, a wall of sound that she hoped would actually cancel out the noise trying to reach them.

It lessened it, and she tweaked it some more until the sound was only coming from inside her mind now.

The hoodoo woman seemed to notice the difference. She glanced at Samantha. "I can still hear her in my mind."

"You have to fight. You have to help me," Samantha said.

The woman's eyes were glazing over, though. "Too strong," she muttered.

"Hey!" Samantha shouted, and the woman's eyes snapped to her. "She's not too strong. You just have to focus."

The woman was trying, but Samantha knew she wasn't going to be able to do it, and she couldn't figure out a way to block the voice inside her head. Had she been a normal human, she knew what she would have done, but then again, this song wasn't meant for normal humans to hear.

She was going to lose her, but she had to learn what she could.

"When did Lilith come to see you?" she demanded.

"It was a couple of years ago," the woman said, struggling with her to get away.

Samantha held tight to her shoulders. "What is it she wanted to know about her past?" She was losing the woman and she had to at least know the answer before that happened.

The woman turned haunted eyes on her. "There was a tragedy ... She wanted to know what became of someone she cared for. She was angry, troubled by what I told her."

"What did you tell her?" Samantha asked. Had this woman seen the events of the massacre? Did she know the truth about what had really happen?

But she had lost the battle; the woman had ceased listening to her at all and was fighting her hard.

Samantha dropped her hands and the woman turned and left.

Samantha just stared into space. Lilith's visit to this woman had set so many things in motion. So many lives had been lost, so much death and chaos. Did she blame Samantha somehow for what had happened to her father and the others? And why, when she found her, hadn't she approached her, attacked her, killed her? Why all the games? Why all the elaborate plots and schemes? It made no sense.

Only Lilith knew the answer to that.

And luckily for Samantha, right now she knew how to find her.

She took a deep breath, walked to the door, and went out onto the porch. She saw the hoodoo woman in the rickety old rowboat, heading up the river at a good clip. There was nothing Samantha could do for her now.

Samantha got into her own rowboat, cast off, and moments later was following behind. She was moving at a slower pace through the water, and the other woman's boat was soon out of sight. That was okay, though, since she could still hear the siren call and it was all the direction she needed.

The mist was just as thick as it had been earlier and it

grew thicker the farther she went. When she came to the fork, she turned down the river away from where the boat captain was waiting for her. Given the fog, there was no way he could see her, which was just as well.

She continued to steer the boat, a tiny nudge here and there. Slowly all other sounds ceased; all the animals and insects fell quiet. It was like floating through emptiness as the mist socked in more and more.

And then, in the silence, she heard the tiniest splashing sound and felt a wave of power wash over her. She turned her head. There, behind her, bobbing up and down, a light appeared in the mist. It drew closer and she heard something moving through the water and it was coming fast.

She moved her boat slightly to the side and a moment later a boat moved past, a man inside staring fixedly ahead, a lantern clutched in his upraised fist. Like her he was steering and propelling the small boat using his powers. Unlike her he was completely mesmerized by the siren song.

She continued to drift along for several more minutes before she could tell that she was close to her destination. She slowed down, wanting to get a sense of what she was about to walk into before she did.

That's when she heard more sounds in the water behind her, very soft, like the gentle lapping of water. She didn't turn, focusing instead on what was ahead of her. She couldn't see through the mist, so she stretched out with her senses, trying to figure out what was in front of her.

And then she saw bits of light in the corners of her eyes. She turned her head slightly.

Dozens of tiny boats were drifting through the water, nearly silent. The mist hung about them and it was an eerie sight to behold. Inside the boats were people of all ages and races, people of power. Their eyes were fixed straight ahead, their destination consuming them completely.

And then in a boat that drifted by she saw a figure she recognized. It was Robin Lightfoot, the girl from Santa Cruz she'd tried to help weeks before.

Samantha bit back a shout and forced herself to remain still in her boat. Tears stung the back of her eyes. She'd asked Trina to check on her, see if she had come to New Orleans. No need to wonder anymore. Clearly she had.

Samantha wished there was something she could do now to help her, to stop her. But even if she sank the girl's boat, she'd just start swimming. There was nothing she could do to stop or restrain her that wouldn't cause a massive amount of noise and draw too much attention to herself.

Then inspiration hit her. She didn't know why she hadn't thought of it with the hoodoo woman. She propelled her boat close to Robin's. Robin didn't even notice, so fixated on her goal.

Samantha reached out, grabbed the girl's shoulder, and sent a mighty jolt of electricity through her, more than enough to knock her out for a few hours while her body healed itself.

Robin fell backward into the bottom of her boat. Samantha sent the boat into reverse, floating back the way it had come. It was the best she could do for now. She just hoped it was enough.

She watched for a moment as it wound its way backward through the flotilla of small watercraft that seemed to still be coming. She couldn't help wondering if somewhere back there were Connor and some of his agents. They had wanted to be nearby when she visited the hoodoo woman, something she'd fought him on. She suspected that they were close, but were they close enough to hear and fall victim to the call?

Just how far did it extend? Could all those with power in New Orleans hear it? Would they all be coming in droves?

From the numbers of people she was already seeing, she guessed it had to be true. All the more reason why she needed to stop Lilith, and fast. She had no idea how many like her were in the city. Dozens? Hundreds? The implications were staggering.

She moved her boat a little faster through the water. Now was not the time for caution. There was too much at stake; she felt it.

Fortunately she didn't have too much farther to go. She saw more and more lights appearing through the mist. Then a few moments later, a small island rose out of the swamp straight ahead. People were abandoning their boats as they reached its shore. Soon there were too many boats floating in the water. The others climbed out of their boats and held candles and lanterns high and waded through the water to get to the island.

A hundred lights bobbed on the water, sickening Samantha at the sight. She turned. There were other lights coming through the mist, too many to count. She had to end this.

She lifted her hands and pushed boats out of the way so she could get close enough to the island. At last she was able to step out onto its spongy surface. Here, too, all sounds of animal and insect life were absent.

At the top of the small island, a rudimentary altar was set up. A woman stood before it who had to be Lilith. As Samantha strained to see what was happening, she saw Lilith seize a man, push him down onto the altar, and then strip his power and life from him before letting him fall to the ground.

She would drain every last one of them unless she was stopped.

"Lilith!" Samantha boomed, making sure her voice could be heard above all else. She was unwilling to see Lilith kill even one more person. "Enough, let these people go!"

Instantly the siren song stopped. Then, one by one, the people surrounding her crumpled in a faint, leaving Samantha standing, exposed. She sent up a quick prayer that people weren't drowning even now in the swamp behind her, but she couldn't turn to look, let alone help.

"So you remember me?" Lilith said. During their last encounter she had sounded twisted, amused, lecturing. Now her voice was filled with anger, hatred.

Samantha walked forward, stepping around bodies when she could and on them when she couldn't avoid them. She wondered where in the tangled heap of humanity the hoodoo woman was and if there was anyone else she would recognize: the Druid, Trina, or Connor? As much as she wanted to know, the whole time she kept her eyes locked on Lilith, waiting for the witch to make a move.

Lilith cocked her head to the side. "You seem . . . you're *her*, aren't you? Samantha?" she asked, spitting the name as if it was hateful to her. "What happened to Desdemona? I worked so hard to get her to come out and play."

"She's still here. They're both me, and it took everything you did to help me see that, accept that," Samantha said.

Lilith was unhinged. Samantha could feel the madness that radiated from the witch. Then again, she'd have to be in order to do the things she'd done.

"What is it you want?" Samantha asked.

Lilith stared at her in disbelief. "Isn't it obvious?"

"Not to me," Samantha said.

Lilith's face hardened even more. "I want you."

"You've got me. Here I am."

"No, you don't understand," Lilith hissed, her rage clearly building. She pressed her hands together and bent over slightly as if she were talking to a child. "I wanted my coven sister."

"I left that life behind after the massacre."

"You think I knew that? You think I could even have guessed that? I knew you were young, that someone had to have claimed you, a relative, someone. I searched for you for years and I couldn't find you. No one had even heard of a witch named Desdemona."

"Because I was no longer either," Samantha supplied.

"All I wanted was to find my coven sister, for us to

hold each other, weep for our losses, and rebuild together. And after years of looking for her, what did I find? A Christian with a strange name who bore her face."

"It must have been a shock," Samantha acknowledged.

"It was an abomination!" Lilith thundered. "How could you betray me like that?"

"I didn't betray you. I remember very little about that night," Samantha said. "What I do remember comes in flashes, in nightmares, all the death, the blood, the screaming." She took a deep breath. "I thought I was the only survivor. I didn't even remember until yesterday that you weren't killed in the massacre with everyone else, that you were away."

Lilith closed her eyes. "You thought I was dead?"

Samantha nodded.

"But the graves—"

"I didn't even see them until I came back from San Francisco. The witch there kept saying something about the last grave, so I went because that was the only thing I could think of, and I found the last grave in the row, and it was mine. I had no idea one was even dug for me. Then I found what you left inside for me."

"So you never knew to look for me."

"No," Samantha said, grateful that it was the truth.

Lilith sat down suddenly and Samantha blinked.

Bloody tears streaked down Lilith's face. Samantha hesitated, not knowing what to do. Could it really be this simple? She took a couple of steps closer, keeping her guard up. "I was alone and I was twelve. I didn't know how to live in the world. My mother kept me so isolated, you remember. I had to adapt. I had to survive. And whatever happened that night, everyone dying, it was too terrible to remember."

"My father was killed that night," Lilith said.

"As was my mother."

Lilith sighed deeply. "My father always said you had the makings of a great high priestess, but he was worried you would never get there because you couldn't find the balance. You were wild, unpredictable when you were little. Then as you got older you were so hesitant, cautious."

"My mother was a brutal teacher, not an easy woman to live with or learn from," Samantha said. She didn't volunteer that Lilith's father had been equally to blame, just as harsh and capricious.

"You really don't remember what happened that night? Because I've been trying for years to get answers about what went wrong," Lilith said.

Samantha took another step closer. "Like I said, snatches of memory in flashback. I know that they succeeded in raising a demon and then the demon killed them all."

"All except you."

"Yes. I wish I knew how, why it spared me."

"You probably think it was your God protecting you."

Samantha was silent. She'd never really thought that, since it was long before she knew God or had the right to claim His protection for anything. Perhaps it had been, though. Maybe she'd never know the truth. "I wish I knew."

"Me, too."

"Was that why you went to see the hoodoo woman, to try to find out?" Samantha asked.

Lilith looked at her and shook her head. "No, I never even thought about asking her that."

"Then what did you ask her?"

"I asked her what happened to you."

Sorrow knifed through Samantha's heart and for the first time she truly felt sympathy for what Lilith must have gone through, just as lost, just as alone, but with no one to help her, no adopted parents to swoop in and show her a better way.

Samantha took another step forward and stretched out her hand. "Maybe together we can find out what really happened that night. Maybe we can make things . . . right."

Lilith gave her the strangest look, as though she actually was having a moment where she pitied Samantha. Then she sighed heavily. "Oh, Desdemona, Samantha, whatever you want to call yourself, that's sweet. It really is. But we are way beyond that."

"What do you mean?" Samantha asked.

Lilith stood up. "There's no going back for either of us. Recognize this?" She pulled something out of her pocket, dangling it from her fingertips.

It was Samantha's cross necklace, the one that had been stolen from her.

"Give that back," Samantha said.

Lilith smiled at her. "Why on earth would I do that? You see, by creating this, by keeping it, by wearing it where anyone could take it off you, you gave me a precious, precious gift."

Lilith closed her hand around the cross, and her

smile turned cruel. "You see, I had your names, all of them, but thanks to this, I have your blood."

The thing that Samantha had feared since the moment she lost the cross. She'd known a practitioner of magic could use that blood against her, and it had finally come to that. She wondered what Lilith was going to do and how she could protect herself against it. Her biggest fear was that Lilith would use her to kill other people and to cause untold evil. She poised herself, wondering how she could regain the necklace before it was too late.

"What do you intend to do?" she asked, trying to buy more time to think.

"You know, I thought about setting your blood on fire, but that seemed too easy, and frankly, it didn't quite suit the situation. And then it hit me. The hot-blooded witch you could have been had her blood cooled by this weak, pale imitation. And I had begun to fear that you were indeed dead and ash somewhere. Now, this cross has your blood all right, but not hot, not even cold. It's old and dried and, frankly, dead. Just like you're about to be."

Samantha lunged forward, made it two steps, and then fell to her knees. Something was desperately, dreadfully wrong.

Her heart stuttered and pain shot through it. It squeezed tightly, painfully, and then shut down completely. Blood began to pool in her extremities as it ceased to pump through her body. Pain roared through her, nearly blinding her. She could feel the moment the blood stopped moving altogether. It just sat, stagnant as the water in the swamp behind her.

And then it began to harden, thicken, pressing against the sides of all her blood vessels until she wanted to scream and scream.

She fell on her side. She came face-to-face with one of Lilith's intended victims, an older black man who was wearing a cross on a chain around his neck. Samantha struggled, trying to move her arm. Now it felt as if her veins were shriveling. She could feel the blood congealing in them and then drying, dying. Just as she was.

She managed to push her pinky finger against the cross. She wanted to speak, but her mouth wouldn't move. She could feel her organs shutting down, and even the pain lessened as one by one her nerves began to die.

By the power of Christ's blood shed on the cross, help me, she thought, the most desperate prayer she'd ever prayed.

The man's eyes flew open and he reached out and gripped her hand, pressing the cross between his hand and hers. He flooded her with energy, trying to jumpstart her body, get it to heal itself.

But how could it when Lilith controlled her blood?

Destroy. Necklace. She. Has. She tried to think to him, barely able to make the words form.

He twisted his head to stare at Lilith. His lips moved, but if he was speaking out loud she couldn't hear it. Everything was fading for her.

She heard a scream and she saw the necklace fall from Lilith's hand. Then she felt the ground shake and people raced by. She didn't know who. She hoped they were there to help, because all she knew as darkness claimed her was that she had failed.

15

Samantha struggled, fighting to come back. There were people who needed her. Around her she could hear a roaring sound and eventually she realized it was screaming.

She forced her eyes open. People were running past her in all directions, panic flowing off them like water. She wondered how it was that she wasn't being trampled to death. Then she realized that the older man was still holding her hand, his cross pressed between their fingers. He was not only channeling energy into her; he was also creating a bubble of safety around them so that people were shying away.

She could see dimly through the mist. There were dozens of fires all over, but they weren't doing much more than sputtering out because of the wetness of the ground. She could see FBI agents running back and forth, some of them trying to direct people off the island, presumably into boats, while others were clearly looking for Lilith or any of her followers.

Samantha was certain the witch would have had an escape route planned. She opened her mouth to try to speak, to get someone's attention, but all that came out was just a squeak.

"You need to gather your strength. You're still in danger," the older man said, his voice strained from the effort of helping her.

I need to stop her, she thought to him since she couldn't speak.

"And you will, but not today."

I can't let more people die.

"It's not up to you to save them all."

It's because of me that she's doing this.

"Any man can only take responsibility for his own actions. She might blame you for something, but what she does, she does for herself, because she chooses to."

My friends need my help.

"You can't help them if you're dead, and you're not out of the woods yet."

She had no argument to give. He was right and he was connected to her; she could feel that he was taking on some of the damage to her body himself. He knew exactly how injured she was, and there was no hiding that fact.

She laid her head down, beginning to be able to pull energy from the earth for herself.

"Good," he said approvingly.

The blood was moving again in her veins, but it still felt slow, sluggish, and somewhat toxic. She winced at the discomfort. Her body was healing, but oh so slowly, and it nearly drove her mad lying there while all around her were people who needed her help.

A thousand questions crowded her mind. Had the FBI agents arrived because they, too, had been lured by the siren song or had they been following the crowd? If so, how had they managed to block the effects of the song?

She watched people scurrying to and fro. Lilith was still on the island; she felt it with a certainty that had to mean something.

The healing process began to speed a little more and finally she opened her hand and freed it from the man next to her. She heard him groan in grateful relief and knew what it had cost him to have saved her life as he had. When this was over she would have to find him and thank him.

She lay still for another minute, watching everything that was happening around her, willing her body to heal faster. They had cleared most of the people off the island now. They were still searching frantically, though, for any sign of Lilith.

She watched as they searched and after a few min- utes it became clear that everyone was avoiding a small area behind some trees to the back left of the island. She watched as yet another agent turned away from it.

She had to check it out. She pushed up slowly from the ground, her arms shaking but ultimately holding her. From there she stood slowly, her legs wobbling and barely able to hold her. She took one step at a time, moving agonizingly slow. Her feet had been asleep and as they came back to life the pain was like being jabbed by a thousand red-hot needles. She gritted her teeth against it and forced herself to keep moving forward, convinced that there was something back there the agents weren't seeing.

Finally she made it back to the spot where everyone had turned aside, and in a flash she knew why. She had an intense desire to turn away, an unshakeable belief that there was nothing back there. It could only mean one thing.

Someone very powerful was hiding someone or something.

She took a step forward and the urge to turn aside became stronger. She took a second step and she could swear someone behind her was shouting her name, telling her to come look at something. It was a lie, she knew. It was just like being back in the basement of Abigail's old house with voices telling her things, whispering them. They weren't real. They were just phantoms designed to keep people away.

She pushed forward, hands at her side, ready to strike if a target presented itself. A moment later she heard a whisper of cloth moving. She parted the leaves of one twisted old tree and saw Lilith, sitting in a boat. On the shore was a person dressed in a suit, and the person was handing the unconscious body of the hoodoo woman down to Lilith.

Samantha raised her hands, preparing to strike, praying that she could do so without hurting the hoodoo woman. Her knees gave way beneath her and she slipped and fell against the tree. The figure in the suit turned, there was a blinding flash of light, and then nothing.

Samantha woke up with a scream.

"Easy, now, you'll be okay," an older male voice said soothingly.

She opened her eyes and the first thing she saw was a cross on a wall. She twisted her head and saw the speaker, an older black gentleman with kindly eyes and white hair. It was the man who had saved her in the swamp. There was power coming off him and after a moment she realized he had his hand on her arm and was sending healing energy through her.

"Where am I?"

"This is my church. I'm Reverend Johnson, but most folks call me Raymond."

"What happened?"

"You were injured in a fight with that devil woman. I was worried. I tried to go after you when you got up, but I was too weak. I saw a flash of light and you fell. That's when I shouted for someone to go get you."

She struggled to sit up as everything came flooding back to her.

He pushed firmly down on her shoulders. "No, you need to rest still."

Fire knifed through her left shoulder and she cried out. She brought her hand up. "What's wrong with my shoulder?"

"It is a very strange wound. I'm not yet sure what she did to you or how I can help heal it. Believe me, I've been trying."

"My cross necklace, the one that you knocked from her hand?"

He shook his head. "I think she took it with her. No one was able to find any trace of it."

"Then why hasn't she killed me?" Samantha wondered out loud.

"Maybe she believes you're already dead. Or maybe she has other plans for you. Or maybe God has smiled upon you."

"I certainly hope He has," Samantha said. "What happened to everyone else?" she asked.

"Some are here, recovering. Some are beyond our help now," he said, looking sad.

She closed her eyes. "We failed."

"You lost a battle, but the war rages on. I am confident that you will be victorious in the end."

"She's so much stronger than I am."

"That's not what I heard. More versed in magic, more diabolical, but not stronger."

"I let everyone down."

He chuckled. "They think it's the other way around. They believe they let you down."

He stood up. "There was someone who wanted to see you once you were able."

"Thank you for saving me, again," she said.

"God wished it. Why else would He have woken me when around us the rest continued to sleep?" he asked.

She couldn't argue with his logic.

He got up and exited the room and a moment later Connor came in, looking ragged. "How are you?" he asked.

"I've been better. I've also been worse," she said. "You?"

"About the same," he admitted.

Something was wrong other than the obvious, she could tell. "Has something else happened?" she asked.

"Yeah, while we were still clearing out of the swamp,

someone hit our base of operations. Killed four agents and burned the place to the ground."

"Do you think it was Martin's demon?" she asked.

"No, but they've disappeared. It was definitely an attack by witches. I just have no idea how they found us."

"I think I do," she said, remembering what she'd seen right before being hit by the flash of light. She quickly filled him in about Lilith and the person in the suit handing the unconscious body of the hoodoo woman to her.

"We didn't find the hoodoo woman, but we figured she made her own way off the island. A lot of locals did," he said. "I just can't believe who you saw was one of my people, though. Could have been any number of businessmen."

"You said it yourself; how did they know where your safe house was? And it's awfully convenient that it was hit so soon after I saw them together."

He shook his head, clearly not wanting to accept it.

"You've put how many moles into other people's covens and organizations and yet you really can't conceive that someone in your organization has been compromised?" Samantha asked.

"It's impossible," Connor said, scoffing "All my people have gone through intensive training in every area, including fighting mind control. There's no way one of them is being used by Lilith."

"The fact that you're that certain makes me more nervous," Samantha admitted. "I'd like to personally question everyone."

"It's a waste of time."

"Yeah, well, Lilith got her information from somewhere, and it sure wasn't from me."

"What about your partner?" he asked.

"Ed's clean. I've checked. And besides, I've taken a page from Lilith's playbook. If anyone tries to enter his mind, *anyone*, for any reason, they'll get one heck of a shock and I'll be instantly alerted," she said, making sure Connor got the point.

"Sound plan," he muttered.

She smirked. He'd been considering doing exactly that, and now he would certainly think twice.

"Did all your agents make it back from the swamp?" she asked.

"Yes."

"Are they're all here?"

"Yes."

"Do they know I'm okay?"

"No, why?" he asked. "Your injuries were extensive. We weren't sure if you were going to make it."

"Excellent. Here's what we're going to do. First off, I want you to tell all of them that I died of my injuries."

He folded his arms across his chest. "Why on earth would I do that?"

She smiled. "Because we're about to play a little game of chicken. It's all a matter of who blinks first," she explained. "Is there anyone whose whereabouts on the island you can account for at every second?"

"Yes, Albert was by my side the entire time, never left it once. We were working to get the people to safety and he was working overtime trying to calm people down enough to prevent them from stampeding into the water."

"Okay, I want you to tell him that in a few minutes you need to see everyone, one at a time. Make up a reason that would be logical to your people. Have him send them in one at a time, but do not have him come in with them."

"I think I'm starting to see what you're getting at. It's clever, but like I told you before, it simply couldn't be one of my people."

"Well, then, prove me wrong and we can both sleep better tonight," she said.

He nodded reluctantly. "I'll set it up."

Half an hour later they were sitting in a small Sunday school room in two folding chairs. Samantha was still far from one hundred percent and her shoulder was killing her. She'd give anything to know what Lilith had done to it. Maybe if they found her accomplice she'd get her chance. She'd also love to find the old hoodoo woman and ask her some more questions before Lilith killed her or got more answers herself.

The door opened and the first agent walked in, someone she'd only seen once. He closed the door behind him, took three steps into the room, and stopped, clearly startled as his eyes fell on Samantha.

"So, tell me," she said coldly. "How much did the hoodoo woman weigh and where is Lilith taking her?"

"Excuse me?" he said, clearly still hung up on the fact that she was alive when he'd heard otherwise.

Next to her she could feel Connor pushing into the man's mind. The guy winced but took it.

"He's fine," Samantha said, and Connor nodded.

"Go out the back door and speak of this to no one," Connor instructed.

The man nodded and did as he was directed.

Two minutes later the door opened again and a woman walked inside. The door had scarcely closed behind her when she gasped. "You're alive?" she asked wonderingly.

"No thanks to you. Now tell me where Lilith's taking the hoodoo woman before I kill you," Samantha said, calling a fireball to her fingertips.

The woman's eyes flew open wide and she took a step backward. "I—I don't know what you're talking about."

"She's telling the truth," Connor confirmed.

They went through ten more agents in rapid succession. After the tenth left, Connor glanced at her. "I told you this was a waste of time. My agents are all highly trained and loyal."

"We're not stopping until all of them have been checked," Samantha said flatly.

"What if it was one of the agents killed at the safe house?"

"How would they have gotten back in time?" she asked.

He scowled. "Okay, let's keep going."

The door opened a minute later and Trina walked inside. She stared at Samantha for a moment and then broke into a smile. "They told us you were—"

"Traitor! I saw you working with Lilith to put the hoodoo woman in her boat. Did you think I wouldn't recognize you?" Samantha burst out, leaping up from her seat.

Trina just stared at her slack-jawed.

Samantha sat down in relief. "It's not her."

"No—no, it isn't," Connor said, raising an eyebrow at her.

"What is going on?" Trina demanded.

"There's a spy," Samantha said. "We have to check everyone."

Trina's hand flew to her mouth. "That's impossible."

"Nevertheless," Samantha said, shrugging, "don't talk to anyone until we're finished."

"Of course not," Trina said, walking to the back door when Connor pointed at it.

They ran through another seven agents. When the last one left, Connor turned a smug face toward her. "I told you it couldn't possibly be any of my agents."

At that moment she shoved her way inside his mind and he shouted and jumped to his feet. She let him go a second later. "You said it was none of your agents, which meant I had to check you."

"Not cool," he growled.

"No," she said, "what's not cool is that leaves only one person it can be, the one person you swore it couldn't be."

She turned and headed out the door. A few feet away was Albert. "That's everyone," he said. "Is there anything else—"

Samantha lobbed a fireball at his head. "Did you think you could hide forever?" she hissed.

He ducked. "Have you gone crazy?" he asked.

"No, but I'm about to," she said. She leaped forward and grabbed him by the throat and hoisted him into the air.

"Drop him!" Connor shouted.

"Not until you scan him!"

"I . . . what the—"

Albert hissed and exploded a ball of light right in front of Samantha's face. She was ready for it this time, though, and managed to reflect it back right at him. He slumped to the floor, unconscious.

"You never checked him," she said to Connor.

"He was by my side the entire time."

"No, you only thought he was. Now let's hope he can give us some answers about Lilith and her coven."

"I know just the agent for the job," Connor said, his lips pulling back in a snarl. "He'll curse the day he ever crossed us."

Samantha didn't doubt that for a minute. She nodded and then went in search of a quiet place. When she had found it she pulled her phone out of her pocket. It was miraculously undamaged.

She called Anthony and felt herself relax when she heard the sound of his voice.

"Are you okay?" he asked.

"Banged up, mostly," she said. "I miss you."

"I miss you, too."

"We found a mole in Connor's organization. He helped Lilith kidnap the hoodoo woman and get away."

"Oh, wonderful," Anthony said. "Just what everyone needed to brighten their day."

"Tell me about it. They're going to be interrogating him here any minute. Hopefully we'll find out something."

"Did the hoodoo woman give you any answers?"

"She didn't have a chance to; we were interrupted."

"Care to talk about it?"

"More than you know. It will take too long, though, and I need Ed to bring me some things."

"I could come along."

"No, it's still too dangerous. I'm happier with you out of sight."

"I understand. I don't like it, but I understand."

"Thanks."

"So, what do you need me to send Ed with?"

"Basically my entire tool kit. It's the gray duffel bag with the red stripe in my room."

"And just how am I supposed to get in there?" he asked.

"Clever man like you, I'm sure you can find a way," she said.

"Uh-huh."

"And if that fails, Ed's got a lock pick."

"Better. Where are you?"

"A church. I'll get the address and text it to him."

"Okay. Miss you."

"Miss you more," she said, then hung up with a sigh.

From the other room she could hear sudden, high-pitched screaming, a sound that should never come out of a grown man. The pastor wasn't going to like that, not one little bit. Connor would have to deal with him on that issue, though. Neither of them was her responsibility.

She would, however, need a quiet place where she could set up her stuff and work once Ed arrived, and she wasn't sure she was comfortable doing it within a church.

Ultimately the pastor offered her the use of a small

gym on the property. It at least felt better to her than bringing some of her witch equipment into one of the other rooms. Ed arrived quickly and once he was inside the gym he held out the bag to her between two fingers, as if it was distasteful to him.

"What have you got in here anyway?" he asked.

"Oh, you know, the usual—eye of newt, heart of rat, wings of bats, shrunken human skulls."

"Very funny," he said.

"I don't know. I thought your expression when I said 'heart of rat' was hilarious."

"Yeah, just so you know, you pull any part of a rat out of that bag and trust me, you won't find my reaction funny."

She smiled. "Don't worry. If a rat comes out of this bag, I won't be laughing."

"Long as we're both on the same page," he said with a nod.

He jerked his hand toward the door. "Sounds like someone out there is getting the once-over twice. I take it that's the spy."

"If it's not I'd say we're all in a lot of trouble," Samantha said grimly.

"I'd hate to be that guy."

"I might have been that guy earlier if you hadn't been there to watch my back," she reminded him.

He shrugged. "What are partners for?"

She loved the fact that he had just waded back into that role with no hesitation. She unzipped the bag. "Well, right now a partner is for making sure no one disturbs us while we work."

"Gotcha. I'll shoot the first guy through that door."

She rolled her eyes. "Again with the shooting?"

He shrugged. "I'm the only guy here who can't do magic. What does that leave me with? My charming personality and winning looks?"

"Good point—better get the gun out now," Samantha said.

"Nice," he responded.

She pulled out some candles and a poppet.

"What is that thing, a voodoo doll?"

"I wish. I know just where I'd like to stick a needle on Lilith," she said. "No, it's symbolic, yes, but that's not really what it's supposed to be used for."

Although back in Salem she had used one to convince a guy that there was a massive spider crawling on his face. She half smiled at the memory. "I'm going to try to use sympathetic magic with the candles and the poppet to help locate Lilith, the hoodoo woman, or any of Lilith's coven. I'm pretty sure they're all shielded, but sometime or another someone's going to slip up, and when they do, I'll know."

Ed rolled his eyes. "You should have just said yes to the voodoo thing. I'd be feeling a lot more confident right about now."

Samantha sighed. "So would I."

In the background she could hear yet another agonized scream. In her heart she knew that at this point if he hadn't given up the information Connor was asking for, then he was going to go to his grave with it. From the sounds of things, that would be sooner rather than later.

"They're going to kill that guy, aren't they?" Ed asked, clearly getting edgy.

"Yes."

"And we're going to let them do it?"

"I suppose—"

She turned around and stared at Ed. "You know what? No, we're not. There's more than one way to skin a cat."

"Don't say 'skin,' because I'm pretty sure that's what they're doing to that guy," Ed said, looking slightly sick.

"Don't worry, Ed. I'm sure they're not skinning him. Whatever it is will be much worse than that," she said.

"Remind me never to give you the job of making me feel better . . . about anything."

"Deal, but only if you'll promise to stay in here and watch my stuff after I finish setting up. I don't want anyone else disturbing it while I'm out of the room. This could take a while."

"Consider your stuff protected," Ed said. "I don't understand it, but if you say it's important, no one will get near it."

"Thank you."

"Now, go do something about all that noise."

"Just one second," she said, turning back to her things. She said a few quiet words, waved her hand, and set things in motion. Hopefully any chinks in their armor would be discovered even if it took some time.

Then she turned back to Ed. "Want to see something cool?" she asked.

"Sure."

She put her head in her hands for a moment, then lifted it after putting a glamour on herself.

He shouted and jumped back, starting to draw his gun.

"Relax," she said, dropping the glamour and returning to her normal appearance. "It's me."

"There for a second you—you looked like someone else completely, hair, face, everything."

"Exactly. Now, to make sure no one comes in here masquerading as me, I'm going to give you a password."

"What is that?"

She smiled. "When I come back in here, if it's me I'll say the name of my boyfriend."

Ed nodded. "I think I can remember that. After all, I know whose legs I'm going to break if you get hurt."

She grinned as she turned to leave the room.

She made her way to where all the screams were coming from. Trina was standing guard outside the door, looking as though she was going to be ill.

"Get Connor for me. I want to let him know what I'm about to try."

Trina slipped inside the room and returned a few moments later with Connor.

"He's not going to crack," he said.

"That's because you're not using the right persuasion," Samantha said.

"You got something better in mind?"

She nodded.

"Be my guest."

"Pull your other guys out first. I don't need them freaking out on me and ruining everything. How much pain is he in?"

"Considerable. He keeps fainting and we have to keep snapping him out of it."

"Good, the more disoriented he is, the better chance this has of working," she said.

A minute later the room was cleared.

"Good luck," Connor said.

"I won't need it," Samantha said as she donned the glamour in front of his eyes.

Even he took a step back and began to swear under his breath.

Her voice even sounded different when she spoke next. "What did I say about proper motivation?"

He nodded mutely.

She turned and walked into the room. She got up close to Albert, who was strapped to a chair, and she knelt down in front of him. When he opened his eyes they widened in shock.

She knew he wasn't seeing Samantha. He was seeing Lilith.

16

"Lilith!" he gasped.

"What have you told them?" Samantha asked, making sure to keep her voice sounding like Lilith's to match her appearance.

"Nothing, I swear."

"How do I know that's true?"

"You know I'd never betray you. I love you."

So that was how she had gotten to him. It was simple enough to trick somebody into believing he was loved or even in love. She lifted her hand and stroked his cheek, sending soothing warmth into his battered skin.

He closed his eyes and leaned into her hand with a deep sigh. "I knew you'd come for me."

"Of course. How could I abandon you once they had discovered you?" she asked.

"You really do care," he muttered.

He was feeling no pain at the moment, glorying in what he thought was Lilith's presence.

"Now, when we leave here, do you know where you have to go?" she asked.

"Of course."

"Tell me," she urged.

"You said never to say it out loud, even to you."

Lilith had covered her bases, Samantha had to give her that.

She thought about pushing into his mind, but she was certain Lilith would have booby-trapped it just as she did to those at the theme park who had seen her. She was in no mood to be sent flying again, and she was sure her body wouldn't thank her for it.

"Then show me. Put an image in my mind."

"You want me to touch your mind?" he asked, sounding somewhat awed.

"Yes."

"I can't."

"Why not?"

"You told us, anyone who touched your mind would die."

"Everyone but you, Albert. Surely you know that."

"I—I," he stuttered.

"Go ahead and try," she encouraged him, stroking his face more.

He blinked and then a moment later his face contorted in pain. "I can't," he sobbed.

Samantha frowned. Lilith had set up outgoing blocks as well as ingoing ones so that he couldn't share the information that way. Samantha would have to take a different approach.

"Do you remember the name of the woman you're

supposed to report to if I'm not there when you reach the coven?" Samantha asked, taking a gamble and guessing that her lieutenant would be a woman since she had chosen women in the other cities.

"Of course," he answered.

"Tell me her name."

"I . . . won't."

He was starting to shut down and they were never going to be able to crack him.

"Tell me!" she barked.

"Her name is—"

He began to scream in pain.

Something was happening, and she knew instinctively that time had run out. She had no choice. If someone was going to have to go into his mind, it should be her. After all, she knew what to anticipate.

She pushed her way in, expecting to be thrown halfway across the room. It didn't happen. Albert continued to scream and thrash around and a moment later there was a blinding burst of light inside and it began to fry his mind like a computer.

Samantha panicked. She could feel thoughts, memories linked to Lilith, and she felt she was scooping them up, seeing them without really comprehending them, looking at everything as though through a strobe effect.

He was beginning to convulse and foam at the mouth. His mind was exploding and Samantha gasped and yanked herself out of it, falling backward onto the floor as she did so.

She glanced up just in time to see blinding white

light pouring out of Albert's eyes and ears and then a moment later his body exploded, sending blood and gore flying all over the room.

She jerked up her hands to block herself from the worst of it even as random images chased one another through her mind. She fought to slow them down enough to focus on them, but she couldn't. She had grabbed everything she could, and her mind was struggling to understand and process the data. It was too much, though, and she felt the images begin to fragment and scatter inside her own mind, as if hiding themselves from her.

She screamed in rage and frustration. This had all been for nothing. Now Albert was dead and the information he could have shared with them was plastered across the walls, floor, and ceiling or else lost inside her own mind.

She pounded the floor with her fist. It wasn't fair. She had worked so hard to get at that information. Agents were running into the room. She knew they had felt what happened, and from where she was lying she could see that there was a camera on a table in the corner. They'd been able to see as well. There was no need to explain, but still she heard herself screaming.

"She left a land mine in his brain! She killed him instead of me! Lost, all lost!"

Connor was kneeling down beside her a moment later, his face inscrutable. "Did you get a look at anything?"

"It happened too fast. I couldn't focus on anything long enough to make sense of it. I think some of the images are in my head, but I can't get at them."

"Do you want me to try?"

"No!"

The last thing she needed was him walking around in her brain. For all they knew he'd get bits and pieces of her life and bits and pieces of Albert's and they'd mesh together in some horrific way that would send them all running off on a wild-goose chase.

She could feel tears streaming down her face.

"You're tired. You've been through a lot. You need to stand down, get some rest," he was telling her.

It was good advice, but how was she supposed to rest after that? All she wanted to do was grab her own head and scream and scream until she couldn't make a sound anymore.

Trina knelt down on her other side. "Let's get you to the bathroom," she was saying. She was white as a sheet, the only indication that she understood just how terrible what had happened was.

"It's useless," Samantha muttered.

"No, we'll get you cleaned up and it will be fine. You'll see," Trina said, and Samantha could tell she was intentionally misunderstanding her.

Together Trina and Connor pulled her up to her feet. Trina helped support part of her weight and walked her out of the room. All along the way Samantha could see horrified faces; the other agents weren't as good at putting on a brave face as Trina was.

"None of you should ever work undercover," she heard herself reproving them. Even as she did she knew that wasn't fair of her. None of them could have anticipated, could have prepared for, what just happened.

In the bathroom Trina turned on the hot water for one of the sinks and grabbed a handful of paper towels. "Let's get you cleaned up," she said briskly.

Samantha grabbed the paper towels from her. "I want to be alone right now."

"I don't think that's such a good idea."

Samantha gave her a look that must have been terrifying, because Trina turned even whiter. "Okay, but I'll be outside in case you need anything."

Samantha nodded. She wanted, needed to be alone. It was her only hope to focus on the memories she so dearly needed to retrieve from her mind, the ones that weren't hers.

Samantha felt shell-shocked. She took a few minutes in the bathroom to clean her clothes and wash her face. Then she walked outside to try to get some fresh air and clear her head. She'd known that Lilith would booby-trap Albert's mind, but she'd assumed the booby trap would be aimed at killing or harming the intruder and not Albert. That only proved that whatever information he'd had, it had been valuable.

Her head was awash with images, none of which made any sense. It was like looking at a picture through a kaleidoscope toy where everything bent and refracted and all you saw was a mishmash of color and geometric patterns instead of a real picture that meant something.

She wanted to scream. She felt unbelievably drained and frazzled, as if insanity was clawing at the edges of her mind. That's what she got for being inside someone else's head when he died.

She shuddered, refusing to let herself believe that she'd been with Albert in his last moment. That way was madness. No, she had pulled out a millisecond before, else who knew what might have happened?

She rubbed her eyes, wishing she could go to sleep. She thought about Anthony. If he was smart he was in bed now and Freaky Kitty was probably curled up with him. At that moment she didn't know which of them she envied more.

Still, the faster she sorted all this out, the faster she could see both of them. Her head didn't want to seem to cooperate, though. No matter how hard she pushed, how she tilted the mental kaleidoscope, it still was just colors and lines. She had the sinking feeling that it could be days before any of it made any sense at all. That was time she didn't have.

She finally decided to go and check in on Ed, make sure he was okay. If she was incredibly lucky maybe there had been some results on that end. Something had to give soon. She couldn't help feeling that they were running out of time, and not just because Lilith was going to be undoubtedly killing more people.

If even we could figure out why she was making a huge power grab now, she thought.

It couldn't all be about Samantha. Lilith could have killed her half a dozen times easily over the last several months. Heck, if she'd really found her a couple of years ago, she could have killed her anytime she wanted with no one ever being able to trace the murder back to her.

No, Lilith had to have some other plan, and it had to tie in to what she'd been doing in Salem and San Francisco.

Samantha blinked.

Demons.

That was the common denominator between the two locations. In both places covens under Lilith's control had been trying to summon an ancient demon. Was it possible that there was another one trapped here? Or was this just a good location because no one was going to notice some extra magic and craziness, at least not until it got really out of hand?

She wondered if Anthony or any of his local friends knew of any legends. She checked her phone. It was the middle of the night. If he was actually able to get some sleep, she didn't want to disturb him. Someone deserved to get some sleep, after all. Plus, if he had to ask his friends, there was no way he was going to be making those calls in the middle of the night.

It could wait until morning. Hopefully by then it would be a moot point because they would already have found the coven. Time to go check in with Ed.

Samantha walked into the gym. Ed leveled a steely gaze at her, a hand on the butt of his gun.

"If I had a boyfriend, it would be Anthony," she said.

"Just admit you like him already," he said.

"What good will that do anyone?"

"More than you think."

"He already knows how I feel."

"Yeah, but the way I hear it, you're a heck of a one for mixed signals."

"Great, now the two of you are talking about me."

"You girls talk about us. We're entitled."

"Guy talk, that's all I need."

"Welcome back, Samantha," he said, letting go of his gun.

"Thanks, Ed," she said, extinguishing the fireball she'd been hiding behind her back, just in case.

"You look like hell," Ed commented.

"Is that all? I must be doing well, then."

"That bad, huh?"

"You have no idea."

"Enlighten me?"

"And depress both of us? No, thanks. One of us, at least, should be able to live in ignorant bliss."

He smirked. "I'd say it's probably a little too late for that in general."

"Thanks for reminding me."

She glanced over at her candles and poppet. Nothing looked different from when she'd left. "Anything change?"

"Not yet."

"Nothing moved?"

"Was it supposed to?" he asked with raised eyebrows.

"Yes, that is the general goal. If something moves, then we have a clue, a possible location on where one of the people we're looking for could be."

"I'll make sure to pay more attention, then," he said.

"I'd appreciate it," she said with a yawn.

She was tired and it was late. She really wanted to get some sleep, but she was pretty sure that wasn't in the cards just yet. She did, however, desperately need to get a little bit of peace, a chance to think about the information swimming around in her head. It was scrambled but she was sure that with a little concentration and a lot of luck, she might make something out of it yet.

"You might want to sit down before you fall down," he noted. "Better yet, why don't you go get some sleep?"

"Can't, too much to do."

"Well, you need to do something before you fall over. Trust me, we've known each other for three years. I've seen that look before. You once face-planted in a plate of mashed potatoes looking like that."

"I don't remember any such thing," she said.

"See," he said innocently, "just goes to show how tired you were."

She sighed. "Do you mind babysitting a little longer?"

"Not if it means you can go get some rest before you fall over or I have to put you down."

"You're always a comfort, Ed."

"Oh, good, because that's what I always wanted to do with my life. You know, every little kid says 'I want to be a comfort when I grow up.'"

"Maybe they should," she said. "I'll check back in a little later. I've got my phone. You can call if you need me or anything changes."

"Ditto."

She waved and headed for the door. Once she exited she debated where to head that wasn't going to be crawling with FBI agents. She wasn't in the mood to deal with any of them. She just needed to be able to find some quiet and some peace if any still existed in the world anymore. She was seriously beginning to doubt it.

She turned and wandered aimlessly for a minute before stumbling onto the sanctuary. That sounded like a good place to start looking for quiet and peace at any rate.

She walked inside. The lights were on, but very dim, and she could feel herself getting drowsy just standing in there. That wasn't good. She needed to stay awake, work stuff out.

She saw movement toward the front of the room. Someone was sitting in one of the pews. She walked slowly forward, curious as to who it was.

She finally got close enough to see that it was the pastor who had saved her. He was praying, his eyes closed, his hands folded.

She should go and leave him in peace, but instead she found herself quietly sitting down in the same pew a couple of feet away from him.

Without looking up he asked softly, "What's wrong, Samantha?"

She was impressed that he had known it was her. Could he tell the difference in her energy or had he just made a rational deduction? It didn't matter, ultimately. She couldn't deny, though, that he fascinated her.

"I need to know something," she said. "I've met a lot of people with the powers. Some use it for good, some for evil, some ignore it altogether. I've yet to meet another Christian who had the powers who used them at all. How can you be a pastor and still use these powers?"

He opened his eyes and looked at her. "And exactly how many Christians with the power have you met?"

"I guess just you."

"Maybe, maybe not. Just because you can feel someone's ability to manipulate the natural world around him doesn't mean you can see into his heart and know anything about him, including his religion. And a lot of very religious people are very private about their beliefs, despite what people often think."

"Okay, that's true, but still, you didn't answer my question."

"The power, where does it come from?"

"I don't know. I was born with it. Everyone that I've met with it seems to have been."

"So it's passed down in families just like eye color or big ears."

"I guess."

"Are blue eyes evil?"

"No."

"Are funny-looking ears evil?"

"No, of course not," she said.

"The power isn't evil. It's natural, with us at birth. It's just another one of God's mysteries, gifts."

"I don't see it that way."

"I know and that is why you are so conflicted. More than that, you're hobbled. You can't be the best of yourself because you refuse to accept all of yourself."

"I'm not sure how I can ever really do that. I've used the powers for evil. And every time I have to use them now, it's just a reminder of that."

"In your past you used them for evil. Everyone makes mistakes. That doesn't entitle you to throw away the gifts and talents God has given you. If nothing else, it makes it that much more important that you make up for the lost time and use those abilities for good."

"But it's so dangerous."

"It's dangerous because you believe it is. Does power like this have the potential to corrupt? Of course it does. But so do many other things, like the ability to speak well, or personal charisma, or even empathy, the ability to feel the pain of others. Because you have let it corrupt you somewhat in the past—and I'm still not convinced you were nearly as corrupt as you believe—you just have to be vigilant."

"I try, but I find myself doing magic when I shouldn't."

He raised an eyebrow. He turned, stretched out his hand, and a Bible sitting on a table halfway across the room flew into his open hand. He looked back at her. "I could have gotten up, walked over there, and picked it up. But why? For me, this was simpler, required less time and effort, and is a way to make sure I keep my skills honed. There was no pressing need for me to do magic other than simple convenience to myself."

Samantha gaped at him and he smiled.

"I can see that I've shocked you."

"Aren't you afraid? It can be a slippery slope. One moment it's calling a Bible to your hand, but where could it go from there?"

"For someone like me, the most natural danger is the urge to convert someone not through logic and truth but through force of will. I've faced my own demons in that area and I've won. I never forget that I have that capacity within me, but I trust myself now to do the right thing." He chuckled. "And I trust God to kick my butt if I don't."

"What if He doesn't?"

"Trust me, the Lord and I have a very special relationship. I know He won't hesitate to let me know if I screw up. And if that day comes, I wouldn't be standing too near me, if you know what I mean," he joked.

She shook her head. "I just can't see things the same way as you."

He patted the Bible. "It says in here in Galatians 5:1: 'It is for freedom that Christ has set us free. Stand firm, then, and do not let yourselves be burdened again by a yoke of slavery.' We were meant for freedom, liberation. Let me tell you, that's something my family knows a thing or two about. You know what one of the craziest things is? Sometimes people don't know what to do with freedom. They put restrictions on themselves that were never meant to be there. Take you, for instance. Christ set you free, He forgave you your past, gave you a new life, a new future. Yet you are so anxious to keep yourself in bondage, in slavery, to your feelings of guilt about the past and fear about what you might do or become. That is not pleasing to God."

"But these powers—"

"Are gifts," he interrupted her. "Some people can jump high. Some people can understand areas of physics and mathematics that look like nonsense to the rest of us. Some people can sing and move an entire stadium to tears. You know, personally, I've often wondered whether or not a few of Jesus' disciples weren't people with powers just like you and me."

She laughed and shook her head.

He wagged a finger in her face. "Laugh now, but think about it. Healing the sick, casting out demons, surviving being poisoned and stoned and heaven knows what else. Sure, God could do it miraculously, but wouldn't it have been easier to pick at least one or two people who could do it themselves?"

"You are the weirdest pastor I have ever met," she said.

"Amen to that. If I wasn't, I'd be worried I wasn't being me," he said. He stood slowly. "You think on what I said."

"I will," she promised.

She watched him leave the room, then bowed her head and tried to pray. Her thoughts were too chaotic, though. She forced herself to take several deep breaths as the pastor's words went round and round in her mind. She thought of how he had compared what they could do to people's other natural abilities.

She remembered meeting her toddler self. She had used her powers as simply and naturally as breathing. There had been nothing evil there, nothing premeditated even. It had just been a part of who she was. Then she thought about her three-year-old self, upset that her mom was going to retrain her because she was "doing it wrong" when in reality she was terrified that her daughter was already far more powerful than she was.

And while she might have been born with more gifts and talents than some, a great deal of that power came from not overthinking it, from just being and letting the energy swirl through her and around her and bending it with the merest thought.

For so long she had thought that it was all evil. In the past few days, though, she had met so many good and decent people with the power who didn't shun it but who used it to fight evil and bring blessings to others.

It was so contrary to how she had been raised, and again she wondered how things would have been different if she'd been raised by someone else.

Her two-year-old self had told her that her father wanted to take her away. What had he been like? Had he been a good man or evil like her mother? What would she have turned out like if she'd been allowed to go with him? She shuddered, wondering if the part about him going away was a lie and that her mother had actually killed him instead. She'd likely never know the truth. She was just going to have to live with that. The pastor was right; she'd spent too much time living in her past already. It was time to embrace the future and the good possibilities there.

Like Anthony. If they made it out of this alive, she would have to make sure he knew just how much he meant to her. Of course, right now that seemed like a pretty big "if."

She rubbed her shoulder, still not fully healed, which was odd. Lilith had to be doing something to keep the wound fresh and painful. If she had recovered the cross necklace, she could certainly be using it to continue hurting Samantha. But if she had it, why not just kill Samantha instead? After all, that's what she'd tried to do in the first place. Could something have changed her mind?

The hoodoo woman. Maybe something she had told Lilith had caused her to be doing this instead of killing Samantha. But what could that possibly be?

Her head was beginning to throb. She definitely needed to get some sleep. She'd pushed her body way too hard and she wasn't resting enough, given the types of injuries she'd sustained.

If only she could find Lilith's coven, she was sure she could find more answers and hopefully even Lilith herself.

The information that she had gotten from Albert was there, inside her head. It just kept dodging slightly out of reach. She was pushing too hard; that was for certain.

She tried to still her mind, empty it of thoughts. The quieter it became, the more she felt her body slump over and begin to relax. Finally she was quasidozing, drifting in and out as her unconscious mind worked hard to sift through all the data that it had been collecting for days.

She was vaguely aware that something was happening, like a giant jigsaw fitting together. Her research, Ed's research, the images she'd pulled from Albert's mind right before he died, Anthony's research.

Anthony's research.

There was something there, something to it, something that connected Anthony and Albert. She could feel it, a common thread between the two. A memory perhaps? No, more than that. A place? No, that wasn't right, either. She drifted deeper, her mind almost dreaming now.

Albert and Anthony. Anthony and Albert. The two kept meshing together in her mind. They had shared something in the last couple of days. What could it have been? She'd heard about it from Anthony and seen it in Albert's mind.

No! Albert had seen Anthony.
When?
Where?
The images meant nothing. They ran together, jumbled and scattered, until one thing came together with crystal clarity.
A person.
A Wiccan.
One of the people Anthony knew and had interviewed was part of Lilith's coven.
And that wasn't all.

She snapped wide-awake as her phone rang.
She had found Lilith's coven.

17

Samantha snatched up her cell phone. It was Ed calling. "You might want to get over here, now," he said, his voice tense, strained.

"There in seconds," she said before ending the call and dialing Anthony.

"Hello?" he asked, sounding completely awake.

"I need you to get over here."

"I thought you'd never ask. I'm at a coffee shop down the street. I'll be there as fast as I can," he said, and hung up.

Seconds later, she was running into the gym. She reminded herself that she had to give the password. "Anthony if I had one and I think I do and he's on his way here," she said all in one breath.

" 'Bout time you finally admitted it. Now get over here. These things are moving around by themselves and scaring the hell out of me," Ed barked.

The poppet had moved to a particular position close to a candle that she had used to signify the St. Louis

Cemetery Number One. She had several candles burning, each representing a major landmark.

"That certainly narrows it down," she said. Someone, somewhere, had let their guard down and it had provided the information she needed. Now they just had to move on it before the coven dispersed again or changed location. She was going to need all the help she could get.

She picked up two more candles out of her bag and set them on the gym floor. "Me," she said of the white one. Then she thought of the Druid. "I name thee Thomas," she said of the red candle. "Come to me." She lit the candle with her mind, set it in motion with a flick of her wrist, and turned back to Ed.

"We'll be leaving soon to go after the coven."

"I'm coming with you."

"It will be dangerous, but I don't think I can stop either you or Anthony. And frankly, you're the two people I trust the most. I want you, need you there."

"Whatever you need, you got it," he said.

Her phone rang. "Where are you?" Anthony asked when she answered.

"I'm in the gym."

"I'm in the church. I'll come get you."

She ran outside and seconds later saw his familiar silhouette. She kissed him hard on the lips, then grabbed his hand and pulled him back toward the gym.

As they ran through the door she said, "This is my boyfriend, Anthony."

"Finally calling things like they are," Ed snapped.

"What is wrong with both of you?" Anthony asked, completely bewildered, but still looking pleased.

"Believe it or not, you're our code word," Ed said, still staring fixedly at the candles. "And that red candle's almost here."

A moment later the door flew open and Connor entered, Thomas in tow. "What is going on?" Connor demanded. "You know this guy? He said he's here to see you."

"He is. It's time to gather the troops. I know where the coven is."

"What?" both Connor and Thomas asked in chorus.

She nodded. "We need to move now, before they change their location."

Connor frowned. "We just got a tip from a credible source, one we've used before."

"Awfully convenient. I wouldn't trust it. Especially not with the timing. I'd say it's a way of throwing us off the scent. They could know Albert's dead and they're nervous."

"Who's Albert?" Thomas asked.

"The mole inside this organization," Ed spoke up.

"What have you got on your location?" Connor asked.

"Frankly, I don't have time to explain. But I believe I found information on Lilith's lieutenant in some of the images from Albert's mind."

"I thought that was all a jumble," Connor said.

"It was, but one thing came clear for me." She turned to Anthony. "I realized there was a connection between you and him and that he'd actually seen you."

"When?" Anthony asked, looking startled.

"When you were visiting one of your contacts in the city. That contact is part of Lilith's coven."

"Who?" everyone in the room asked at once.

"One of the Wiccan women that you said was scared to death."

Anthony turned pale. "I knew there was something wrong with Jo," he said. "She was just acting so much stranger than usual. And it was the first time I've ever known her to be scared of anything. I mean, Helena, sure, but not Jo."

"We find Jo, we find the coven. They're together now. I can feel it."

"I can't go on your feeling," Connor said.

"Why not? It's been working so far," Ed pointed out.

"I have to trust my source."

"Fine, you follow your wild-goose chase, but give me five agents," Samantha said.

"I'll give you two."

"Okay, but one of them needs to be Trina. Let her pick the other one."

"Done," Connor said. "I'll go alert her and then we're heading out."

"So are we," Samantha said, glancing at the table. She didn't like that they were dividing their forces like this. It was the fastest way to be conquered. But short of hijacking his mind, she wasn't going to be able to get Connor to see things her way, she could tell. Best to just let him go and do his thing. At least she'd get Trina, whom she was sure she could trust.

"How about someone tell me anything that's going on?" Thomas said.

"You said there were others with powers willing to rise and fight. Anyone you can get here in the next ten minutes?" Samantha asked.

"No," he admitted.

"Okay, we will need them later, though, if Lilith isn't with the rest of the coven."

"Um, I'm pretty sure we're going to need them now if Lilith is with the rest of the coven," Ed interjected.

"No time," Samantha said. "We have to go now."

The door opened and Trina and one of the guys whose name Samantha didn't know walked in.

"We're with you," Trina said.

"Excellent, then the gang's all here. Time to go," Samantha said. "I've narrowed the location of the coven down to a four-block radius that encompasses St. Louis Cemetery Number One."

"Jo's shop is in that area," Anthony said.

"Then I'm certain that's where they are. Lead the way. We have no time to get there and try to figure out where the power is coming from. We've got to hit fast and hard."

"We're with you," Thomas said.

Samantha turned and headed outside.

"There's six of us. We'll take my car," Trina said, pointing to the dark sedan.

They all piled in, Anthony and Samantha in the front with Trina and the other three in the back. Samantha was about to go into battle with a Druid she hardly knew, a complete stranger, a woman who didn't remember her, and two people without powers. It was far from ideal, but it was what it was.

"No time like the present," she muttered to herself.

They peeled away from the curb and Trina floored it after muttering a spell designed to put a glamour on the car so they could pass unseen. They were soon doing over ninety on streets designed for less than half that speed. Trina turned out to be an excellent driver, though, and she knew how to handle her car.

Anthony began barking directions. From the backseat she could feel the tension building.

"What's the plan?" the other agent finally spoke up.

"What's your name?"

"Pat."

"Pat, you, Trina, and Thomas are going to guard the exits, make sure no one gets in or out. Ed, you and Anthony are going to be keeping a lookout, call one of them if you see anything. I'll be going in alone."

"That's crazy!" Trina protested.

"This whole thing is crazy. We can't let anyone escape, though. Also, we have no idea if Lilith is there and I'm not willing to risk anyone else inside that building with her if she is."

"We have no way of knowing how many witches will be in there. You can't possibly kill them all yourself," Thomas protested.

"If everything goes according to plan, I won't have to kill them all, just the ringleaders. Trina, you remember Santa Cruz? Not everyone there was evil. A lot of them were naive and duped or just stupid. It was the same in Salem. Hopefully some of these people can be shown the error of their ways and let go. We can sort that out when it's all over. If I willingly let a person leave the building, I will burn a mark on his skin."

"What mark?" Trina asked.

"You will know when you see it," Samantha assured her.

"This plan sucks," Ed said.

"I agree," Anthony echoed.

"This is not open for negotiation," she snapped.

They were getting close; she could feel it. "Ed, your dog's name is the password. Anyone comes out of that building looking like me who doesn't know his name, you shoot him, got it?"

"I got it," he said grimly.

"Turn left. We're almost there," Anthony said through gritted teeth.

Trina spun the wheel, sending the car into a slide that she recovered from quickly.

"When we get there, everyone scatter. Move as fast as you can before anyone can break and run," Samantha said. "There is no backup coming. It's just us. We have to get this job done."

She was grateful that Trina and Pat didn't even question whether they were headed to the right site. That, at least, made things easier.

"Straight ahead, two blocks on the left," Anthony said. "Red neon sign of a moon out front."

"Here we go," Samantha said.

A moment later the energy wave hit and she could hear the gasps from the other three magic users in the car. There were a lot of people dead ahead of them. They were most certainly in the right place.

Trina slammed on the brakes, bringing the car to a screeching halt directly in front of the building. Samantha leaped out, seeing the others doing the same in her peripheral vision. She ran straight for the front door, flinging it open from three feet away.

She raced toward the back of the shop where there was a curtain and flung it aside. There, in a large room lit with overhead lights, were about forty people, gathered together into a circle.

She had found Lilith's coven, and she could tell in a moment Lilith wasn't there. She stepped forward, trying to push her disappointment out of her mind. It was enough for now that they disband her coven, remove this power base from her.

She had caught them in the middle of performing some sort of ritual. A portly middle-aged woman stood in the middle of the circle, hands raised.

"Jo, I presume?" Samantha asked, demonstrating that she knew the woman's name already.

Jo slowly lowered her arms, an arrogant look plastered on her face. The members of the coven fidgeted, some clearly shocked by the interruption, others angry, others frightened. It was as Samantha had expected.

"It was stupid of you to come here."

"It was stupid of you to try and send me somewhere else."

"Not so much," the woman said. "I understand most of your friends are wasting their time far away where they are of no help to you."

"I have all the friends I need right here," Samantha said.

She looked around the room. Some of the witches were wearing cloaks; others were not. She met every eye that she could see. "I will give each and every one of you one chance, and one chance only, to leave this place in peace. Anyone who chooses to stay will die."

There was sudden, anxious muttering among the ranks. She could see a couple of people struggling to break free, but those on either side were holding them fast, refusing to let them break the circle.

Just as her mother and Mr. Black had once refused to let her leave.

She blinked as that memory came clear. Anger built in her as she saw those who would prevent the ones who had the good sense to leave and save themselves.

Jo laughed, loud and long. Her confidence was starting to get on Samantha's nerves.

"Let those people go who wish to go or you will feel my wrath," she warned.

"Oh, I very much doubt that. You're the lame witch after all, the one who can't harm anyone, the one who won't use her powers. I've heard all about you," Jo said, sneering. "Magic and faith can't abide in the same person. You have chosen your pitiful God over true power. There's nothing you can do to us here."

Samantha shook her head. "You know nothing of me and the things I've done to stop witches like you. It doesn't matter, though, because what you say is a lie. That I have to choose between my powers and my faith. It's not true. I don't have to choose. I can be who God created me to be and praise Him through what I do with the gifts He gave me."

And in her mind she let go of the fear, the pain, and even the knowledge of how the energy and power worked. She opened her mind, embraced everything she had known as an infant by instinct. She could feel God deep in her soul, and she opened her mouth and fire spewed forth, setting the entire room ablaze in one single instant.

There were screams of fear and people began fleeing past her. She held out her hands so that they had to push past her. She could feel their essence, the good, the evil, everything. She let a man and a woman run by her, but not before she had reached out and seared crosses into their flesh. Then she ripped the powers from the next man because his heart was black as night. He collapsed in an instant, dead, and the power shimmered through her, merging with her own.

She let three more flee with the cross burned into them and then tore the power out of a woman who tried to race past without touching her. Samantha closed her eyes and let her spirit take over. Many she let run free, bearing her brand, some more innocent than others, but a few she could not allow to leave and continue to spread their evil throughout the world. She was God's vengeance poured out on them.

At last it was done. All that was left were the dead. She opened her eyes and beheld the fire that was racing up the walls and dancing across the ceiling. It was beautiful in its destructive capabilities. Fire purified as well as laid waste. She would let it burn this place to the ground and she would salt the earth afterward so that nothing evil could return.

In that moment she remembered at last that terrible day so many years ago that had seen the destruction of her coven.

She stood in the basement of Abigail's home, her cloak and athame left at home since her mother had insisted she would not need them for this ritual. She felt uneasy as she seemed to be the only one without them. Around her the others had their hoods up, masking their faces. Since they were all known to her and it was not their normal custom, it just put her more on edge. Something didn't feel right. She was wearing a white dress, one her mother had just made for her. She was barefoot as well and the cold concrete of the basement made her shiver.

Through her feet she could feel everything, the blood that had soaked into the concrete from so many sacrifices, the excitement that Abigail was feeling, and the mixture of excitement and fear the others were giving off as well. She could feel everyone's emotions, heightened, intense, everyone except her mother, who felt colder, more detached than she usually did.

Abigail had an altar set up tonight in the center of the circle, another rarity. On it rested a large book and a chalice. There were a variety of objects surrounding the chalice, and Abigail was chanting and adding them one at a time into the goblet.

After the last item was added, Abigail looked up, a look of triumphant expectation on her face. "Tonight, we achieve ultimate power," she boomed to her followers. "For tonight we raise a creature who will be chained to us, who must do our bidding, an ancient demon, one of twelve that ruled this realm ages ago before they were banished. We will claim his power, his allegiance for ourselves."

Desdemona shook her head violently from side to side. This wasn't right. They were messing with something far stronger and smarter than them, and it couldn't end well. She didn't want any part of it. Something terrible was going to happen; she could feel it.

"Mother, we must leave," she whispered.

Her mother didn't answer, didn't even look at her. She just tightened her grip on Desdemona's hand. Mr. Black did the same on her other side. The circle must remain unbroken, that's what he would probably say. But this was different. They were all in danger. She didn't know how she knew, but she knew it with all her soul.

She had to stop this, had to make them see reason before it was too late for all of them.

"Only one last ingredient remains and then we shall see him come forth," Abigail crowed.

Suddenly she fixed her laserlike stare on Desdemona. "Come here, child," she said.

Her mother and Mr. Black pushed her forward and then linked hands behind her, resealing the circle.

No one ever dared contradict Abigail. Her wrath was legendary, her punishments swift and cruel. But with every moment that passed, Desdemona was more intensely aware that they were all in grave danger. "Please, please, don't do this. That creature will kill us. We need to leave now."

Abigail chuckled. "You really believe that, child? Fear not, this spell will give me control over the demon. We will be quite safe."

"I don't think so."

Abigail smiled. "I would be less worried about us than about yourself."

"I'm sorry to question."

Abigail cackled again. There was a look in her eyes that sent terror through Desdemona. "Child, you know why I called you up here?"

"No."

"Do you know why you alone are not dressed as the others?"

"No."

"*Let me tell you. There is one final thing needed for this to work. The blood of a witch must be spilt. And we have chosen to sacrifice you.*"

Desdemona stared at her in disbelief. She turned and looked at her mother, and the woman's cold, cruel face told her all she needed to know. She turned back and saw the athame in Abigail's hands.

"No!" Desdemona shouted.

Abigail swung the athame toward her and Desdemona raised her hands, trying to protect herself, block the knife somehow, but then her mind seemed to go blank and she felt a mighty pulse of energy burst from her.

She would kill her first.

And suddenly the knife spun in Abigail's hands and the witch plunged the athame into her own breast. Her eyes opened in shock. "You! How?" And then Abigail was crumpling to the floor, flecks of her blood spraying everywhere.

Around her witches began to shout. The high priestess was dead. But Desdemona knew that wasn't what they should be worried about. They should be worried that the whole room was shaking violently. The demon was coming.

She turned, shock still coursing through her. Abigail had meant to kill her and the others . . . the others knew.

She locked eyes with her mother.

"The devil take you!" Desdemona shouted.

There was a mighty roar and the room shook so hard it knocked everyone down. A blackness shimmered in the middle of the room, darker than the darkest thing she had ever seen. And through it stepped a giant creature. Its skin was the red of blood but shimmering, slippery, as though there were things swimming through it. Its shiny black horns scraped the ceiling. Its back was covered with curved black spikes. Its yellow eyes burned with a hatred that she understood all too well.

The demon laughed, the deep sound making the room shake more and making her breastbone reverberate. It twisted its right hand and the witches on that side of it lifted off the floor and hung suspended in midair, screaming in terror. Then they ripped in half, torsos flying one direction, legs another.

The remaining witches scattered, several trying to run for the stairs. They were foolish, stupid. There was no escaping the devil they had called forth. He lifted a foot and stomped it on the floor. The witches scattering before him were flattened by an invisible force, their blood painting walls and ceiling as their pancaked bodies oozed into the floor.

Desdemona turned and looked at Mr. Black. Only he and her mother remained.

"Where is your circle of blood?" she shouted.

The demon flicked its finger in Mr. Black's direction. The man who had tormented her for as long as she could remember exploded. Hot liquid flew in all directions, but not one shred of flesh remained.

She turned and looked at her mother. The woman actually looked frightened. Desdemona sneered. "What's wrong, Mother? Isn't this who you wanted me to be? All I ever wanted was for you to love me."

Her mother crumpled to the floor and Desdemona knew that the woman's heart had stopped beating.

Desdemona turned slowly. The fools hadn't listened; they hadn't understood. They had raised the demon that would kill them all.

And slowly she began to understand that because she had caused Abigail's blood to be spilled, she had sacrificed the *witch who would sacrifice her; she was the demon's master. There was more to it, though. It had something to do with her power and her ability to wield it without thinking. That's how she could ultimately control the beast.*

She turned to it. It was hideous. It couldn't be allowed to live. But she didn't know how to get rid of it.

She glanced at her mother's body, and sorrow ripped through her. Things should have been different. Tears stung her eyes.

"What do you want?" She heard a deep rumbling behind her.

She turned and screamed, "I want you to go!" She felt a mighty pulse of energy leave her, and the room was filled with blinding white light. When it ceased the demon was gone, but all the destruction it had caused was still there. The stench of blood and death filled her nostrils.

She felt numb, confused, terrified, and yet unaccountably relieved at the same time. She felt as though her mind was descending into a fog even as she turned and ascended the stairs. When she made it to the top, she closed the door firmly.

"I will never return," she vowed.

Samantha stood as the fire raged around her. She hadn't remembered what had happened to her that day, because so much of it had been her unconscious mind acting to protect her, save her. She had called on her natural abilities that her mother had tried for years to retrain and suppress.

It had been she that had killed Abigail and, inadvertently, everyone else who had been intent on seeing her murdered and a demon raised. She let out the breath she had been holding, turned, and walked slowly from the building, the fire springing up all around her but not touching her. When she finally walked outside, she was a different Samantha Ryan, whole, complete for the first time in her life. *And the truth shall set you free*, she repeated in her mind over and over.

"Samantha! Are you all right?" Anthony demanded as he came rushing up to her. Over to the side of the building she could see Trina, Pat, and Thomas checking brands and eventually letting people go.

She nodded slowly. "For the first time in my life, I think I really am."

She turned to Ed. "You have no dog, never have," she said.

"What happened in there?" Ed asked.

She turned and glanced over her shoulder. "Judgment day came a little early."

They were both looking at her as if they thought she was crazy. All she wanted to do was laugh and enjoy the feeling of lightness in her chest.

But first she had something else she had to deal with.

"Lilith, I'm coming for you," she whispered, willing the witch to hear her.

18

"Do you know where she is?" Anthony asked.

"No, but I just figured out how to force her to come to me," Samantha said.

"Care to share?" Ed asked.

"Not just yet."

She glanced over at Trina. "Stay here. I'll be right back."

She hurried over and Trina looked up at her approach. There was awe in the other woman's eyes. "I don't know how you did it," she said.

"I got in touch with my inner child," Samantha said, not caring to explain any further. "Are you about finished here?"

"Yes, most of them don't know anything of value. The couple that might, I'm afraid they could be booby-trapped like Albert."

"They are," Samantha said. "Get their information and see if you can do anything for them when this is all over. If I'm still feeling generous."

"Already done," Pat spoke up.

"What now?" Thomas asked.

"Now we bring Lilith to us. First, though, we need to get out of here before fire and police show up, and we should call Connor and tell him he missed the party."

Trina nodded.

A minute later they were all piled back in Trina's car and heading away from the scene. Pat was in the back on the phone to Connor, who Samantha could tell was going through various stages of shock and rage over the events, and the fact that he had been wrong and she had been right. She had a feeling there was one informant who was going to be seeing the inside of a jail cell for a long time.

"Where do you want to go, anywhere in particular?" Trina asked.

"No, just drive. I'll tell you when to stop," Samantha said.

She wasn't sure what she was looking for; she just trusted she'd know the place where she wanted to have her final standoff when she found it. "Tell him to be ready to meet us where we tell him to," she called back to Pat.

He relayed the information and she could tell it went over like a ton of bricks. That was fine. Looking out for Connor's feelings was not her job.

Next to her Anthony slipped his hand around hers and gave it a squeeze. She could feel his anxiety, practically hear all the thoughts colliding in his brain. The same was true for Trina and Pat. Thomas's mind seemed strangely quiet. From the backseat she could hear Ed think, *Samantha, are you okay?*

Better than ever, she reassured him. *Just ready to end this once and for all.*

That seemed to satisfy him because his mind fell quiet as well.

Trina just drove, waiting for a sign from her. That was fine, because she was gathering her thoughts, her strength, for the final showdown. Because it was coming and she knew it was going to be nasty.

"There!" she said at last, pointing to a large warehouse.

Trina pulled over and then around the back, where she parked.

"What is this place?" Ed asked.

"It's a warehouse where they store Mardi Gras floats," Thomas said.

"Isn't that about to start up?" Anthony asked.

"Yes," Thomas said, "the warehouse should be filled with all kinds of interesting things."

She didn't know why, but in her gut she knew this was the place. And if the last several days had taught Samantha anything, it was to listen to her gut. She nodded and turned to Pat.

"Okay, call Connor and let him know where we are," she said.

She climbed out of the car and the others followed behind. She walked up to a side door, twitched a finger, and it flew open.

As she walked through the door, she turned on all the lights in the building so it was ablaze.

"Not exactly inconspicuous," Ed noted.

"It's not meant to be," Samantha said.

Around them were more than a dozen brightly colored floats, just waiting for their big debut. Samantha inspected them while she waited for reinforcements to arrive.

One of the floats had a giant jester head that made her grimace. Garish purples and greens abounded. At last she found what she was looking for. Three of the floats were designed with large spaces for people or performers to stand on top of and they had rubbery surfaces that made for comfortable standing and extra spring for anyone doing any kind of acrobatics.

Minutes later Connor and his crew arrived, looking exhausted despite the fact that they'd had nothing to do for the last hour other than drive around and raid an empty office building. It was almost laughable.

"Okay, people, listen up," Connor began.

"Samantha's in charge," Trina said quietly.

"Yeah," Pat added, backing her up.

Connor looked as if he was about to burst a blood vessel but in the end realized he had nothing he could argue otherwise. "Fine, what's the play?" he asked.

All eyes turned toward Samantha. "When things start and get ugly, which they will, get yourselves and as many people as you can onto these three floats," she said, indicating them. "They have thick rubber matting that Lilith won't be able to pull energy through to drain people and use them as human batteries."

Connor blinked. "I thought you said you disbanded her coven."

"Oh, we did. But when she comes, she'll be bringing everyone she hasn't killed yet with her. Everyone with power will be here. Whatever she's got planned, it's big, and somehow I'm now a part of it since she ceased trying to kill me. I have a suspicion I know why, but we'll find out soon enough."

"You have got to be kidding me," he muttered.

"I wish I was," she said.

"All those people will be coming here?"

"Yes. This is it. The last battle. We have to be prepared for it. I've seen what witches can do when they want to use a whole lot of people, the whole human battery thing. It's important that we cut her off for two reasons. First, we can't let her accomplish whatever she's trying to accomplish. Second, if she drains a person of too much energy, it sucks the life from him and he dies. I've actually seen people turn to ash."

"Salem," Trina whispered. "Randy said it was terrible, and he was powerless to stop it. He was one of the ones being used."

"That's true," Samantha said. "We can't let that happen here, which is why I need as many agents up there to start with as possible. And seriously, get as many people up there as possible without endangering yourselves. Trina and Pat will be in charge of that."

They both nodded and after a long moment so did Connor.

Samantha turned around. "Anthony, Ed, I want you to take three agents and hide. Once Lilith is in the building, I want you to try and stop and turn around everyone else who will be following. Knock people out, make barricades out of their unconscious forms, do what you have to to keep as many people out of this as you can. It's possible her reach will extend far enough to use them as batteries. If you feel her starting to drain you, run, get as far away as you can. Do not ignore me on this, understood?"

Both men nodded.

"Great. Grab your people and go find a good spot to wait, preferably behind the warehouse so she doesn't find you guys before she comes inside and finds me."

Anthony hesitated and she knew he wanted to come to her, to hug her and kiss her one last time, and she wanted that, too, but it would have to wait.

Besides, she didn't want to kiss him right now. She was afraid that if she did, it would be good-bye, and neither of them could afford to think that way. No, they had to focus on fighting, surviving, winning.

He gave her a strained smile as if he understood but didn't like it.

"And where will you be?" Ed asked, clearly not going to go as quickly or as easily.

"Right here, in the middle of the warehouse, waiting to greet her," Samantha said.

"And I'll stay with you. She'll know there's more than one person here, but depending on how many are coming right on her heels, she might not be able to determine more than that. Seeing another person might buy the others a few seconds of anonymity," Thomas said.

Samantha nodded. "Agreed. All right, everyone, get in position, because I'm about to summon her."

Ed stared at her for a long minute as everyone else began to scramble for cover. His thoughts were transparent to her and she could tell that he was afraid, but not of dying. He was afraid of letting her down the way he felt he had in Salem.

It will be okay, Ed, she told him silently.

He nodded, turned, and left with Anthony and the agents that were going with them.

The others were still scrambling for cover, trying to conceal themselves on and around the floats. She didn't know how long they'd actually be hidden, but at least she knew it made them feel better, more courageous. That was important, because she couldn't have anyone freaking out on her now.

She waited until she knew for certain that Anthony and Ed were both outside the building. Everything grew quiet. She said a quick prayer for the safety of all involved, particularly Anthony and Ed, and then she focused herself. She took deep, cleansing breaths and tried to clear her mind, preparing for what she was about to do.

"How do you plan to get her to come to you?" Thomas asked.

"Simple," Samantha said. "She attacked me and she kept the connection open, trying to be the thorn in my side. She injured my shoulder and she has something of mine that is allowing her just enough control to keep me injured. But there's something she hasn't thought of."

"That door swings both ways," Thomas said.

"Exactly."

Samantha reached up and touched her shoulder. She closed her eyes. And through the distance she could feel Lilith and the cross that she was carrying on her body. She was using it to stay connected, to keep agitating the wound. And that thin thread of connection was all Samantha needed. She reversed the flow of the energy and then yanked as hard as she could.

She felt a flurry of activity but realized within seconds that Lilith had no idea how to break the connection now that it was flowing the other way. It was her own arrogance, her own need for control that would be her undoing. All she would have had to do was get rid of Samantha's cross.

"She's coming," Samantha said, opening her eyes.

Thomas nodded. "Well played. Before things get crazy I just want to say that it is an honor to stand beside you. You have become an amazing woman."

She turned and looked at him, really looked at him. Each encounter with him had been strange, almost as if he was watching her, sizing her up. Now the sound in his voice, the pride, was disproportional to what you'd feel for a stranger.

Unless she wasn't a stranger to him.

She stared at Thomas and suddenly in a flash she knew. "You're my father," she whispered.

He inclined his head, a sad smile playing over his lips. "Not exactly how I planned on telling you, but you're right, and you deserve to know the truth before whatever comes next."

All these years of never knowing and now he was standing next to her as if it was the most natural thing in the world. She hadn't thought herself capable of being surprised anymore, but this did it.

"I never thought I'd meet you," she said simply.

He smiled at her. "Whereas I dreamed of seeing you again every night. When you showed up in my city, I couldn't believe it. But when I saw what was happening to you, I was afraid."

Lilith was on her way, but it would take several more minutes for her to get there.

"I'm ready for this battle. I don't need to prepare anymore. We have a few minutes."

"And you have questions," he filled in.

She nodded.

"Your mother and I met and fell madly in love. She was a beautiful woman. You have all her best features. And some of mine," he said, touching her red hair. "Alas, you can't tell that one anymore," he added, referring to his own gray.

"What happened?"

"Magic never came easy to your mother. She had to work hard at it her whole life. For you, from the moment you were born, it was as natural as breathing, and that scared her like nothing else. I kept telling her that she had nothing to be afraid of, but she became obsessed with the idea that someday you were going to kill her. So she wanted to change you, force her structure on you, try to control and manipulate you more and more."

Samantha nodded. "And the more she did all that, the tragedy is she never realized that she was turning it into a self-fulfilling prophecy."

Thomas looked more closely at her. "I always suspected, but I never knew."

Samantha nodded. "I finally remember what happened the day the entire coven was slaughtered. I let the demon we raised kill her. I wanted to be free of her and the fear and the pain so badly."

"I'm not surprised. You mustn't blame yourself," he said, touching her shoulder.

"I know. So, what's your story? Until recently I didn't even know that you were there for any part of my life. Now I remember that you apparently gave me the name Samantha."

"Your grandmother's name. Your mother and I went round and round about it. Desdemona Samantha or Samantha Desdemona. While I hated the name Desdemona, I personally thought that Samantha Desdemona O'Donnell had a nice ring to it. It was what was on your birth certificate until your mother destroyed the record."

"O'Donnell?"

"Yes, that's my last name."

Samantha shook her head. "So my real birth name was Samantha O'Donnell?"

"Yes."

"So even Desdemona Castor is a lie?"

"I will admit you've got more names than anyone I've ever heard of."

She took a breath. "Knowledge is power."

"And names are power. Hopefully this will help you a bit, knowing this. And hopefully it will slow Lilith down as well."

"I'll just be glad to leave Desdemona behind. It's a horrid name."

"I must admit, 'of the devil' or 'ill-fated' never seemed to suit you. Well, except for the time you set fire to the new drapes. Oh, I'd never seen your mother that mad before. She was claiming you were of the devil that night, and I was sure you were fated for a very short life."

"Why did you leave us?"

He looked at her with so much sadness in his eyes it was hard to keep looking at him. She had to know, though. All her life she'd assumed that whoever her father was, he never even knew she existed. As it turned out, not only did he know, but he'd left her with her mother, knowing what the woman thought of her.

"I didn't want to," he said. "I know that sounds like a stupid answer, but it's true. When your mother and I were married, we both had the power. I came from a Druid upbringing. She was Wiccan—well, in name only really. She didn't believe in anything, no higher power, nothing beyond herself. But she was funny and passionate and before I knew it I was in love, we were married, and you were on the way.

"I'm not sure if she started to change at that point or if I just started to notice things that I hadn't before. You know how they say love is blind? Sometimes that can be true. She was very greedy and obsessed with power. She kept wanting more and more even though there was no good reason for it. We were happy, comfortable, and we had an adorable little girl."

He closed his eyes as if reliving the memories, and for just a moment Samantha felt she could see the images, too, the young happy family. Although clearly not so happy as he had thought.

After a moment he continued. "The more power she had, though, it seemed the more she wanted. It's always a slippery slope and it's especially dangerous for those who don't have a strong moral code, an authority other than themselves that they're answering to. She met a few other people and joined their coven over my objections.

"She became more and more paranoid about your powers, about the ease with which you used them, like breathing. Then, one day, I met her high priestess, a woman named Abigail, and I knew she was evil. I told your mother straightway afterward, but she wouldn't listen."

"Mom never listened to anyone, except maybe Abigail," Samantha said softly.

He nodded. "That's when I began to sense those currents of danger flowing around me. I knew it was only a matter of time before she decided I was in her way. I decided to take you with me. I was sure she would agree, given her paranoia, but she refused. There was a fight, and she won. I refused to harm her and I barely escaped with my life.

"A few weeks later I tried to come back for you, to take you, but Abigail was waiting for me. She knew how much power you had, and she was intent on using it. By the time I woke up in the hospital, four weeks had passed. I still don't know why she didn't kill me or if she thought she had and I miraculously survived. When I got out, you, your mother, Abigail, and the others had all vanished. I searched for months, but they had powerful spells to hide you all and eventually I had to give up. I didn't learn until years later that they'd taken you to Salem."

Samantha blinked. "So, where was I born?"

"Right here in New Orleans. So was Lilith. Her father was part of that coven from the start."

Samantha took a deep breath. It felt as if her entire life was a house of cards that had been crashing down around her the last couple of days. Everything she had known or thought she had known about her life was either an outright lie or a distortion of the truth.

"I'm sorry. I really am. By the time I found you, you were with the Ryans and you seemed happy. I wasn't about to interfere with that."

"Thank you," she said. She was truly grateful that he hadn't. The Ryans had helped her find God and build a semblance of a normal life. She could only imagine what would have happened if Thomas had come to take her away at that point.

"It seemed the best thing I could do for you. I tried to keep tabs on you from afar, but it was difficult to do because I didn't want to pull you back into the world of magic when it was so clear that you wanted nothing more to do with it. I resigned myself to what little I could glean. I was proud that you became a detective, that you were building something with your life."

"So, what else is it I should know that I don't?" she asked.

He shrugged. "It seems like you're pretty well caught up."

"So, that day in the alley, you knew who I was?"

"Of course. It wasn't exactly how I'd wanted our first meeting to go. Then there was the dead body, and I could tell that there was something seriously wrong with you. Glad to see that's been taken care of."

"Good as new," she said. "Actually, better, I guess."

"Fantastic. So, nothing like I've been planning, but, yes, hi, I'm your father," he said with a sheepish grin.

Samantha stepped forward and threw her arms around him. She was going to need a bit of time to process how she felt about everything he'd told her, but it sounded as though he'd truly done his best. And she remembered how much her two-year-old self had loved him and wanted to go with him. That was enough for now.

He hugged her back and she could feel his surprise and gratitude. His emotions were threatening to overwhelm him and they started to get to her as well.

"Hey, I'm your daughter," she whispered.

She could feel his tears on her cheek and that was just fine. After a long minute she finally pulled away, wiping at her own eyes.

He cleared his throat. "I have to admit. All the times I thought about this moment, I never imagined it going that well."

"I guess it's your lucky day. If we live through this, maybe I'll even introduce you to my boyfriend."

"That guy with the dark hair, no powers whatsoever? Not the cop, the other one."

"That would be him."

"Seems nice enough."

She thought of how compassionate and forgiving and patient Anthony had been with her. "You have no idea," she said.

He nodded. "Good to know. Although somehow I have a suspicion that he'll be the one giving me the 'hurt her and I'll kill you' lecture."

"I wouldn't be at all surprised."

"Understood," Thomas said. "Now that that's settled, let's get down to it."

Samantha nodded. As much as she wanted to spend time with her father catching up, getting to know him and learning more about the rest of her family, if there was one, there was business at hand that couldn't wait. Lilith was almost there.

"Whatever you need me to do, I'll do it," he said.

"I'm so glad you said that," she said.

"I mean it."

"Lilith has my cross necklace. It's what's connecting her to me. It has a few drops of my blood that I placed in it the day I turned my back on magic."

"Then that necklace has to be retrieved so the connection between you can be broken."

"But only once she gets here, which is soon," Samantha said. "Who knew? The thing that she meant for my harm will ultimately work for my good and be her undoing."

"Put another way, 'The Lord works in mysterious ways.'"

She glanced at him.

"What? I'm Irish. You think I grew up and didn't go to Sunday school?"

She shook her head. So many questions, so little time. Hopefully they'd both survive this for there to be answers to those questions.

"I'm proud of you," he whispered.

"Thanks for being here," she said.

Around her she could feel the others, their nerves strung tight, nearly to the snapping point. Everything hinged on what happened in the next few minutes, because as Lilith drew closer, as Samantha felt the connection with her more strongly, she became more sure that she knew the other witch's plan and if they didn't stop her now, tonight, the whole world would burn.

She threw back her head and waited. That was all that was left to do. Around her the crazy Mardi Gras floats stood, eerie in their size and stillness with their macabre depictions of people and creatures, a symbol of all that was wild and decadent about the city.

And if tonight didn't go as planned, there would never be another Mardi Gras ever again. Somewhere on one of the floats somebody coughed. The sound echoed like thunder through the warehouse and she could feel the tension ratchet up another notch.

Just what they all needed.

In the silence that followed she could actually hear Thomas's heart pounding. He was terrified, but he was standing his ground. She should be frightened, but she wasn't. Instead, an unnatural calm settled upon her. Maybe it was her accepting her destiny. Maybe it was reassurance from God that she would be victorious.

Or maybe it was the relief of knowing that the waiting was finally over.

Because just then a wave of energy rippled through the building, strong and powerful.

Lilith was there and she had brought hell with her.

19

The front door of the warehouse flew off its hinges and Samantha felt the ground shake as it crashed somewhere outside. It was an impressive use of force. Lilith had to be really ticked off. Samantha smiled at the thought.

Lilith stormed into the warehouse. "How dare you summon me!" she shouted.

"Oh, hello," Samantha said. She lifted a hand into the air and suddenly all the moisture in the air condensed and baseball-sized hail pelted the witch, who fell to one knee, startled.

Samantha followed it with a dozen fireballs, which flew off her fingers effortlessly. Lilith worked hard to extinguish a couple and was forced to deflect the rest. One landed on a parade float and set some of the decorations on fire.

Samantha stomped on the floor, sending a massive tremor through it to Lilith, knocking her off her feet.

Samantha ran forward just as she heard the sounds of many feet running. She looked past the witch and saw people coming out of the darkness, racing forward, eyes wide with terror.

Lilith had compelled those with power to come, just as Samantha had feared she would.

The first dozen streamed into the warehouse, flowing past Lilith.

Then several shapes hurtled out of the darkness, tackling others to the floor before they could make it inside. Ed, Anthony, and their team.

Samantha hissed, wishing they weren't as close to Lilith as they were.

The witch leaped in the air, twisted, and made a yanking motion. Ed came sailing into the room and ricocheted off one of the floats before hitting the floor with a grunt. Samantha made a similar yanking motion to pull Lilith to her. Lilith laughed and hit herself in the shoulder, sending shock waves of pain to Samantha's injured shoulder and driving her to her knees.

From all around her, agents began to drop from the floats and were literally tossing the people arriving inside the warehouse up onto the floats as requested. Thomas leaped forward and sent fireballs at Lilith, which she deflected.

Samantha reached up and pulled lightning out of the sky and through the open warehouse door. Lilith spun out of its path and it hit the giant jester on top of one of the floats right in the middle of the forehead.

Suddenly a familiar figure staggered through the open door. It was Martin. Samantha blinked in surprise. "You have to stop her! I saw what she's going to do!" he was shrieking. She couldn't tell if it was him or his demon.

Before she could react, Lilith snapped his neck. Something black and foul began to slither out of his nose and ears, and Samantha rained fire down on the body, destroying it and the demon as well.

More people came streaming in. Anthony and the three agents were losing the battle outside to keep them there.

And then Samantha felt the energy suddenly being sucked out of her. Lilith was pulling energy so hard and so fast that it nearly sent Samantha to her knees. She'd worried the witch would use them all as human batteries, but she was so much better at it than her lackeys in Salem had been. As everyone else grew weaker, she visibly grew stronger. The witch laughed and walked past her with a little wave until she was a few steps beyond her in the warehouse.

Samantha saw Robin run into the warehouse with some of the others and she screamed in frustration because there was nothing she could do about it.

The agents on the floor were scrambling back on top of the floats. She had told them not to risk themselves and they were listening.

Samantha tried to move, tried to fight, but it was as if she were frozen. Finally she discovered that she could slide one foot slowly ahead of the other, though it took all her willpower and concentration to do so.

Around her people started to collapse, dropping like flies. She prayed that outside Anthony was able to run to safety. She dared not spare a glance at Ed. She didn't know what she'd do if she saw him die that way.

She saw Robin fall and she cried out, but there was nothing she could do for her. Trina saw, too, and she leaped down from the float. The moment her feet touched the floor, Samantha could see her start to crumple as the energy was pulled out of her. Still, Trina fought her way over to Robin. She picked the girl up and moved back to the float, where hands reached down to pull them both to safety.

Samantha returned her attention to Lilith.

The witch had a chalice and she was chanting and throwing various ingredients in it. She might not have come willingly, but she had come prepared. It all looked too familiar and Samantha knew her hunch was right.

Not again! something screamed in the back of Samantha's mind.

"You're crazy! Did you learn nothing from the past!" she shouted at Lilith. Lilith was about to summon a monster she didn't understand and had no hope of controlling.

Lilith looked at her. "I learned long ago that those who don't learn from the past are doomed to repeat it. I had hoped you could help me learn from the past, but then I found out you didn't even remember that night, so how could you help me figure out what went wrong when they raised the demon?"

Samantha kept silent, refusing to admit that she now knew the truth. She was also focusing on being able to move her feet forward, one step at a time, in a painful shuffle. It was, nonetheless, bringing her ever closer to Lilith even though the witch seemed oblivious of it.

"That's when I knew I might as well kill you. I mean, what use were you to me at that point?" Lilith asked.

"Why did you stop trying?" Samantha asked as she

continued to slide ever closer. She wanted to weep because of how long it was taking while around her she knew people were still dying. But she had to at least be grateful that Lilith either didn't notice or didn't care.

"When she woke up the hoodoo woman was very helpful. At least, she was until I killed her. She was able to tell me what you couldn't."

"And what was that?" Samantha asked, sliding ever closer. She was not surprised that Lilith had killed the woman after she had gotten what she wanted from her. At least she, Samantha, no longer had questions that were unanswered.

"She told me that the only person who could control the demon once it was summoned was you."

Samantha hissed under her breath, wishing that Lilith didn't know that. Of course, it could have been worse; the hoodoo woman could have told Lilith that Samantha was directly responsible for killing her father.

"That's when I knew I had to keep you alive, that you still had a purpose for me," the witch said. "With your necklace I control you and you control the beasts."

Beasts.

Lilith had used the plural, and something told Samantha it hadn't been an accident.

"What do you mean *beasts*?" she asked, desperate to keep her talking if nothing else.

Lilith cackled. "That's the best part! The demon Abigail tried to raise? The thing chained under the mountain in Santa Cruz? They're brothers! There were twelve originally. One was chained, eleven slain by magic users ages ago. Abigail only tried to raise one. Then again, she always lacked vision."

Samantha's blood felt as if it had turned to ice in her veins. "You're trying to raise all of them!"

"That's right. And you'll help me use them to destroy the world."

Samantha felt sick inside. She'd always worried that Lilith would try to use the necklace to control her, and now it looked as though she might actually accomplish that. It was too horrible to even think about.

Lilith dropped in the last item she was holding, and the chalice began to boil and bubble. All she needed now to complete the spell was a sacrifice.

And as Samantha glanced behind Lilith, she had a terrible sinking feeling she knew who it was going to be.

Thomas was also managing to move slightly and had been sneaking up behind Lilith. Suddenly Lilith spun and threw him to his knees. She yanked an athame out of her robes and held it to his throat while with the other hand she pulled something else that Samantha recognized all too well out of a pocket.

The necklace was dangling from the witch's hand. She was prepared to use it to compel Samantha to control the demons as she poised the tip of her knife above Thomas's throat.

Samantha looked around frantically. There was no one who could reach them in time. She was so weak, she couldn't snatch either athame or necklace from the witch's grasp from where she was.

Suddenly a black blur streaked past her and she stared in amazement as a giant black panther slammed into Thomas and Lilith, sending both dagger and necklace flying.

The panther jumped after the necklace and picked it up in his teeth and turned to Samantha. Only then did she realize that it was Freaky. How he was there and how he had changed himself back into a panther she didn't know; she was only grateful that he had.

And the impact with the panther had been just enough to break Lilith's concentration and she stopped pulling energy from everywhere.

Samantha sprang forward just as Freaky bared his teeth and Thomas snatched up the athame and both turned toward Lilith.

"No! No blood will be spilled. Blood is the final ingredient in the spell," Samantha shouted. She came to a halt in front of Lilith, who was rising onto her knees, and she stared down into her eyes. "So I rob you of your final act of terror." She put her hand over Lilith's heart and took her power. Before her eyes the witch withered and turned to dust with a scream echoing in the air all that was left of her.

Samantha ran to the chalice. She plucked a strand of hair from her head and dropped it into the mixture, anything to throw the mix off, ruin the reaction.

It worked; the liquid ceased to bubble. She waited a moment and then hurled the chalice onto the floor, shattering it and sending the contents leaking into the floor.

Above her, the jester head teetered for a moment, fell, and smashed onto the floor at her feet.

"I think that pretty much sums it up," Ed said drily.

Half an hour later they were all sitting in the sanctuary at the church except for the wounded. The pastor and a few other volunteers were tending to them in the other room. Once they had made it back there, Samantha had destroyed her cross necklace. It had been a little bit sad, but she could never risk it falling into the wrong hands again. On top of that, she realized the vow she had made when she had sealed her blood inside was obsolete. As she destroyed it she promised God instead that she would no longer fear her magic and that she would use it to help others.

Finished, she joined the others and sat down, surrounded by Ed, Anthony, and Thomas. Both Ed and Anthony were eyeing Thomas warily as though expecting him to suddenly turn on them.

For her part Samantha felt a little bit as though she were floating. It was over. They had saved the world.

Again, she thought with a shake of her head.

"You should call Vanessa and tell her that everything's okay, and that you'll be coming home," she told Ed.

His face lit up. "Yeah, I can." He stood up and pulled his phone out of his pocket and called.

"Hey, no, don't worry—everything is great. We saved the world. Yes, again."

Samantha bit her lip. She always had liked Ed's wife.

"When will I be coming home? Tomorrow if I can manage it. I might have to stick around and help a bit with the cleanup, but the FBI's here and I'm hoping I can slough that job onto them."

Samantha certainly thought he should. He had done more than his part.

"Yeah, Samantha will be coming back with me. What? I miss you, too," he said.

He moved off quickly as the conversation clearly started to take a more personal tone. Samantha was so relieved that he was okay and that he was going to be getting back to Vanessa soon. She was a good woman and deserved to have her husband by her side.

"You are going back to Boston, right?" Anthony said.

"Of course," she answered. She had no idea if it would be permanent, if the police department there really wanted her back, but she had to try.

She wanted to see her adoptive parents, and frankly, she needed a very long rest.

Connor had been sitting quietly, his head in his hands, still trying to absorb everything that had happened. Finally he looked up at her with tired eyes.

"You ever want a job working for the bureau—" Connor began.

"I know who to look up." She smiled.

He nodded. He stood, weaving slightly on his feet.

All of them were exhausted beyond belief.

"I'm going to go grab a section of floor and get some shut-eye while I can," he admitted.

"Sounds like a good idea," Samantha said. Personally she was still a little too wound up, but she knew that when the crash came it would be hitting her hard. Better to get wherever she wanted to be when that happened. And she, for one, was not looking forward to grabbing crash space on the floor.

"I think I have just enough energy to drive us all back to the hotel," Anthony said. "I'm still not sure how Freaky got out of the room."

"At least you have the answer to your question of whether or not he can track me," Samantha said.

"And it's a good thing he did," Anthony said.

The kitten was back to his regular self and passed out on one of the pews, lying upside down on his back, his belly exposed, as though he had not a care in the world. She had no idea how he'd managed to transform himself into the panther form, but she was intensely grateful that he had. Maybe the bond between them was growing. Maybe he could access some of her powers because of it.

"Take care of your pets and they'll take care of you, that's what I always say," Thomas said with a gentle smile.

"You heading out?"

Samantha turned and saw Trina. "Yeah, I've got to get some sleep," she said, standing up.

Trina hugged her. "Thank you for everything. I'm sure I'll see you before you go back to Boston."

Samantha nodded.

"And don't worry. I'll make sure Robin gets safely back to her mom in California."

"I'd appreciate it," Samantha said, stifling a yawn. She turned to Anthony. "We'd better get going quick before I fall asleep here."

He took her hand and started to lead her toward the back of the sanctuary, where Ed was still talking on the phone to Vanessa.

Thomas got up and trailed after them to the car.

"Can we drop you somewhere?" Anthony asked at last.

"No," Thomas said, turning to Samantha. "It was good getting to know you. I'd like to continue the conversation."

"So would I," she said. She gave him a quick hug and then slid into the car.

"I know this is a few years overdue," he said, "but I think it's time I took my little girl to the most magical place on earth."

"Where would that be?" she asked with a raised eyebrow.

He grinned. "Why, Disney World, of course."

"I can't think of anywhere else I'd rather go," she said with a laugh.

20

Samantha and Thomas had spent a week together in Disney World, which had actually turned out to be perfect. They could talk when they wanted to and busy themselves with rides and activities when one or both of them weren't in the mood. When they finally posed for a picture with Sorcerer Mickey, it was all she could do not to laugh hysterically.

She had texted with Anthony for a few minutes every night before going to bed, but otherwise he'd given her space to deal with her father and all the new things she had to process. She loved him for that, but she had also begun to miss him so much it was unbearable.

When the week ended she and Thomas said goodbye as friends and made plans to get together again in a few months. It was beyond strange to her that the father whose name she had never even known was now going to be a part of her life. Even stranger, though, was the realization that she could finally return home to Boston and possibly pick up the pieces of her life that Lilith's machinations had destroyed months before.

As she stepped out of the terminal and onto the sidewalk at the airport, she felt the bag in her arms begin to wiggle. Freaky had not appreciated being cooped up in the bag underneath the seat in front of her. She had discovered that for some reason she could no longer dispel Freaky's energy and re-create him when she wished. He had become too real, too sentient; that was the only thing she could figure. Fortunately he was still pure energy and had no need for food, water, or the other things a flesh-and-blood kitten would have. She had not been prepared, though, to buy him a cat carrier and his own ticket on the plane. Clearly if he traveled with her by plane in the future, these were things they were going to have to work out.

A car pulled up to the curb and she felt a surge of joy as her adoptive mom hopped out and threw her arms around her. Her dad was smiling from behind the wheel.

She climbed into the backseat and quickly unzipped her bag. Freaky bounded out with an irritated mew.

"You got a kitten?" her mom said, raising an eyebrow.

"It's a long story," Samantha said.

"We look forward to hearing it," her dad said, smiling at her in the rearview mirror.

"I love you guys," she said.

"Not half as much as we love you," he assured her.

"We were planning on going right out to eat, but does he need to get home?" her mom asked, eyeing Freaky.

"No, he'll be fine in the car. I'm starving."

"Won't he overheat?" her dad asked.

"Not this kitten. He's sort of . . . indestructible."

"Okay . . . well, to the restaurant it is," her dad said.

He drove right to one of her favorite seafood restaurants, a place they usually reserved for special occasions like birthdays. They went inside, were seated at a table, and she didn't even bother picking up the menu since she already knew what she wanted.

"Let me guess," her mom said with a smile. "Mahi-mahi in lemon caper butter sauce."

Samantha grinned. "You know me so well."

"True, but you seem different, happier," her dad noted.

"A lot has happened," she said.

"So we've gathered. Ed's been over to visit twice in the last week," her mom said. "Glad to see he's mellowed out."

Samantha nodded and picked up her glass of water.

"And the second time he brought around a young man by the name of Anthony," her dad said, looking at her over the top of his menu.

Samantha nearly spewed her water. She choked it down and set the glass carefully back on the table. "He did?" she asked.

"Yes, although frankly, I always assumed that when a young man came to be introduced, you'd be the one bringing him and not Ed," her dad said with a twinkle in his eye.

She shook her head. "I don't know what I'm going to do with him," she sighed.

"Which one?" her mom asked.

"Both," she said with a laugh. "Well, what did you think of Anthony?"

"Nice, incredibly nervous, but nice," her mom said.

"He's clearly got some emotional baggage, but he seems to be working through it," her dad added.

"Leave it to the psychologist to come up with that assessment," she mocked.

"Careful, now, or I'll start in on you and this change I'm noticing," he teased.

The waitress came to take their order and as soon as she had left, Samantha leaned across the table. "Believe it or not, I finally found peace."

"Praise the Lord," her mother said softly.

"A pastor actually helped me put the last piece of the puzzle together. He helped me understand that the gifts aren't evil. It's what you do with them that is good or evil or even neutral."

Her dad reached out and squeezed her hand. "I tried to tell you that years ago, but you just weren't ready to listen or accept it. I'm so glad you've finally come to the place where you can."

The waitress came back with their drinks. As soon as she'd left, Samantha's dad took a sip of his coffee and grimaced. "Too cold," he said with a sigh. "No one knows how to do real hot coffee anymore."

"Have you really come to peace with everything?" her mom asked.

Samantha grinned. "Let me show you."

She reached out and put her hand on her dad's mug. A moment later it was boiling. She pulled her hand away. "It should be hot enough now." Her dad had always taken his coffee scalding.

"I think I'm going to hug you," he deadpanned. "Also, you must go with us to all restaurants from now on. I can have truly hot coffee again."

She laughed. "Anytime you need hot coffee, I'm your girl."

"You're always my girl," he said with a warm smile.

She felt herself beginning to tear up. Thomas might be her biological father, and she was looking forward to spending more time with him, getting to know him more, but these people were her mom and dad, the ones who loved her unconditionally and would always be there for her no matter what.

"I love you guys," she whispered again, just because she felt it couldn't be said enough.

They both beamed at her and took her hands. Then her dad took her mom's free hand so the three of them were joined in a circle.

Samantha smiled. This was the circle she had always wanted, a family, not a coven. She had it, and she knew, thanks to them, that love was thicker than blood.

"Now, tell us all about this boy," her mom said after a minute.

"And all about New Orleans. Ed's narrative was exciting but lacked some perspective," her dad said.

"And don't forget to tell us why it's okay that our grandkitten was stuffed inside a duffel bag."

Samantha laughed. "Okay, but we're going to be here all night."

"That's okay. We'll order dessert," her dad said.

"Twice," her mom chimed in with a grin.

Samantha started laughing and she wasn't sure she was ever going to stop and it felt so good. Slowly over dinner and what ended up being triple desserts all around, she explained everything that had happened, and even about Freaky.

Finally the restaurant closed and they had to leave, but they continued talking in the car all the way home and late into the night before they all had to retire to bed.

Samantha went to her old room. They had decided that she would stay with them for a couple of weeks while she looked for a new apartment. And to be honest, they were all looking forward to some quality time together. Plus, despite what Ed had told her, Samantha still had her doubts that she was going to be welcomed back at her old precinct. In the back of her mind she kept thinking that there was a very real possibility she was going to have to leave Boston again if she wanted to find work as a cop.

She just knew there was no way she was going back to San Francisco or New Orleans. She'd had her fill of the particular crazy both those places had to offer. Maybe she'd opt for somewhere nice and laid-back. Hawaii sounded good.

Her old bedroom held so many memories for her and she relived several of them as she got ready for bed, particularly the pivotal one when she had foresworn magic altogether and dripped her blood into the cross.

At last she lay down and forced herself to close her eyes. Her mind was still racing, though, and she had a hard time falling asleep, even with Freaky curled against her side purring and snoring all at the same time. It still amazed her that he'd managed to take on such a life of his own that she could no longer disperse his energy. It would make it harder to hide him when she wanted, but she was still actually quite glad.

"You're a real boy now," she whispered to him. Fortunately, though, he still didn't come with the higher-maintenance functions of a real boy such as injuries. She could only imagine trying to explain that one to a veterinarian.

It was far into the night before she was finally able to fall asleep.

When she rose in the morning, she dressed for her day, feeling butterflies in her stomach. She left Freaky in her bedroom and then headed downtown. When she parked she said a silent prayer before getting out of her car.

Samantha walked back into her old precinct, fear prickling at the back of her mind. The last time she had been there, it was far from a happy experience. Ed had reassured her, though, that things would be different, that everyone was willing to welcome her back with open arms. She hadn't asked him just how many of those arms he'd had to twist to guarantee that that would be the case.

She'd spoken briefly over the phone with Captain Roberts the night before and he had reassured her that, yes, they wanted her back and her badge and gun were waiting to be collected the next morning in his office. Still, she couldn't help wondering if it was all some sort of mistake, if she'd get there and people would have changed their minds about having her around.

She should have made Ed come in with her, but he'd said he had a doctor's appointment that couldn't wait.

Personally she wondered if he just didn't want to be there in case there were unexpected fireworks.

She walked into the hallway and was surprised that she didn't see anyone around. Normally there were officers busy heading in all directions. Something seemed off about the whole thing. It was unnaturally quiet as well. Had they heard she was coming and made themselves scarce? She really wasn't sure how long she wanted to be working in a department where most of the other cops avoided her like the plague. When she finally entered the squad room, she was tense, braced for anything.

Anything but what she saw.

Every officer was standing there beneath a huge banner that proclaimed WELCOME BACK, SAMANTHA, OUR SECRET WEAPON.

She blinked in shock and then her eyes found Ed's. He was grinning from ear to ear.

"Surprise!" he said.

Everyone began to applaud and then to cheer. Captain Roberts approached her with her old badge and gun in hand. She felt a lump in her throat as she accepted them from him.

"The way we figure it, every department needs a secret weapon. We're just glad we found ours," he said with a grin.

"I don't understand. I thought no one here wanted anything to do with me."

He shrugged. "I told you to give it some time. When Ed came around, it was like opening the floodgate." He chuckled. "Course it doesn't hurt that since you've been gone there've been a couple of cases that we definitely could have used your expertise on."

She nodded. "Well, whatever the reason, I'm grateful," she said.

"I'm sorry this was so long coming."

He stepped back and the other officers swarmed around her, patting her back, shaking her hand. A few of them even hugged her.

"Drinks tonight at O'Doul's in honor of Samantha!" someone shouted.

Ed rolled his eyes. "Well, there go my and Vanessa's plans to take you out to dinner tonight."

Samantha smiled. "There'll be plenty of time for that. When was the last time any of these guys even asked me to go out celebrating?"

He shrugged. "That's what you get for being so darn unlikable."

She smiled at him.

"Hey, don't forget the cake!" someone shouted.

The crowd parted and someone wheeled a cart up with a large cake on it that said WELCOME HOME. There were some unlit candles on it.

She grinned.

"Okay, who forgot the matches?" the guy with the cake shouted.

"Don't worry, boys. I've got this," Samantha said.

She snapped her fingers and the candles lit.

There were gasps all around. She stepped forward, stared at the cake for a long moment, and then bent low and blew out the candles.

There was more cheering and anyone who hadn't already patted her back surged forward to do so.

Great, you know they're going to want you to do that at

all the parties from now on, Ed said, thinking the thoughts at her.

As long as they keep inviting me to the parties, I'm good with it, she thought back. Then with a happy start, she realized that she truly was.

The rest of the day was crazy. Captain Roberts needed her to fill out some paperwork. Ed made a great show of reintroducing her to her desk, then took almost fiendish glee in piling it high with open-case files.

"So this is why you really missed me," she finally quipped.

Everyone who hadn't been able to make it to her welcome party dropped by at some point during the day to say hello. Then, when it was quitting time, she was swept up by a crowd of people heading for the bar down the street.

Samantha limited herself to soda, but no one cared what she was drinking as long as her glass stayed full. She realized that there was so much she had missed out on in life because she had always kept herself so closed off, and the simple joy of blowing off some steam with her coworkers was a new experience, one she vowed she'd repeat.

Ed left early to get home to Vanessa after making Samantha promise that she'd let them take her out to dinner later in the week. She knew that sooner or later all the attention would die down, but she decided to enjoy it while it lasted.

If the guys had had their way, the party would have lasted all night at O'Doul's. As it was she managed to bow out at midnight. She made it back to her parents' home and tumbled into bed in her old room, where Freaky already was asleep. He glared at her for waking him and she grabbed him and hugged him close as she fell asleep.

She slept through the night without a single nightmare and in the morning she woke with a smile. She and Anthony had made plans to do a late breakfast together at Red's in Salem. It was the first time they were going to have seen each other since parting ways in New Orleans, and she could hardly wait.

Driving into Salem felt different this time. There were no witches to fight, no good-byes to say, and the past could no longer haunt her as it once had done. A burden seemed to lift off her shoulders and she felt truly free. It was such a relief, such a blessed feeling, that she wanted to sing out loud. She actually flipped on the radio. The Eagles' song "Witchy Woman" came on a moment later. She laughed and then began to sing along for joy. The world was a new place. A song she would have shunned before for all the pain and guilt it would have reminded her of was now instead something to celebrate.

She parked on one of the streets ringing Salem Common, got out of her car, and drank in the sights and sounds. She walked slowly up Essex Street, smiling at all the shop windows filled with their touristy witch paraphernalia. For the first time she was able to see it as others saw it and not as a mocking reminder of her own grisly past.

At last she turned the corner that led to Red's. It was appropriate that she and Anthony were meeting at the same restaurant where they had first met. She glanced at her watch; she was actually a couple of minutes late. She'd taken her time strolling down the street when she hadn't expected to. When she got there she was shocked to see a sign on the door that said the restaurant was closed that morning for a private event.

She stood for a second, feeling deeply disappointed and a bit unsettled. Why had Anthony not called to tell her and to suggest an alternative meeting place? He was usually quite punctual and she had a hard time believing she had beaten him there. He couldn't be having second thoughts about them, could he?

Maybe with the danger finally now past he'd had time to think and realized he just couldn't be with her. She had started to turn away when the door opened and a waitress stepped out. "Come on in, miss," the lady said.

Samantha pointed to the sign. "You're having a private event."

"Yes, and I believe it's in your honor," the woman said with a smile.

Startled, Samantha followed her inside. Anthony stood up from the table, *their* table, and gave her a smile that melted her heart. She moved quickly over to him and he kissed her heartily before waving her to a seat.

"What's going on?" she asked.

"Well, I realized that it can be so hard to get a table here in the mornings and so noisy with all the crowd, so I rented the place for the morning. It seemed the thing to do somehow. After everything, I thought we could use a little peace and quiet and time for just us."

"You are a genius."

"And don't you forget it," he said with a grin.

The waitress came and put food on the table. There were eggs and bacon and sausage and heaping plates of their famous pancakes.

"It would take an army to eat all this," Samantha observed.

"Well, then, we'd better get started," he said with a grin.

The food was even better than she remembered and she was surprised at how hungry she actually was. For the first time maybe in her entire life she actually felt at peace. It was a unique feeling and she savored it even as she savored every bite.

"So, I hear that you met my parents," she said.

He nearly choked on his bite of pancake. "I thought I was going to kill Ed. That had to be one of the most awkward few hours of my life."

"Well, they liked you, so you don't have to worry too much. My dad psychoanalyzed you, of course, but the results were mostly favorable."

"*Mostly?* Great," he said.

"I wouldn't worry. Mom thought you were nice."

"Oh, *nice.* That's even better, because that's what every guy likes to hear," he said sarcastically.

She laughed at him and continued eating. At last they both began to slow down and the waitress came back and cleared away all the dishes and refilled their coffee mugs.

Samantha sat back with a contented sigh. "That was really good."

"Yes, it was. You remember the last time we were here together?"

She nodded. She had seen him before she left for San Francisco. It had been a much more somber occasion.

"Do you remember what I told you?" he asked, smiling wistfully.

"How could I forget? You said we had a good story. You know. Boy meets girl. Boy falls for girl. Boy tries to kill girl."

"Yes, but it needs a better ending," he said.

"Boy rescues girl. That's pretty good."

"I've got a better one. Boy proposes to girl."

Samantha's heart began to race. Anthony was no longer smiling. He was dead serious.

"Girl says yes," she whispered.

A moment later they were in each other's arms, laughing, crying all at once. He kissed her, and the world swept away. This was what was real. This was what mattered. It made all the pain and sacrifice worth it.

At last Anthony pulled away. He reached into his pocket and took out a ring box. "I, um, had this made for you a while ago."

He opened the box and inside was a thick gold band with a diamond on it.

"You had it made for me?" Samantha breathed as he took it out of the box.

"Yeah, and believe me, it took some doing to find a jeweler who would do it to spec."

"Why is that?" she asked.

"Well, the band has a hollow core that runs all the way around. Before it was sealed shut underneath the diamond, I filled the core with a few drops of my blood. So this way, you'd have a circle of my blood always surrounding you, always protecting you."

He slid the ring on her finger and the metal felt warm to the touch. "I can feel it," she whispered in awe.

He kissed the ring on her finger. "That's my love, my life, everything that I am."

"It's perfect."

She kissed him with tears of joy streaming down her cheeks. In all her life, Samantha had never dreamed that a circle of blood could be so beautiful or make her feel so protected and so very, very loved.

Don't miss the first novel in the
Witch Hunt series by Debbie Viguié,

The Thirteenth Sacrifice

Available from Arrow.

1

Everywhere she looked there were shadows. Somewhere far away a man was chanting in a deep voice, and with each word a new cut appeared on her arms, until she was bleeding from a dozen wounds. The blood rolled down her arms and dripped off the tips of her fingers to land in pools on the floor. She began to shake.

"Turn!" It was one of the grown-ups, the one with the pale blue eyes.

She spun slowly, the blood continuing to drip onto the floor, forming a circle around her.

She stopped when she had gone all the way around. She began to feel faint and the smell of her own blood made her sick.

"It must be unbroken."

She looked down at the floor, at the blood spatters that formed the circle. Except it wasn't perfect; there were three spots where the line was broken.

The man stopped chanting and a moment later several women started a different chant.

"Close it—now."

She stared down in terror at the breaks in the circle. The circle kept her safe. The circle protected her from what was outside, but only if it was unbroken. A sulfurous smell filled her nostrils and she could hear screams nearby. She began to spin in a circle again, trying to drip blood on the gaps, but no matter how hard she tried, the blood went everywhere but where she wanted it to go.

She started to get dizzy and she thought she was going to fall down, but she had to stay inside the circle and she had to finish it. The screams grew closer and she didn't know what made them.

"You will die!"

She began to scream herself, trying to block out the other screams. She dug her fingernails into her arms, tearing at her skin until the blood flowed faster and fell all around her. Two gaps left.

She heard the sound of claws scratching the ground, running toward her.

One gap left.

Growling and snarling, they were upon her, on every side. She shook her hands, watching her own blood fly through the air, covering her, the ground, the things beyond the circle with red eyes, and then the last gap was closed.

And something hit the circle and sent shock waves through the air and the screaming got louder.

Samantha Ryan shrieked and sat up in bed. Sweat covered her and she could still smell the blood from her dreams. She switched on the lamp on her end table and saw that she had scratched several deep grooves into her arms, and her sheets were bloody.

She wrapped her bleeding arms around herself and

began to rock back and forth. "Just a nightmare, just a nightmare," she told herself over and over again.

Only she knew it wasn't a nightmare. They never were. It was another repressed memory from her childhood, bubbling to the surface to haunt her and shatter the peace she had tried so hard to achieve and hold on to.

Finally she got up and made her way to the bathroom and did her best to stanch the flow of blood. The scratches were across the insides of her lower arms. Cat scratches— that's what she'd tell anyone who asked. Scratches from a phantom cat who didn't exist, who got blamed for a lot she didn't want to have to explain.

Once she got the bleeding stopped, she applied Neosporin to the cuts. As her fingers stroked the scratches, she fought the urge to mutter a healing incantation over them. The pain was great but not unbearable. Far better to feel the pain.

She reached up to touch the cross she wore around her neck. It wasn't good to wear it to bed. She risked injuring herself while she was unconscious. Still, she couldn't bring herself to remove it. Her arms began to throb and she said a silent prayer as she swallowed some Tylenol.

She straightened and looked at herself in the mirror. Green eyes that looked far too old to belong to her stared back. Her shoulder-length red hair was damp with sweat and she ducked her head under the faucet, letting the cold water wash away the last clinging tendrils of the nightmare memory.

A few minutes later she toweled her hair dry and walked back into her bedroom, where she looked at the clock. It was almost four in the morning. She knew from experience that she wouldn't be able to go back to sleep, and that even if she could, she wouldn't like what she saw. She stripped her bed, dumped the sheets in the washing machine, and then got ready for work.

Black pants went on first. A gray button-up shirt suited her mood. A small Swiss Army knife she'd carried with her since her first day on the job and her detective's shield went into a pocket. She hesitated only a moment before clipping her holster onto her belt and sliding her gun inside it.

After leaving her house, Samantha drove downtown, parked, and headed to her favorite coffee shop. The city was just beginning to wake up and she savored the sights and sounds. Every city had its own character and Boston was no exception. The city that had witnessed so many historic events had not forgotten its past even as it pushed boldly forward into the future. It felt old and young all at once.

Just like me.

A jogger passed her, throwing an admiring glance her way. She ignored him. Samantha was twenty-eight but often felt much, much older. With her red hair and green eyes betraying her Irish heritage, a gift from the father she had never known, she caught the eyes of a lot of guys her age. It was admiration she found hard to reciprocate because they all seemed so very young and so very, very naive.

She walked into Jake's Eats and settled into her usual booth. Claudia, the motherly brunette waitress who never forgot a customer, appeared with a glass of orange juice in her hand.

"Rough night, huh?"

Samantha smiled at her. "You could say that."

"You're in luck. We've got corned beef hash this morning."

"Sounds like a winner."

Claudia smiled, patted her on the shoulder, and headed back toward the kitchen. Samantha wrapped her hand around the glass of orange juice, feeling the cold of it against her fingers, inhaling the smells coming from the kitchen, feeling the squishiness of the red vinyl upholstery, and remembering, as always, her first visit to the restaurant.

She had been twelve and a police officer had brought her. It had seemed like a haven from the horrors of her childhood, and the bloodbath she had just witnessed. It was where she came whenever she needed to remember that the past was the past. *When I need to feel safe,* she thought, briefly closing her eyes.

She heard the chimes on the door and opened her eyes to see a man a few years older than she was, with short black hair, a square jaw, and a brown trench coat, and he was heading her way with a determined stride.

"Morning, Ed," she said in greeting as he slid across from her into the booth.

"Samantha. I knew I'd find you here."

"Did you call the house?"

"Yeah, and, surprise, you weren't there."

"You could have called my cell," she said.

He rolled his eyes at her. "I could have, if you ever had it on."

She resisted the urge to check, but knew he was probably right. Her cell phone spent more time off than it did on. She told people she was forgetful, but deep down she knew that she really just didn't want to talk to anyone.

"I think you must be the worst partner I've ever had," he grouched.

She smiled. "I'm the best partner you've ever had and you know it."

He gave her a defiant look and then grabbed her orange juice. "Whatever," he said as he took a swig. She had long before learned not to let his occasional lack of boundaries faze her. He knew she kept secrets from him, but he didn't push. In exchange, she didn't gripe when he mooched her food. It was a tenuous truce at best, but for two years it had worked well for both of them.

Ed was her second partner. Making detective so young hadn't made her popular, and everyone knew that her family was close to the captain. Her first partner had spent more time griping about her age than helping her learn the ropes. It hadn't mattered to him that she had a degree in criminal science, had worked her tail off, stepping up and taking responsibility wherever she could, and had earned high praise from her supervisors. The whole partnership had been a disaster. After three months Captain Roberts had assigned Ed to be her partner. Fortunately Ed had been willing to overlook her inexperience, and she had learned a lot from him. But she prided herself on also having taught him a thing or two.

"Why are you here, Ed?" she asked as she retrieved her orange juice.

"Why else? We've got a body—college coed turned up dead in her apartment off campus."

"We're not on duty for another couple of hours."

"Yeah, but there's some local color involved."

Claudia reappeared with the promised corned beef hash. Samantha shoveled several forkfuls into her mouth as Ed grabbed a piece of her sourdough toast and headed for the door. She put money down on the table and followed him outside to his car. They drove for ten minutes in silence before parking outside an apartment complex.

"Local color" was what the other detectives called it when there was anything weird about a call. As soon as they walked inside the apartment, Samantha saw why the phrase had been applied.

A girl was standing, talking to a uniformed officer. Her hair was dyed an unnatural black, and she was dressed like a Goth, in a black velvet dress, black boots, and fishnet tights. Nearby, the crime scene photographer was taking pictures of the body of a young woman dressed in white who had a bloody pentagram drawn on her forehead.

When Samantha and Ed approached, the uniformed officer explained that the live girl was Katie Horn, that she lived there and had discovered the body. The dead girl was Camille. He then moved away.

Samantha turned to Katie and studied her, taking in everything from the pentagram necklace to the crystal ring on her finger. *Wiccan?*

"What's with the getup?" Ed asked.

"I'm a witch," the girl said defiantly.

Wannabe.

Samantha suppressed the urge to roll her eyes. "When is your coven meeting?"

"I don't have one. I'm a solitary practitioner."

"What you are is full of crap," Ed said. "You see, my

partner here, she has witch-dar. If you were a witch, I would have known it ten minutes ago."

Samantha sighed and contemplated kicking him, but he continued. "Friend of yours?" he asked, indicating the body.

"My roommate."

"You don't seem too shook up," he noted.

The girl shrugged. "Didn't know her until three weeks ago. I put an ad in the campus paper, and she was the only one who answered who wasn't a freak."

"Good one," Ed said, as if she had just made a joke.

"Was she observant?" Samantha questioned.

"Huh?" Katie asked, a confused look on her face.

"Did she practice? Was she Wiccan? Pagan?" Samantha clarified.

"No, nothing like that. She was like Mormon or something."

"And she didn't have a problem with you being a . . . witch?" Ed asked, choking on the word.

"No, some people have, like, religious tolerance, you know," Katie said, glaring at Ed.

"Right." He snorted.

"Did she have a boyfriend?" Samantha interrupted.

"Yeah, Brad, a real frat brat," Katie said, wrinkling her nose. "They just started going out."

"Did she have any enemies?" Ed asked.

Katie shook her head. "She wasn't interesting enough to have enemies."

Samantha's eyes swept the room. They weren't going to get anything useful out of Katie. The way she stood, all defiant and rebellious posturing, was mostly a front, but if she knew something more, she had no plans to spill it.

Ed continued to question Katie while Samantha inspected the environment for anything of interest. Aside from the bloody pentagram on Camille's forehead, there didn't seem to be any blood on the body or anywhere else in the room.

She walked into Katie's room, which had vampire-themed posters on the walls. Stacks of vampire and witch books cluttered her desk and nightstand. A handful of mythology and comparative lit textbooks teetered precariously on the edge of her desk.

A pentagram had been marked on the floor underneath and around her bed. Samantha raised an eyebrow and wondered if the guys Katie brought home found it as dark and sexy as Katie clearly did.

From there she moved to Camille's room. By contrast, this room was all delicate pastels. A stuffed bear sat lonely in the middle of the neatly made bed. Posters of horses and kittens decorated the walls. If Camille really was Mormon, then Samantha was surprised that she would have tolerated a roommate like Katie. Her parents would no doubt have been even less thrilled.

"Why were you here, Camille?" she whispered to the room. She closed her eyes and could almost feel the younger woman's spirit, her essence.

She opened her eyes and shook herself hard. She moved over to Camille's desk and went through the drawers, finding only school supplies. The textbooks on the desk were neatly stacked and revealed that Camille had been taking biology, chemistry, and French literature.

After gathering all the names and information they could, an hour later they left the scene. Once in Ed's car, Samantha's irritation with him returned. "I don't like it when you do that."

"Get sarcastic with the suspects? You know I can't help myself."

"Not that."

"What, say you have witch-dar?"

"Yes."

"But you do."

"No, I don't."

"Okay, was she a witch?"

"No!"

"Was she a Wiccan?"

"I seriously doubt it."

"I don't know. I think she might have been—after all, there were all those candles around," he said.

She couldn't tell whether he was serious or he was baiting her. "You saw that apartment. There was no place she could cast a proper circle, not easily."

"Maybe she worships outside."

"In the dirt and the mud? Hardly."

"What makes you say that?" he asked.

"Let's just say her boots weren't made for walking."

"Okay, but the candles . . ."

"All black. She's a Goth. You know, darkness, death, tragedy. Wiccans celebrate the whole cycle—birth, life, death. Not just one aspect. Besides, you can't do candle magic with all black candles."

"Witch-dar," he said smugly.

Samantha turned to stare out the window, annoyed that she'd walked into it. She fingered her cross and tried not to think about how her need to touch it to make herself feel better was not much different from ceremonial magic.

"Sorry," he said, growing serious. "What do you think about the dead girl and the pentagram on her forehead?"

Samantha shrugged. "I think it's a red herring. Wiccans take an oath to do no harm. Human sacrifice isn't their thing."

And the types of people who do believe in human sacrifice don't use that symbol.

"Still, it's freaky."

"Do we know what the cause of death was?" Samantha asked. She hadn't been able to see any trauma to the body—no gun or knife wounds, no strangulation marks either.

"Coroner's gotta run some tests. It could be poison or something like that."

"Or she could have had a medical condition. Neither of which points to the supernatural."

"No witches, then? So, all that and it's just going to be a standard investigation," he said, sounding disappointed. "Remember last month it was that fake vampire murder and six months before was that woman who swore the ghost of her dead husband was the one who killed her boyfriend instead of her?"

"Your point?" she asked.

"Mark my words—one of these days there's going to be something supernatural actually going on."

"You really believe that, Ed?" she asked, carefully keeping her tone neutral.

"Where there's smoke there's usually fire. Plus, Vanessa saw a ghost when she was a kid and I believe her."

"It's always a good policy, believing your wife."

"And you don't believe her?" Ed asked.

"Of course I do. She's one of the most grounded, practical people I know. If she says it happened, I take it as gospel."

"So, off to chase down an ordinary killer. Let's go see the boyfriend."

"Frat Brat Brad," Samantha said. "What more did you get on him besides a nickname?"

"Brad Jensen. His name was in Camille's cell. According to Goth girl, he belongs to an honors fraternity. Apparently that's how he and Camille met."

Ed pulled up outside the fraternity house. They walked up to the front door, knocked, and the door was opened by a tired-looking guy with three-day-old stubble and coffee breath.

"We're looking for Brad Jensen," Ed said.

"Come in. He's in the kitchen," the other guy said before yawning.

They walked into the kitchen just as someone picked up a backpack and began to head out.

"Brad?" Samantha asked.

"May I help you?" he asked, open curiosity on his face. "If this is about pledging, maybe Harry can help. I'm just on my way to class. Sorry."

Samantha looked him over. He was tall and slender with a gentle smile and innocent eyes partially obscured by glasses. He was wearing slacks, a long-sleeved shirt, and a tie and seemed comfortable in them. He didn't look like someone who was into drawing bloody pentagrams on girls after he killed them. Samantha flashed Ed a sideways glance and could tell he was thinking the same thing.

Brad left the kitchen and they followed him into the common room.

"Brad Jensen?" she specified.

"Yes. Why?" he said, turning to look at her. There it was in his eyes, the sudden dawning that something might be wrong. She had seen that look dozens of times. Most people could sense when they were about to get bad news.

"We're Detectives Ryan and Hofferman," she said, flashing her badge. "We need to talk to you about Camille."

"Is she okay?" he asked, going completely white.

"I'm afraid not," Ed said, his voice softening. "She's dead."

"Dead?" Brad asked as he sank down into a green velvet armchair that had seen better days.

Ed nodded. "We understand the two of you were dating."

Brad's eyes had glazed over and he didn't respond. Samantha knelt in front of him and put her hand on his shoulder. "Brad?"

"What? Sorry. Yeah. We had just met, but she was special, you know. We had so much in common." His voice caught in his throat and he looked away.

He doesn't want to cry in front of us.

"I told her to be careful when driving around here, that people were crazy. She wasn't used to all the traffic, and it scared her."

"She didn't die in a car accident," Samantha began.

"She was murdered," Ed finished.

And she watched Brad's eyes as the news shattered him. Grief, pain, and disbelief flashed across his face in quick succession. Rage would come soon enough. It was a critical moment, the one when you realized the world wasn't safe and that those you loved could be ripped from you by evil. It would likely be a defining point of his life. She wondered, as she always did, what it was like to be innocent and then to lose it. Her own innocence had been destroyed when she was too young to even remember it.

"Was she religious?" Samantha asked.

Brad nodded. "Very. She's Mormon. I am too. That was one of the things that was so great. You don't meet as many Mormons out here as you do back home."

"Was she interested in Wicca or anything like that?"

"You mean witchcraft?" Brad asked, looking somewhat shocked.

Samantha sighed. Wicca and witchcraft were two different things, especially in the way he obviously thought.

"Yeah," Ed said, pressing on.

Brad shook his head. "No. I mean, I know her roommate was into some weird stuff, but not Camille. She was only staying there until she could find a better place to live. The fraternity is coed. She applied for a spot in the girls' building. I was really praying she'd get it so she could get out of there."

"When was the last time you heard from her?" Samantha asked.

"Three nights ago. We went out to dinner. We were supposed to go to the movies tonight . . ."

The tears he had been trying to stop started to flow.

"Did anyone ever threaten her in any way?" Samantha asked.

"Who would do that? It was Camille. She was so . . . nice."

The guy who had answered the door and two others had gathered at the far side of the room. Samantha stood and nodded, and one of them moved over and sat down next to Brad, putting a hand on his shoulder.

"If there's anything we can do to help you find her killer, let us know," he said, looking Samantha straight in the eye.

Brad had begun sobbing uncontrollably. Samantha and Ed took the names and phone numbers of the others in the room and then left.

"That got us nowhere," Ed complained when they were finally back in the car.

Samantha wished she could disagree, but Brad didn't know anything. She was sure of it.

"Someone wanted her dead. There had to be a reason, right?" Ed continued.

"Well, we'll just have to keep looking until we find it."

Samantha's phone rang.

"Look at that—it does have an ON button."

Samantha grimaced as she went to answer it.

"Let's hope that's the coroner with some good news for us," Ed said.

"And that would be what? 'Oops, our bad—she's still alive'?" Samantha snapped.

Ed looked at her, clearly startled, and she turned away to answer the phone. She could tell by the caller ID that it was George at the coroner's office.

"Do you know the cause of death?" she asked with no greeting.

"Hello to you too," an older male voice said. "No. There's no easily discernible cause. I'll be running a tox screen."

"If you don't have anything, why are you calling?"

"Wanted to let you know that the pentagram was drawn in nail polish."

"Not blood?"

"Nope. Looks like it was applied several hours *after* she was dead."

"Thanks, George," she said, and hung up.

"What is it?" Ed asked.

"Pentagram was drawn in nail polish, not blood."

"I think we need to go back to the apartment and do some color checks to see if it might have belonged to her or Katie," Ed said, steering into the right-hand lane and preparing to turn.

"Agreed."

It felt morbid, going through a dead girl's bathroom, looking for her makeup. Three flavored lip glosses, a pale pink blush, and a bottle of clear nail polish turned up in the third drawer Samantha checked. That was it. No eye shadow, no mascara, no liners, not even any powder. The nail polish bottle was nearly full. The blush looked like it had been used only a couple of times.

Samantha searched the other drawers, but she knew she wouldn't find anything else. It fit with the picture of Camille that she had been forming.

Camille's bathroom was the one shared with guests.

Katie had the master bedroom with her own bathroom, which Ed was searching. Samantha exited Camille's bathroom and headed for Katie's room.

Katie was sitting on the couch in the living room, arms folded across her chest, clearly upset that as soon as forensics finished their job she was going to be locked out of her apartment for the next couple of days to preserve the scene.

A couple of days on a friend's couch won't hurt her, but a couple of days in prison might, Samantha thought.

Samantha walked into Katie's bathroom just as Ed was whistling and bending over the trash can.

"Look what we have here," he said.

"Red nail polish." Samantha confirmed it as he used tongs to pull the bottle out of the trash can and deposit it in an evidence bag. They returned to the living room and Ed held the bag high.

"Care to explain?" he asked.

"Duh. It's nail polish," Katie said.

"Why did you throw it away?"

"What? I didn't throw it away."

"Then why was it in your trash?" Samantha asked.

"It . . . I don't know," Katie said.

"Did you put it in there, or drop it accidentally, after painting the pentagram on Camille's forehead?" Ed asked.

"What? That was blood, and I didn't do it!"

"It was nail polish, not blood, and you need to start talking to us before this gets any worse for you," Samantha said.

"Worse for me?" Katie squeaked, her eyes widening in fear. "But—but I didn't do anything."

"So who are you covering up for?" Ed demanded.

"I . . . uh—no one. No one!"

"Who are you protecting?"

"I'm not protecting anyone!" Katie said, beginning to sob.

But she was. The question was, who would someone like Katie protect? She seemed more the kind to be loyal to herself first. What would someone have to do to gain her loyalty? What would someone have to be?

Samantha stared hard at Katie. The girl was scared and she was hiding something. "Tell us about your boyfriend," Samantha said suddenly.

"Kyle?" Katie asked, blinking at her in confusion. "Why do you want to know about Kyle?"

"Is he the kind of guy that likes pentagrams a little too much?" Ed asked, gesturing first to Katie's necklace and then mimicking drawing a pentagram on his forehead.

"What? No. He's, like, a normal guy. Anyways, he's not even my boyfriend. We broke up, like, six months ago."

And yet on some level she still thinks of him as her boyfriend, Samantha thought.

"I mean, he and Camille never even met."

"Are you sure about that?" Ed asked.

"Yeah."

"Do you have any enemies?" Samantha asked.

Katie went pale. "I hope not," she whispered. There was fear in her eyes, a fear that was much deeper, much more primal than her fear of the detectives.

Ed's cell phone rang. After a few seconds he moved several feet away. Samantha turned her attention back to Katie. She wanted to know what the girl was hiding from her, what she was afraid of.

You could make her tell you. It would be easy, a voice whispered in her head.

She set her jaw and tried to ignore the promptings, the urges. A spell of revelation perhaps . . . Samantha shook her head fiercely. She didn't do that anymore, not for years. She took a deep breath, struggling to control herself. It had to be because of the nightmare. Every time she had a nightmare she had to remind herself that she wasn't that person anymore. No spells. But convincing Katie to trust her would be so very easy.

Samantha squatted down slowly, bringing herself to eye level with the girl. She tilted her head slightly and waited for Katie to meet her eyes.

"Look at me, Katie," she said, dropping her voice into its lowest range. "You're going to trust me. You're going to tell me—"

A hand descended on her shoulder and Samantha gasped and nearly fell backward onto her rump. She caught herself with a hand on the floor and took several quick breaths. Guilt rose up in her at what she had been about to do.

She glanced up and saw Ed looking at her with raised eyebrows.

"What?" she snapped, more forcefully than she meant to.

"We need to go. Now."

She stood up.

"Don't leave town," Ed said to Katie. She nodded, eyes wide, still looking at Samantha.

"Joe," Ed said, turning to one of the officers still on

the scene, "make sure you drive her to her friend's house, see that she gets settled, and get all the contact info for her and her friend."

Joe nodded his understanding. Ed turned and headed out of the apartment, Samantha trailing behind him. As soon as they were in his car, he turned to her. "What was that? Trying to hypnotize her? Watching too much television again?"

"Yes, that was it exactly," she said, letting sarcasm drip from her voice. "I was just trying to calm her down and get a better look at her eyes when I asked her questions."

"Did it work?"

"I didn't have long enough," she said. *Thank God*, she added silently. "Where are we going?"

"Across town. St. Vincent's Cathedral."

"Can't they put someone else on it?"

"No, we're the go-to guys for this one."

"Let me guess," she said with a sigh. "Local color?"

"Worse. There's a dead nun with a pentagram on her forehead."

The 13th Sacrifice

Debbie Viguié

THE PAST CAN KILL

Samantha Ryan is plagued by nightmares. Horrific memories lie in wait – of dark magic and chopping meat, of strange creatures and blood-soaked walls. Because Samantha grew up a witch, coven, enslaved by power and greed.

But now, Samantha must age undercover to confront the horror of her terrible past, and protect her home town against a newly awakened heart of evil.

'One of the most beautifully written and scariest books I've ever read' – Nancy Holder, author of *Buffy the Vampire Slayer*

'Dark, bloody, emotional and scary and so damn well written that it's almost impossible to put it down . . . this novel is an insanely good read' – *USA Today*

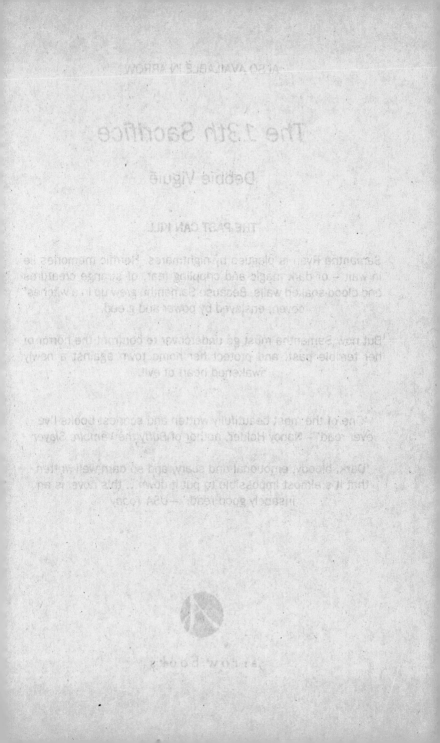

Arrow Books

ALSO AVAILABLE IN ARROW

The 13th Sacrifice

Debbie Viguié

THE PAST CAN KILL

Samantha Ryan is plagued by nightmares. Horrific memories lie in wait – of dark magic and crippling fear, of strange creatures and blood-soaked walls. Because Samantha grew up in a witches' coven, enslaved by power and greed.

But now Samantha must go undercover to confront the horror of her terrible past, and protect her home town against a newly awakened heart of evil.

'One of the most beautifully written and scariest books I've ever read' – Nancy Holder, author of *Buffy the Vampire Slayer*

'Dark, bloody, emotional and scary, and so darn well-written that it's almost impossible to put it down… this novel is an insanely good read.' – *USA Today*

arrow books

The Last Grave

Debbie Viguié

'Fans of Buffy and Charmed will love it … I enjoyed it immensely.'
Sunday Independent

Police Detective Samantha Ryan is doing whatever she can to
forget her terrible childhood in a dark and evil coven.

But escaping who you are isn't easy.

She is called in on a bizarre and horrific murder case, one that
is steeped in the occult, and Samantha is soon led deep into a
powerful coven. As she works to uncover the connection with the
murder, an earthquake rocks the Bay Area.

That's when Samantha has a premonition: Something is coming.
Something evil.

One of the most beautifully written and scariest books I've ever
read' – Nancy Holder, author of *Buffy the Vampire Slayer*

'Dark, bloody, emotional and scary, and so darn well-written that
it's almost impossible to put it down… this novel is an insanely
good read.' – *USA Today*

arrow books